ROGUE COURIER

BOOK THREE OF THE THOMAS YORK SERIES

ALSO BY SHIRLEY BURTON

UNDER THE ASHES
Book One of the Thomas York Series

THE FRIZON
Book Two of the Thomas York Series

SECRET CACHE
Book Four of the Thomas York Series

RED JACKAL
New Release 2016
Suspense and action in Istanbul and Mediterranean

shirleyburtonbooks.com

ROGUE COURIER

BOOK THREE OF THE THOMAS YORK SERIES

SHIRLEY BURTON

To Roy,
Shirley Burton

HIGH STREET PRESS
CALGARY

HIGH STREET PRESS
Calgary, AB
highstreetpress.com
shirleyburtonbooks.com
First printing 2014

Printed in the United States of America and worldwide under licence
Available in eBook formats.
Production and edit Bruce Burton
Cover Bruce Burton, photo licensed Shutterstock.com.

Library and Archives Canada Cataloguing in Publication

Burton, Shirley, 1950-, author
          Rogue courier / Shirley Burton

(Book three of the Thomas York series)
Issued in print and electronic formats.
ISBN 978-0-9919531-5-8 (bound).—ISBN 978-0-9919531-4-1 (pbk.)—
ISBN 978-0-9919531-8-9 (kindle)

     1.   Title. II.Series: Burton, Shirley, 1950-. Thomas York series; bk. 3.

PS8603.U778R63 2014   C813'.6   C2014-907035-7
                                           C2014-907036-5

10 9 8 7 6 5 4 3 2 1

Dedicated to my grandchildren,
Abigail, Andrew and Marcus

ROGUE COURIER

PROLOGUE

Emily and Joseph knew how to outwit danger. In Albany, New York, he had been a hunted witness in a murder case against lawyer David Sanderson that ultimately brought them to France in a witness protection program.

In Paris, their new world was turned upside down as they were drawn into the art market, uncovering a world of forgery. But their true identities, Thomas York and Rachel Redmond, were left behind in America.

At his friend Daniel Boisvert's urging, Joseph spent seven weeks in an Interpol Recruitment boot camp in the French Alps.

Alone on the side of a mountain, Joseph's survival skills were challenged by night wolves at his campsite, and the infection that racked his body. No longer able to walk or crawl, he drifted in and out of consciousness, barely able to press his rescue beacon. Found on the mountain, he had advanced into delirium. By air ambulance, he was lifted to a Paris hospital and treated for malnutrition and dehydration.

In those weeks apart, Emily endured a broken heart in a first real test of their relationship, the test of being apart and out of touch. Most puzzling to her, he missed his promised rendezvous.

A week later, Joseph hobbled up the stairs and turned the handle on the loft door; his surprising arrival spiralled Emily's world into a powerful romance. He held her like he would never let her go; days later they were married in a private ceremony, a few days before Christmas.

Joseph's expertise in military training was pivotal in leading them out of past traps and detours. Uniting his tactical approach and Emily's talent in art and passion for research and solutions, they started the Harkness Detective Agency in Paris.

Daniel Boisvert's life had become intertwined with Joseph and Emily in Albany, and followed them mysteriously to Paris.

But Daniel's purpose in Paris evolved, emerging from the shadows from being a friend to becoming an inexplicable figure in their lives.

The secrecy of Daniel's passionate mission has been known only to himself and his organization. Behind the backs of Joseph and Emily, he set in motion a plan to reproduce and sell high-price counterfeit Frizon clocks, intent on taking millions of euros from unscrupulous buyers.

Daniel's disappearances and reappearances since Albany have become an ongoing enigma to Joseph and Rachel, built now on a shaky question of trust.

ONE

Daniel didn't expect an intruder but was prepared if it might happen. Cursing and grunting, the two men heaved against the steel vault, forcing it inches at a time down the rollers onto the armored truck. They froze at any sound.

At the cry of a tomcat, they stopped to listen. One paced outside the truck with a gun in hand while the other secured the shipment inside with chains and padlocks.

At 4:00 a.m., their heavy van rolled silently from the Clock Collector's building in La Wast in Normandy.

Daniel turned down his window to take in the crisp air. He cranked up 'Ils Sont Cools' on the radio.

Leaning his elbow out the passenger window, he puffed on his briar pipe, but lowered his head to watch a movement in the side view mirror, a remote outline in the distance.

He reached to turn the volume down and looked at Pascal.

"I think it's a car beam. Do you see it?"

Pascal stretched to watch out both side mirrors.

Daniel asked. "Did you tell anyone we'd be taking the Frizon tonight?"

"Non non, Daniel! We have been so secure with our plans. Absolutement!" He looked again. "But, yes I do see it."

"We'll pass through the village in a few minutes. Take a detour and we'll wait and hope they overshoot. Left at the intersection near the brick post office; it goes to a back lane behind some shops."

Pascal turned the running lights off and veered onto the side road into an alley behind a bakery's loading area. He rolled to a stop but nudged a stack of crates allowing them to career down over the truck. Shutting off the engine, they sat in silence.

Moments later, a Benz Cabriolet sports car passed within sight, with two occupants and an open roof. Daniel snapped photos with his cell. As the engine roar dissipated, they found their way back to the thoroughfare.

"Cut over to Bacqueville, Pascal, I'll arrange a decoy vehicle from my brother."

Daniel fumbled in the darkness to reach his cell.

"It's me Amelard! No small talk—it's urgent. I need your intervention. We're heading to Port de Bordeaux with a discreet shipment. Can you find us on the highway and misguide a Mercedes Benz sports coupe? If we time ourselves, we should intersect about 50 kilometers south of Dieppe."

Amelard hopped on one foot as he put the other into his boot. His phone was tucked between his ear and his shoulder. "I'm up for the chase. Andrew is awake, I'll bring him too." His voice roared. "We'll force the Benz to a ditch! No problem!"

The pickup spun gravel from his yard as Amelard set the GPS for Dieppe.

Pascal was barely back on the pavement, when high beams veered into his lane. He swerved off and fishtailed to the side but held the wheel and watched the car disappear.

Neither spoke for a moment. "It had to be a coincidence," Daniel said.

"This route will add maybe ten minutes, but we'll still be on time." Pascal calculated.

A text came from Amelard twenty minutes later. "You're in my vision, Daniel." He flashed his lights from behind, tooted and passed.

At Port de Bordeaux, Daniel cruised the tarmac and spotted Amelard's pickup waiting behind a row of transport trucks. He pulled up beside, commandeering a rolling dolly to hoist their cargo.

"Bonjours, Amelard! Trouble with the sports car?" They both laughed.

"C'est domage. Daniel, the traffic was too thick as we approached the terminal and they must have turned off. We kept our eyes sharp and they didn't double back."

Daniel said, "We've been militant about our shipment. Not even Basil knows our precise coordinates, so there has to be a bug somewhere in our office or camera surveillance. Whatever the source, we'll be all the more diligent."

"What do you suggest?" Amelard asked.

"Check out these pictures; track these men. They must be known around La Wast."

"Daniel! When do we see you again?"

"The Atlantic crossing will take eight days, then I have to take care of arrangements in New York before returning to London. Let's hope we'll be together next month at Bacqueville. Thanks for covering in a pinch. You okay on your return?"

Amelard chuckled. "Sure, the hooligans in the coupe don't have a chance with me. Besides, Andrew slept most of the way so it's his turn to drive."

The brothers did a cross arm handclasp. As Amelard drove out the service road, he passed an abandoned cottage nestled in overgrown ancient yews. It was minutes from the shipping yard, and he didn't see the sports car lying in wait.

The binocular man said, "The vault looks heavy. Boisvert and the other man are struggling; they've secured it with a crank and padlocks. I'll get closer so you can smuggle yourself aboard. The GPS device will soon be out of range. Stay out of sight!"

"What do we do with Boisvert?"

"Just keep in close contact, there's no need to come face to face with him. Go now."

The passenger latched a heavy backpack over his shoulder. Stuffing a revolver into his pocket, he set out across the road and through the field. Finally with Daniel in sight, he found a niche spot between the loading containers.

Two days out of Port de Bordeaux cargo docks, Daniel stood at the ship's rail watching the moonlight dance over the waves of the Atlantic. France disappeared on the horizon behind.

For the first few days the waters were rough. Although now acquainted with his co-workers, Daniel took extra effort to remain private, a style accustomed to his occupation.

He was enjoying the solitude of the ocean and the moonlight while he pondered his arrival in New York. He was looking forward to seeing his counter-partner Jacques again.

Most of the men were below playing poker or gin rummy, with only a sparse night patrol. On deck near the aft, a stack of crates was lashed down and covered with a canvas tarp.

Daniel stopped to listen, and a noise pulled him closer to the canvas.

There's definitely something there. A scratching sound.

Inching toward the heap, he bent in the darkness. A steel-toed hiking boot moved, then a leg, struggling to get free of the ropes. On his knees, to see the cause of the commotion, Daniel was confronted by a snub-nose revolver.

"Back away or I'll shoot!"

Daniel was unarmed and had no choice.

From under the tarp, a young man climbed out, his hand shaking with a gun. He was slight but wiry with a wisp of a beard indicating his youth.

In the light, Daniel saw his familiar features.

"You're one of the fellows tailing us from La Wast?"

"That's irrelevant. Give me the code to unlock the container." He pointed the gun at Daniel's head with one arm.

"Come on lad, use common sense. We are stuck at sea for another week, unless you have an escape boat waiting on the lea."

Daniel stepped closer calculating each step.

The freighter was steady except for a few sweeps into the swell. Daniel counted the seconds between each dip and when they came to the crest he lunged.

Under-estimating his opponent, Daniel was grabbed by his legs and tossed into the crates. He retaliated with a hard chop to the shins.

Inching to the edge of the deck, Daniel smashed his fist to the man's jaw. With the roll of the ship, the revolver slid toward the railing. Daniel tried to reach for it when he heard the whip-o-will of a lasso.

Daniel pulled out a knife and shouted, "Laddie, I'm getting tired of this. You have nothing to gain by giving me a few bruises."

"Just like you, Daniel, I have my orders. Your troupe from La Wast isn't invincible; we know about your smuggling of fake Frizons."

"Who do you work for?" Daniel asked.

"What makes you think you have the upper hand to ask these questions?"

"The fact I have a switchblade in my hand gives me reinforcements." Daniel swung forward with a pretend slash, and surprised himself with a laugh.

The kid backed up, his feet tangled in the ropes. Daniel rushed him, slamming his head against a steel foot post. He hoisted him over his shoulder and returned him to the tarps.

A storm stretched into the sixth day, tossing the ship like a cork. Despite the rough seas, Daniel walked the deck continuously passing the cargo area to observe the area of the stowaway. But it remained quiet under the tarp giving him an uneasy feeling.

As the freighter rumbled under the shadow of the Statue of Liberty toward Ellis Island, the crew took their debarkation posts. A surge of pilot boats escorted the ship until it idled into port waters, and the containers in the hold heaved one last time as the engine shuddered and shut down. In the distance, fireboats and tugs approached from the New York Port Authority to bring them into dock.

Daniel went down to check the container lashings, but stopped and jolted back up the steps at the sound of running and shouting on the deck.

A crewman was in a frenzy at the chaos.

"Mon dieu! A fellow is trapped between two containers. He's not crew. Let the captain know we have a stowaway. C'est domage. Il est mort!"

Another cargo man bellowed, "Ahoy guys, give us a hand over here!"

Daniel called out, "What do you need?"

"The stowaway is pinned between these two containers, we need a forklift to free him."

Three men including Daniel pushed the two crates aside. It was the man who accosted him on the upper deck the night after sailing. The gash to the back of his head was bloodied and dried. His bruises had healed well enough, and he didn't appear to have been dead for more than a day or two. The man was clearly deceased, with a pair of chain cutters at his feet. It was Daniel's container he'd been working on.

Who is he? How did he know about the Frizon?

Daniel was baffled, but uncharacteristically relieved at the assailant's demise.

Daniel's cargo was released for unloading after the coroner's examination.

Several hours later, Daniel changed into his business suit and removed the fragile crate from inside the metal vault, loading it onto a delivery dolly.

Pascal was waiting in the immigration clearance zone. "Glad to see you had a safe trip. You've lost a few pounds!"

"There was a hiccup we should be concerned about, Pascal. A stowaway died trying to get into our container. The seal remained intact, however his ID said he was from La Wast—name is 'Manon'. Send a message to Basil to vacate the Frizon space and relocate in Bacqueville. Amelard can help them move after dark."

Pascal nodded. "I'll fly back to Paris once the cargo has been delivered."

"No, this can't wait. They must move immediately, Pascal. They'll need to scour the property for transmitters and receivers, and monitor the painters and workmen. There is a leak we must find! Basil knows the stakes and I have total trust in him."

"Mais, oui." Pascal moved to the corridor for the call.

The buyer paced back and forth near the revolving door of the Park Plaza lobby on High Park. He tugged at his tailored sleeve again to check his Rolex.

Daniel got out of the airport limo and greeted his client at the door. The man didn't have the American accent from the Sauliere's London auction where the original Frizon clock had been sold, but was shorter and refined.

The two adjourned to a private room. Daniel lifted the fraudulent Frizon from the case and removed the velvet cloth. He had taken every effort to add a luxury touch in his handling of the clock, and the buyer equally admired it, even knowing it to be a counterfeit. The fake Monett, painted inside, was still unknown in the art market and would bring him a healthy profit.

The buyer examined it quietly, then lit up in his praise. "This is truly remarkable, Monsieur Pinchot. A perfect copy of the clock and the painting in it."

Using the undercover alias, Daniel accepted the compliment. He'd been careful in selecting this man from Robillard's list of clients who had knowingly previously bought and sold forgeries illegally.

Daniel didn't want to be overconfident until the exchange was complete. The buyer opened the briefcase and presented ten pouches of polished cut Amsterdam diamonds.

Withdrawing a Firescope viewer from his pocket, Daniel set a single diamond on a scrap of velvet. Searching for the eight symmetrical arrows and the specific patterning of the hearts from above, Daniel determined the polishing was exquisite and accepted the diamond value his client offered.

"Here is the amount, we discussed. I have one question, Mr. Pinchot. How much for the genuine Frizon?"

The client unwittingly committed himself on tape.

Waiting for the concierge to wave a limo to the door, Daniel felt the burden of the supreme blue diamonds in the briefcase.

He made two calls: the first to Nigel Baker at the London foundation, then to an FBI contact to advise them of the Frizon forger's transaction. Daniel placed the microchip in an envelope marked 'F. B. Ingram' and left it with the desk clerk.

Daniel was tempted to wait and see the FBI take the American in the hotel lobby, but his incognito presence would be compromised.

The limo took only minutes to reach the Trump Tower and the plush offices of Jacques Simpson, the powerful magnate of the international consortium.

Daniel stepped from the elevator and opened the heavy double doors.

'Angels of Providence' was etched in glass.

"I'm Daniel Boisvert. I have an appointment."

The receptionist greeted him formally then rang through to announce his arrival.

A tall man with a commanding presence strode toward him with his hand extended.

"I'm glad to see you made your transaction safely, Daniel. Come, we have much to talk about."

The American wore a crisp white shirt with three buttons open revealing a chain with a silver engraved medallion.

"Jacques, it's been too long." Daniel said. He looked at the man's shirt.

Curious about the medallion. I've seen it somewhere before; looks like a family crest.

The courier syndicate and Angels of Providence shared the entire floor. It was adorned with marble and a surround of immense glass windows looking over Lincoln Centre and 5th Avenue, walking distance from Central Park.

Jacques turned up the lights in the boardroom, and Daniel placed the briefcase on the desk. The sparkling blue stones glittered.

"You've authenticated the diamonds?"

"Yes, the hearts and arrows test was flawless." Daniel said, "Not a wrinkle. Everything went as planned, however there was a kid from La Wast on board. Could your connections check the cargo area's surveillance at Port de Bordeaux?"

Daniel asked, "Sir, who will be the benefactor on this one?"

Jacques said, "It'll be off the radar, Daniel. We're sending a charity shipload of rice, beans and dried milk to an aid organization in Somalia. This will feed many villages and orphanages for a while."

Daniel nodded.

Jacques said, "Counterfeiting valuable Frizon clocks and selling them to criminals and forgers for a fortune. It's good indeed to feed mouths with the proceeds."

Daniel laughed. "Like Robin Hood, but it feels honorable to rob crooks to benefit the needy. Is this really a crime?"

Jacques shook his head. "We don't want to find out. But Angels of Providence is well hidden behind our international courier operation. It's unlikely to ever be seen.

"Besides, the return far outweighs the risks. There aren't enough Samaritans in the world. Big potential dollars are at stake, Daniel."

The sun shone through the ceiling height windows, and Daniel looked down on the honking horns. Everyone was in a hurry. "What's wrong with society down there? Don't people have important priorities and values?"

Jacques fingered the silver medallion. "Sit down, Daniel. I have another mission for you. But this one is not so cut and dried. Our London lead, Winston Metcalf, was contracted by a South African diamond mine owner to track down a diamond thief. We've intervened and directed Metcalf to assign it to Scott Marchand, our agent.

"Metcalf has already drawn our suspicions of his honesty and we need to test his loyalty. He is in serious debt to the Italian mafia and desperate for money. With our plan, we can kill two birds as we also suspect our courier, Scott Marchand, is skimming from us. He might be in collusion with Metcalf as they both have financial motives.

"Your role, Daniel, will be to oversee the operation to test and hopefully catch Winston Metcalf and Scott Marchand red-handed.

"Shouldn't be hard; you'll plant clues for Scott, each with numeric values leading to a safety deposit box code. You'll lay these clues in London. You can be as inventive as you want."

Jacques held up a sealed envelope. "The number in here is the solution, and will be revealed to the person who opens the vault in Amsterdam.

"This quest for truth and honesty among our own colleagues will clean house. With millions of charity dollars at risk, it is imperative that our consortium is built on faith. The danger level is high but I trust in your abilities." He laughed.

Jacques opened the wall safe and removed a black pouch filled with diamonds. He then carried a second pouch to the table.

"He placed the superb counterfeit diamonds in the briefcase, Daniel. Their quality will fool anyone but the most astute expert. We'll toss a few genuine stones into the vault, but be assured our investment is secure. Our inside man will vouch that the fakes are genuine diamonds.

"Can you leave right away, Daniel?"

Daniel looked up from the instruction sheet. "Do you have a reliable contact where I can borrow the needed theatrics?"

Jacques pulled a business card from an envelope in his desk. Daniel was satisfied with the contact.

"Yes, Sir. I can go tonight."

The tassels on Jacques's leather jacket swayed in the handshake as he passed the pouch to Daniel.

He remained standing as Daniel left. Returning to his desk, his eyes went back to the wall safe behind the portrait. He gripped the silver medallion around his neck and fingered the engraved 'C'. He stared at the wall trancelike, then reached for the intercom.

"Trisha, I need you to do some research. You'll find it interesting, I assure you."

"Of course, I love a new challenge." Trisha settled in a chair beside his desk, pen in hand.

"Jefferson Ducharme. He lived in California years ago. There's a little winery somewhere near Vallejo. See if you can find one using the name 'Ducharme'.

"I'll give it my best shot, Mr. Simpson."

TWO

Scott Marchand had been given his secretive courier instructions by phone at his home in Branly Quai. A terse message ordered him to be at the London Victoria Suites on New Year's Day. A contact would locate him there with further clues.

A sneer crossed his face. He tapped #06 to activate the reverse phone number triangulation—it was from Hyde Park International Couriers. Scanning Google Earth, he zeroed in on a visual of the London location.

Whenever these calls came, he felt a knot in his stomach. Although his mission directions were always confidential, it never changed his aversion to the process.

At thirty years old, Scott looked forward to the day when he might have a son of his own to take to a baseball game, as many American men dream. A quiet house in the suburbs of Pennsylvania with a garden for Eloise was only a fantasy.

He had flown in from Paris the day before. Eloise was angry and disappointed at the urgency of the trip but as usual asked few questions. Before leaving, Scott stopped at a local florist and ordered a dozen red roses.

True to his promise, he phoned Eloise to confirm his London arrival and hotel.

After the call, he left the hotel for a walk in the night air to clear his head. He looked into the night sky searching the stars for the Big Dipper. It was a juvenile habit he'd had since a boy, but was his own personal sanctuary when he was frustrated.

Most of his New Year's Day was spent hanging around the lounge waiting for his contact, but none came. A cluster of overstuffed high back arm chairs provided privacy in the center foyer. He moved to the sitting area with his newspaper and cognac for the evening.

At nine o'clock, he retired to his room.

Ordering a pot of tea and a glass of warm milk from room service, Scott tried to relax hoping sleep would come. He spent a fitful night thinking the worst of skepticism. Was he being set up as a lame target or an insignificant decoy?

In the morning, Scott went for breakfast before settling in an armchair in the lobby to read the Times.

A young bellman approached waiting to speak to Scott. The boy held an ivory envelope sealed with wax.

"Mr. Marchand, this was delivered to the hotel by hand for you."

"Thank you." Scott scanned the lobby, then called to the bellman to come back.

"Can you describe the man who delivered it?"

"He was a regular looking business man wearing a black fedora and fine houndstooth coat. Dark glasses and a ponytail are the only distinctive features I can tell you."

"Thanks, lad. If you recall anything else, let me know."

He opened the envelope.

Where Isaac Newton sleeps; nature's law lay hidden.

Surprised the message was delivered in this manner, it was clear he needed to go to Westminster Abbey to find the monument of Isaac Newton.

I've been to the Abbey before and recall a number of statues. That must be it.

He spent the morning replaying scenarios of the clue and the Abbey through the cobwebs.

Buying a folding umbrella and a silk scarf for Eloise, Scott was unaware of the distance he'd walked, and found himself near Buckingham Palace before retreating. Taking Buckingham Gate, illuminated by padded lamp-posts, he worked his way back to the Victoria Street hotel.

Scott scarfed down a bowl of barley soup with a beef dip sandwich, chips and a brown ale. Sitting in the hotel's main floor café, he checked his watch, anxious to get on with the task.

Returning to his room, he pulled out the hotel's stationary folder from the desk, and copied the note. Tearing it into a narrow strip he removed the desk drawer and taped it to the inside back panel.

Trained as an international courier to be invisible, he calculated on the probability that no-one would back him up, but liked the reassurance of leaving a vague trail when he felt danger looming. Something to suggest he were still alive.

Satisfied the evidence was secure, Scott returned to the lobby. It was a cold January evening and nightfall had descended on London. He stepped onto the hotel's valet platform and waved to the doorman for a taxi.

Ten minutes later, the cab pulled up in front of the formidable cathedral of Westminster Abbey. He got out and stood to admire the amazing edifice, with tall spires and magnificent stained glass reigning over the graves of royals and nobility buried beneath the floors.

As Scott entered through the enormous gates at the north entrance, he was struck by the foreboding silence. A podium inside the lobby held a donation box for the privilege of entering, with a stack of maps of the Abbey.

Scott dropped twenty pounds in the box, took a map and proceeded to the nave of the Choir section in the inner sanctum, the location of Newton's statue.

The white and grey marble monument in tribute to the great inventor was easy to find in front of the choir screen, inscribed 'Here lies that which was mortal of Isaac Newton'.

The imposing statue by Michael Rysbrack stood atop a sarcophagus, but at night with the dim lighting, the statue's base remained in the shadows.

A group of tourists loitered by the monument, and Scott paced back and forth a few feet until they disseminated. Two nuns walked past and stopped twenty feet from Scott at the pillar. He stiffened up and considered his options.

Their eyes are on me, I know it.

Scott fidgeted with the map, ready to bolt. His eyes had adjusted to the dimness, and he edged into the monument's shadow.

His fingers fumbled around the base feeling for the plaque, and ran his hand across undiscernible etched numbers. In spite of the glare of the nuns' burning curiosity, he pulled out a penknife flashlight. Deciphering the brass plate, he put it to memory, '173'. The rest was Latin gibberish to him.

The nuns inched closer to Scott.

His heart stuttered as his eyes fell on Nike shoes, with blue jeans visible below the hemlines of their habits.

They were inches away, and he was breathless with limited options now, needing a miracle to escape.

Spotting a priest walking in the outer corridor, he flung an open map into the air. As it fluttered to the ground, Scott darted toward the main aisle to the north entrance.

The assailants calculated his next move and were on him with the strength of men. He struggled to lay a punch but his arms were pinned from both sides.

A gravelly voice grunted out, "Don't make this difficult, Marchand, just continue walking out through the front door." Scott knew he couldn't overpower them, and he let them drag him forcefully out to the fresh air.

A Land Rover was waiting close to the door. The second man thrust Scott into the back seat, a sacrilege in nun's clothing in plain view of the Queen's own church.

THREE

Fondling the handrail, Rachel bounded up the circular staircase to the second floor. She stopped at the first door on the right.

"Here it is, Joseph. Number 204."

Joseph took a deep breath and closed his eyes, then smiled at Rachel and inserted a brass key into the lock. Rachel ran her fingers over the painted signature on the window.

"Harkness Detective Agency," she whispered.

The offices were compact, with only one window to rue Euler below. They were officially open for business.

Joseph stood in thought, his hands in the pockets of his business suit. He watched the traffic chaos on the street and the woman's efforts below to cross against the light.

The screech of tires and blaring horns were oblivious to Eloise as she crossed rue Euler. Her mission to find her husband brought her directly to the Harkness Detective Agency.

Her high-heeled shoes clattered on the stone sidewalk as she hurried from the Champs-Élysées. She was dizzy with terrifying thoughts of why her husband had disappeared.

She had stealthily planned and rehearsed every word she would say at the agency.

On this brisk January morning, Eloise tightened her coat collar close to her neck, plunging her hands into her pockets for warmth. In her haste, she had left her scarf and gloves on her counter at Branly Quai.

In front of the building, she stopped and pulled a slip from her handbag to confirm the address. Numb and tired, she climbed to the second floor.

Eloise Marchand was twenty-four, five foot five with a braid of strawberry blonde locks threaded by a blue twist. Her pale freckled complexion hinted to the mischief of her Pippy Longstocking appearance. Contrarily, dark circles under her eyes revealed she had been sobbing.

With her hand on the door knob of commitment, she straightened her back and entered. The door swayed inward and as the man at the desk looked up, she thought he was strikingly handsome.

"Hello, may I help you? I'm Joseph Harkness."

He rose from his fifties style oak pedestal desk, and came around to clasp her hand. Stretching out her hand she was comforted by his warmth and old-fashioned charm.

"Eloise Marchand."

The door burst open, their formality broken by Emily's singing and laughter, with two coffees balanced against her coat.

Emily stopped abruptly at the sight of Eloise. Flushed with embarrassment, she put down the cups and removed her glove to greet their first client.

"Hello! I'm Emily."

Eloise fidgeted with her bag.

"Please, I need your help," she said.

Seeing her agitation, Joseph asked Eloise to sit, not wanting to delay her with pleasantries.

Emily tried to recover. "How do you take your coffee, Eloise? I'll just be a jiffy."

"Black would be fine, thanks!"

When Emily returned, Eloise was seated close to Joseph's desk. Emily wheeled her chair to join them.

"My husband went to London on business nine days ago. I thought he'd taken another courier contract agreement needing signatures. The first three or four nights, he called right after dinner like we agreed. In our last phone conversation, he seemed tense and stressed I shouldn't worry."

She stopped and refocused her script.

"But I'm worried, Mr. Harkness. Can you find him? I'll pay you two thousand euros up front and then whatever else you need. I'll have to pay you next week when Scott's paycheck is deposited. We have a joint account."

Eloise's behavior became more erratic, shifting in her chair and wringing her hands.

"What kind of business is your husband involved in?" Joseph asked.

"It's some kind of international courier operation. I've never understood it as he took pains to ensure I wouldn't know too much. He travels frequently on short trips, but has never told me the name of his boss.

"Scott assured me his business was highly confidential but he hasn't been away this long before."

"How long have you known Scott?" Emily asked.

"We've been married two years. I met him the year before that in the States."

"Does he have any other family connections in Paris?"

"No, we keep to ourselves."

Joseph needed something, even a basic clue to find a starting point.

"Is there other information that might help us, Eloise? Notes, dates in his calendar, airline tickets, hotel receipts, phone calls?"

"Scott was careful and impeccably neat. The only thing I found was in the last suit he wore, this piece of paper."

Eloise pulled a crumpled paper from her coat and opened it on Joseph's desk. He read it several times and passed it to Emily.

Embedded numerical codes will lead you to the conquest.

"Does this mean anything to you, Eloise?" Emily prodded.

"Not at all."

"Do you have a photograph of Scott we can keep?" Joseph asked.

"Yes, I thought you'd need it." Eloise reached to a manila envelope in her handbag and handed a portrait to Joseph.

Joseph studied Scott's features. A tall, handsome man, chiseled cheek bones, weathered tanned complexion, green eyes and light brown hair and a hint of grey, with a natural wave over his forehead. Joseph silently guessed him at about thirty-five.

"What hotel was Scott at when you spoke?"

"The London Victoria Suites."

"Eloise, do you have a number for his cell and any other means to contact him? Has he sent any text messages?" Joseph asked. "We might be able to do a GPS tracking."

"In the event of a crisis, I have a phone number that doesn't answer but I can leave a message. Otherwise, he was to call me after dinner each night."

"If you don't mind, I'd like the number where you could leave a message. It might help."

Eloise jotted it for him, squirmed and looked at her watch.

Joseph nodded for Emily to join him to discuss it in their boardroom. He had come to a decision to take the case, but wanted Emily's opinion. In moments, they returned.

"Well, Eloise, I'll be honest. The trail is already cold and we don't have a lot to go on. I can't guarantee we'll be successful in finding Scott, but we're willing to try. There will be expenses involved; do you have any other means than Scott's paycheck?'"

"Yes, we sold property recently back in the States. The closing funds should be in our account within days. I can cover your expenses without difficulty."

Eloise was lying and Joseph knew it.

"Emily, I'll go with Eloise to Branly Quai. I shouldn't be more than an hour."

The Marchand's garden suite looked out onto the Seine not far from Place de la Resistance. The street was lined with quaint brownstones, each unique with colorful shutters and wrought iron balconies.

Joseph followed Eloise down a five stair walk-down to an open patio framed with planters; boxes of winter herbs and snowdrop bulbs peeked through the rich soil.

Her entrance was locked by a grated frame gate in front of a French pine door and peek-a-boo window. Eloise explained the previous owners had extensive security.

"Come in Mr. Harkness. This is our humble home. Scott's desk is by the window and his dresser is the hi-boy chest. I don't know where else you'd want to look. Maybe check his coats in the front closet, and of course the bedroom."

Joseph felt her eyes were locked on him and wondered her motive.

"Thanks, if you don't mind, I'll shuffle around a bit."

"Help yourself." Eloise watched with her arms crossed.

Joseph opened the front closet and lifted Scott's shoes, all polished and wiped clean on the mat. It nagged him that they had no personal photos on display.

Something about this place. It's too organized. Do they really live here?

The search seemed futile but Joseph remained diligent and thorough. Taped to the back of the top chest drawer, he found what he needed—a business card, visible when removed from its tracks. The card had a UK phone number and a sequence below it: 13 03 17 21 01 09 04. Behind the top desk drawer he found another note.

Eloise steeped a pot of Earl Grey tea and invited Joseph to sit with her for a few minutes. It was for her benefit; she didn't want to be abandoned.

"I don't know what I'll do if any harm comes to Scott." She wrung her hands.

"There isn't any reason for you to entertain those kind of thoughts. Stay positive."

Joseph was anxious to leave but stayed to be polite.

"Eloise, do you have any family in Paris or a relative who could stay with you for a few days?"

Eloise shifted closer to him.

"Like you and Emily, we are newcomers. Shortly after our wedding, Scott was unexpectedly reassigned and we quickly put the house in Allentown, Pennsylvania up for sale and packed our bags. An older landlady upstairs looks in on me and a university student next door drops in for tea when Scott is away. I'm not totally alone."

Joseph eased out of his chair.

"I need to return to the office and make inquiries. Before I leave, can I have a look at Scott's bank statements? It's surprising what secrets can be deciphered? I'm sure you understand the importance of the smallest of clues."

"Of course, they are here in the desk."

Eloise opened the middle drawer of Scott's desk. It was empty. Her face was crimson and she closed the drawer gently without searching further.

"That's odd. They were always here before Scott went away. I can't imagine where they'd be, but if I find them I'll bring them by." Joseph detected that she was unconcerned.

Eloise had dangled a clue then cleverly snatched it away. Without looking at Joseph she stared toward the front window, her fingers drumming on the table.

"Has anyone else been in your apartment since Scott left?"

"Yes. A phone repair man came to check our land line; I wondered why the landlord hadn't warned me. He was uniformed with ID and claimed another tenant in the building was having interference." She looked away as she created her falsehood.

Joseph checked the phone workings for a sign the alleged repairman had intentionally placed a bug. He was rewarded finding a digital chip.

Someone's listening.

Without disclosing his find, he left it in place to trip up the con.

"Thanks for the tea, Eloise."

At the front door, Joseph took Eloise by the elbow and pulled her outside, at the same time casing the street.

"Eloise, I don't want to be overheard but have you noticed any unfamiliar vehicle parked nearby?"

She stretched to survey the pavement.

"I'm not sure. Maybe the telephone truck. What does that mean, Joseph?"

"Probably nothing to be concerned about, but if you notice it again, call me right away."

Joseph was more than suspicious about the truck. The type of bug used in the phone required a receiver in close proximity.

Without warning to Eloise, Joseph returned to Branly Quai by metro, stationing himself a half block from the garden suite. He was certain the repair truck spies now had ample reason to tune into Eloise's further conversations with the Harkness agency.

Two hours later, Emily dialed Eloise.

"Eloise, if you'll be home, Joseph wants to stop by with an update regarding Scott."

Eloise was happy with the attention she imagined she was getting from Joseph.

From his vantage point, at a bus bench near some honey locust trees, Joseph waited. In minutes, the white van wheeled back into the curb three townhouses from Eloise.

Joseph's Qphone intercepted the conversation in the van.

"This Harkness fellow doesn't know anything." The first voice said. "And the Marchand woman can be easily manipulated, it's a joke."

A lower voice spoke. "What are we waiting for this time?"

"A phone call from either her husband or the detective."

Joseph stayed out of range of the van's rear view mirror and attached a transmitter to the back window frame. He crouched and released the air valve on the rear tires.

The second man saw the slight movement.

"We've got a tail!" Neither man moved, but the second pulled out a knife and continued to watch.

"It's the detective bloke."

"Don't sit there! Go after him," the driver said.

Hearing it, Joseph took off toward the metro station but didn't get far.

The man tackled Joseph from behind, plunging him to the ground. He held Joseph's face into the soil, catching his own breath, then yanked him back to his feet.

"Harkness! Keep your nose clean and stay out of other people's business."

The knife was pressed against his jugular.

With the man still panting from the run, Joseph prepared for a head assault. Butting his challenger backward with his head, he hit him squarely on the nose. Reeling, the man dropped the knife, and Joseph didn't wait for the outcome.

Eloise sat alone at her kitchen table. Preparing for Joseph's return, she changed to a burnt tangerine dress with a Hermès scarf that Scott had sent, posing for herself in the mirror.

She was relieved to hear a tap at the back door.

"Oh, come in."

"Sorry, Ma'am. He got away but we threatened him good. Here are the uniforms and the knife." The assailant had turned into a pumpkin. "You'll need to get the van towed, the tires are punctured."

"I knew I couldn't count on the two of you. But a promise is a promise so here's what I owe you."

Eloise was about to say something else, but changed her mind. As she pushed the door closed on the errand boy, he jammed his foot in.

"Ms. Marchand, you know we can get more if we go straight to the Harkness guy?" He waited for her nod.

The shock on her face declared she had underestimated the league she had joined. The man with the nosebleed glared at Eloise.

"You'll be seeing us again soon!"

FOUR

By the second Tuesday of January, London routines had fallen into place after the holiday break. Heathrow's morning flight was heavily booked and the weather forecast for a London downpour came as scheduled.

Emily insisted that Joseph take his waterproof waistcoat. He had argued it but was glad now.

His first stop was the Victoria Suites in the heart of Mayfair and Knightsbridge, close to Buckingham Palace, Big Ben, Madame Tussauds and Trafalgar Square.

Joseph shook his trench coat free of water and entered the hotel lobby.

Two male uniformed clerks stood guard behind the granite counter, one seasoned with a moustache and shiny head, the other an apprentice.

Joseph approached the older man.

"This might seem unusual, but would either of you have been in attendance over New Years?"

The clerk shook his head and ran his finger through an employee log, "I'm sorry sir, but I can't assist you."

Joseph continued to press. He pulled Scott's photograph from an envelope and showed it to both clerks.

The balding employee insisted he'd never seen the man before. But the apprentice's eyes looked down, and Joseph sensed he was about to hear a fib.

"I've never seen the man either. Sorry we can't be of help." The deception had been committed. Without moving, the witness had stepped forward.

Joseph watched their faces before speaking.

"If something comes to mind, call me. It is important, gentlemen."

Looking at the reluctant clerk's badge, he laid his business card on the desk. He looked in Randy's eyes long enough to make him squirm, and the young man's pain and discomfort told him their dealings were far from over.

"Thank you Gentlemen. You've been a help to me already."

Joseph took a plush lobby seat to look through his files and observe the scene longer.

Am I paranoid or is Randy making a call?

Joseph returned to the desk.

"Randy, I'd like a room for tonight. Joseph Harkness."

After Daniel delivered the clue to the Victoria Suites, he parked across the street to observe Scott leaving the hotel, and parked across from the Abbey to watch him enter.

He watched in disbelief as the men in the Land Rover intercepted.

Who would be following Scott? No one is aware of the clues and the diamonds, except . . . Metcalf knows about Mugabe's diamond shipment.

Joseph used his cell from his room, aware their conversation might be heard.

"Emily! We'll keep this call short. Buy a disposable phone and call me on the house phone in an hour? I need an update on Eloise. Love you, Babe!"

He hung up and stood at the window to think about her. They had knowingly selected a dangerous career and he knew the risks for them.

He loved her more than anyone in his life and dreaded any possibility they could get into something that could cost them their lives.

He pulled his jacket from the closet.

There's something yet to be found at this hotel.

Joseph skipped down the stairs to the lobby. The fidgety clerk, Randy, saw him approach and retreated to the office. Joseph called him back out and twisted his mouth to show his annoyance.

"Randy, what room did Scott Marchand occupy on his last visit?

The clerk was a lad of barely twenty, lanky with a surfacing thin mustache. He hesitated and checked over his shoulder to see if he was being watched, then huffed while searching the computer for the expired reservation.

He darted glances to the office.

"Relax, kid, you're not doing anything wrong" With a slight of hand, Joseph slapped a twenty pound note in front of his face. Now in cahoots with Joseph, he stepped up his search.

"Mr. Marchand occupied Room 804. He didn't actually check out. His room hadn't been used for two days so the manager ordered that his things be put into storage. They are still in the concierge's baggage room." The clerk stood taller asserting an effort of firmness.

"Well, Randy, can I move into Room 804?"

"That's a highly unusual request, Sir."

"Yes, I would agree, but it will need to be Room 804." Joseph was persistent.

"As you wish. Please, Sir, I could lose my job for doing this. I trust you'll be discreet."

"Don't worry Randy, we both have our secrets, don't we?" Joseph noticed that Randy's face reddened. "Please send my luggage over to 804."

The room viewed Buckingham Palace in the distance but otherwise was a typical junior executive suite with a corner desk. Joseph knew Scott was fastidious about neatness and neurotic about details.

A man with those quirks would have left some security in his room.

Joseph lifted the mattress and checked the water tank of the toilet. He thumbed the pages of the Bible in the nightstand looking for loose papers and unscrewed the light bulbs for microchips.

The desk drawer! Scott might be a man of habit.

Removing the stationary folder from the drawer, Joseph laid it open under the bright light of the desk lamp, detecting slight impressions of handwriting.

Taking the drawer from its lodgings, he nodded. Scott had not let him down. The cryptic note directed him to go to Westminster Abbey in search of Sir Isaac Newton.

Joseph texted the Westminster message back to Emily's new phone and asked her to raise it to Eloise.

From the conversation with Randy, he calculated the last day Scott Marchand was at the Victoria Suites would have been January 4, but was checked out on January 6. Eloise had come into the detective agency three days later.

I'm already five days behind.

Joseph figured he could pry more details from Randy with financial persuasion and went back to the desk.

"Mr. Marchand called down to inquire about the hours for the Abbey. One thing was peculiar. Mr. Marchand usually waited in the armchairs over there. But on the night he came down and took a taxi to Westminster, a man was here watching him. He pretended to read a newspaper but I could see he was looking over the top."

"Did he follow Marchand's taxi?"

"I think so. He had a Land Rover waiting by the curb."

"Have you seen that same man again since?"

"I did, just once; the morning after. He came to the front desk and asked if Mr. Marchand had returned."

"Did you catch a name?"

Randy looked at his desk and shook his head.

"A description? Was he tall, old, or what?"

"He was a tall and muscular with shaggy dirty blonde hair. He had a scar over his right eye that pulled his lower eyelid down. It was uncomfortable to look directly at him. I'm sorry I can't tell you more, Mr. Harkness."

"Thanks. Back in America, I could use you well as my 'brown shoe'. It's an expression for detective or sidekick."

Joseph turned away without an explanation.

Randy stood proudly at his post, not sure if he had been complimented or corrected.

Joseph answered Emily's call. He knew he could rely on her for attention to detail. Her literary acumen might see something he had overlooked.

"Emily, Babe!"

Before he could say anything more, she jumped in with her own news.

"Joseph, I've taken on a new case. A Mrs. Webster has employed me to follow her husband, a dentist in the Eiffel

Tower district. The good part—she paid cash for the two thousand euro deposit.

"Mrs. Webster suspected her husband of an affair and wants photographic evidence for the divorce court. She's already convicted him in her mind and was angrily on the warpath. She has hopes of financially ruining him and damaging his professional reputation.

"Last night, I followed Dr. Webster from his office with his nurse, until he exited her apartment at 6 a.m. I've delivered the infidelity pic this morning, and Mrs. Webster is satisfied.

"I barely had a couple of hours sleep and I have an appointment with Eloise. I'll be looking for pretty strong coffee when I hang up."

"I know you can do it, Emily. Has Eloise come up with anything useful?"

"I don't know. She seems to be an emotional wreck right now."

"The case is complicated but at least we are keeping pace and maybe today I can close in a bit."

"Do you expect to find him alive, Joseph?"

"I do. He obviously has something the other side wants. It would help if I knew what that could be. I'll be in London for another few days. Might be longer than we thought."

"Do what you have to; I'll manage business in Paris. I'm a tough bird."

FIVE

Winston Metcalf stared from his tenth floor penthouse executive office. Traffic bustled below him but his eyes couldn't focus on anything. The motion on the street was like a daze. His brow was furrowed and his hand rubbed his chin after the terse and disturbing call.

Metcalf had earned his position as a successful financier in a venture capital firm, dealing in international markets and multi-level marketing schemes.

This call was rare. It was seldom that his American boss called. Assignments normally came by email, usually clandestine deceptive missions and always described in detail.

Something doesn't feel right. Manny and Winch have to step it up so I can get closer to Marchand.

The American man's accent on the call left him with the same misgivings that he'd had in the past.

Who is this man in the dark?

The international courier network reached far beyond Metcalf's knowledge; he didn't know who was monitoring him and despised the control on him.

His respectable reputation in the business community was bona fide, and secured by his connections with the police department.

His instincts were usually correct. The talk amongst his minions told him a diamond shipment was on the street in London.

Wandering to his desk, he picked up a portfolio: 'Scott Marchand, Level 4 Confidential and Classified'.

It should be up to me to choose my own agents for these jobs.

Metcalf's greed was paramount; he was disgruntled, adamant that he should have been the one to oversee the clues given to the courier.

Metcalf mulled. *Who's the black sheep in this operation? I think I'll make a wee barter with Marchand.*

Rain drizzled on his window and a grey fog hung over London. He squinted to see the spires of Westminster Abbey, now barely visible in the haze.

SIX

Scott opened his eyes, unaware of his surroundings or how he got there. His eyes were still covered by the hood that had been placed by the nuns, but he listened for any clue.

He'd spent the night in an abandoned factory in Kent on the outskirts of London, with his arms bound to a straight-back chair.

Scott felt the periodic vibrations of trains rumbling through the yard, and listened as the morning factory whistle echoed between the limestone buildings.

It has to be about six o'clock.

The residue of chloroform had kept him asleep in the wretched chair overnight. As he attempted to stretch, pain surged through his limbs, with stiffness taking its toll in his joints.

The wiry bonds cut into him as he tried to wriggle free. His wrists were becoming stained in blood and a trickle of water from the roof dripped onto his jeans.

He heard low voices nearby, but was unable to decipher the conversation. Scott figured they had entered his area of the room.

Raising his shoulder to ear level, he tugged slowly on the hood. The room was stark and silent with the nuns' habits lying in a heap. Metcalf's men had scarcely spoken.

In his past assignments, this had never happened. He'd been given anonymous clues before, but this time the tables had been turned. He was usually the pursuer, not the pursued.

Scott replayed the Abbey events in his mind.

They were ready and waiting. Who do they work for? How would they know I'd be at the Abbey?

He glanced at his jacket on the floor with the pockets inside out. The men were watching him.

What do they want from me?

Every courier in the organization understood the costs and risks; each was left to his own devices without any backup.

The older of the two men spoke, the one with a two-day old beard.

"Mr. Marchand, what did you recover at the statue?"

"I have nothing to say."

"That's where you are wrong." The man bristled at Scott's boldness.

"You are going to tell us who sent you to Westminster Abbey. And…the objective of your mission?"

"Who are you and why were you following me?"

"You are mistaken, Mr. Marchand, we weren't following you. We were sent to watch the monument and lo and behold you appeared."

"Who sent you?" Scott was doing the questioning now.

"You'll find out soon enough."

The second man leaned close to Scott's face. His breath was obnoxious.

He shouted, "Answer our question! I'll repeat it once more. What did you retrieve at the Abbey?"

The inquisitor poked Scott hard in the chest with his index finger and held the pressure on him.

"I need my hands free to find the flash drive. It is a tiny shred with a broken grip. I haven't had an opportunity to make an inspection."

The two men talked briefly. The younger one inspected Scott's jacket again and slashed the lining with a pocket knife.

He tossed the jacket to the floor and came to Scott's chair.

"We'll give you a chance," he said. "Find it!"

As the man knelt to cut the wrist cords, Scott thanked him and reached for the jacket to wipe his bleeding wrists. The young man stepped aside, and Scott reached down bracing his hands on the front legs of the chair.

He swung it upward knocking the man to the ground. Before the older man had time to react, Scott slammed him with the wooden chair.

A revolver lay loose on the floor. Scott kicked it away before charging at the door. Heading toward the stairwell, he left his pursuers lagging. Grabbing a two by four he jammed the door, but heard the splintering of wood behind him as they smashed their way.

Scott scrambled to a manual freight elevator, barely dodging a shot fired over his head.

Exiting the factory, he fled across the multiple tracks to a cargo train crawling through the yards. A loading door was ajar and he jumped into a railcar landing on a pile of shipping pallets. Whatever the direction, the further away from his attackers was the right direction.

He jumped from the train as it entered a tunnel under the highway and flagged a truck driver for a ride into London.

It was obvious it wouldn't be safe to return to his hotel. Instead he found his way to Marylebone in London's West End.

He walked the last five kilometers to the Marylebone Hotel on Welbeck Street between Oxford and Bond. The desk manager hesitated at Scott's torn jacket and blood soaked wrappings on his wrists, but agreed to give him a room on the fifth floor.

Scott sat at his desk to refocus on his assignment—to seek out four numerical codes, then to follow the next delivered instructions. Recalling the first group of numbers, he recorded them on a strip of paper and taped it to the back of the desk drawer.

The phantom voice that ordered him to London stated the mission would find a diamond thief and a safety deposit box code. Anything else, he surmised, was a result of his own fabrication.

The thugs who hassled me must be connected to the caller, or the man who ordered this fantastic ruse.

He thought it through one more time, about Randy's description of a man in a houndstooth coat and moustache.

The clue handed to me at Victoria Suites lobby led me to Newton's monument. If there's a pattern, I'll spend some time in the Marylebone lounge. I'm guessing the mystery man will track me here.

Scott found the hotel bar off the lobby, settling into a comfortable booth where he could observe the comings and goings. When he took his seat, a bloke in a brown leather jacket was at the bar chatting with the barkeep. Scott assessed him from across the room; he looked like a foundry worker with his woolen cap pulled over his brow.

The factory worker was alone, but in time spoke to the man at his elbow. Their voices grew louder with each joke, seemingly intoxicated.

Scott gazed at the two men and watched as other patrons arrived. He was interrupted by a desk clerk with an envelope.

"Mr. Marchand, this was delivered for you. The man asked that I bring it to you straight away and personally."

"Thanks, lad." Scott struggled to find a suitable gratuity. "What did the man look like?"

"No one unusual. One of those men at the bar, the man with a brown leather jacket and toque."

Scott's head jerked back to the bar. Daniel's stool was empty. He signed his bill and went through the lobby to the front entrance. As expected, the man had gone.

The envelope included a full sheet of hotel letterhead and the message handwritten in backhand.

He's probably left-handed.

Fare Windsor to Uxbridge; lions roar above the Colne.

He retreated to his room and wrote the adage on a strip of paper, taping it to the back of the desk. Meticulous and obscure, he felt this tactic gave him an edge.

What does this mean?

Scott used the lobby internet to look up the train schedule, discovering that the tube station at Uxbridge was a meagre eight mile journey west from the core of London.

A daily commuter with four stops. It would be better to rent a car, but I know better than to waiver from the directions.

The accumulation of clues was a challenge. Scott opted for a hot shower to clear his mind.

He thought first of Eloise but resolved to maintain a safe forum.

After ordering his nightly port, he watched the local news on television and fell into a slumber.

Scott woke with a start. The hotel room was dark as he fumbled for his illuminating watch on the nightstand. It was 4:00 a.m. and the puzzle rushed back. He knew he wouldn't find sleep again this night.

Turning the desk lamp on, he surveyed the clues.

At 6 a.m. Scott called his room service order, a full breakfast of bacon, sausage, eggs, toast and a pot of coffee. He knew in this business you could never count on your next meal.

Breakfast was delivered with the morning paper Financial Times and his laundered shirt from housekeeping. He had abandoned his luggage at the last hotel, and needed to be cautious before returning for it.

Scott tore a scrap of paper and wrote out the most recent clue. He walked the five floor staircase to the lobby and surveyed the sitting area suspicious of anything and anyone.

Waiting at the reception desk to extend his stay for another night, everything seemed normal. The clerk gave him directions to a menswear store to buy some shirts. He stopped at a florist shop to send bouquet of colorful gerbers to Eloise.

After frequenting a few shops, he returned to deposit his parcels with the hotel concierge for delivery to his room, then walked the few blocks to the metro in search of his clue 'over the Colne'.

SEVEN

Joseph walked under the streetlights, arriving at Westminster Abbey an hour before closing. He didn't see Daniel's black sedan arriving in the traffic stream, and Daniel didn't see him.

The statue of Sir Isaac Newton was straight ahead. He passed tables of lit votive candles and an Anglican nun on her knees in prayer. The day's crowds had dispersed and the height of the ceiling created an echo chamber of remaining voices and footsteps on the stone floors.

Joseph walked quietly but briskly in search of an altar boy or priest to make an inquiry.

The nun rose from the worship table and passed close by him.

"Excuse me, Sister, may I ask you a few questions?"

She had the smile of an angel. "Of course you may. Please call me Sister Clara. What can I do to help?"

"Could I ask if you were here last Thursday about this same time? I'm looking for a lost friend who hasn't been seen since his visit to the Newton monument."

The Sister nodded at the question.

"Well, it's odd you ask about that night in particular. Sister Katherine and I were here for vespers—we always come at this time on Thursdays. Two men approached us asking for help, but instead attacked us, knocking us out. When we came to, we'd been dragged to a side room and our habit robes had been taken."

Clara's face flushed. "It was most upsetting. The head priest called the police; however he also conducted an internal investigation. An altar boy, tending to the candles, saw two nuns forcing a man from the building in habits."

"Does the Abbey keep security footage?"

"Yes, the Abbey has clear images of the car, a Land Rover, and the two fake nuns with the stranger."

"Your recall is impressive. Who can I ask to view the tapes? Perhaps there's a license number."

"Wait here . . . I'm sorry I didn't catch your name."

"My apologies. I am Joseph Harkness."

"Please wait here. I'll find Father McLennan; he can answer your questions."

Father McLennan wore a priest's hat over his groomed grey hair. He walked tall in his Cossack robe and crisp clerical collar. The Father led Joseph to a tiny office lined with books and cabinets.

"Please take a seat, Mr. Harkness."

"Thank you Monsignor."

"Sister Clara said you'd like to see the license plate on the kidnap vehicle. It was unfortunate that our security system failed to protect your man, and even worse the indignity to our dear servants, Sisters Clara and Katherine."

The Monsignor fumbled with his keypad to download the security tape.

"Here it is, Mr. Harkness."

In slow speed, Joseph watched the Thursday kidnapping. Scott Marchand was definitely the victim being coerced. Although Joseph couldn't identify the photos of the two nuns, he recorded the license number of the vehicle.

The cleric pulled a manila envelope from the file. "You can take these photos as we don't have any further use for them. Our investigation is over and the police have no other evidence to pursue."

"Thank you kindly." Joseph pulled out his check book and wrote a generous donation toward the maintenance of the Abbey.

He flagged a passing cab back to the hotel. The black sedan had waited for him and followed at a distance, pulling up across from the hotel.

With binoculars, the driver watched Joseph exit the cab to enter the lobby.

"Holy Cow, it's Joseph!" Daniel blurted. "How did he get involved in this? I didn't expect this. I wonder where Emily is."

From the car, Daniel dialed New York. "You didn't tell me the Harkness people would be involved. I know these people. This complicates my end."

"Calm down, Daniel. We didn't know that Marchand's wife would hire them. You know how the Harknesses work. Let Joseph do his own thing—it might even be useful."

Back in the room, Joseph phoned Emily on her disposable cell.

"Babe, it's me. I've got some details from the Abbey. Can you quickly run the plates of the escape car?"

"This might take a few minutes, Joseph, as the bureaus are closed. I'll see what I can do."

"Tell me what's going on while I search."

"I'm sending you photos of the two thugs. The pictures are grainy but see if you can come up with any matches."

"You are assuming I am Aladdin, so what is your third wish?" Emily teased.

"Third wish . . . to see you."

"Well, if you are still there tomorrow, I could fly to London for the weekend to give you a hand with the case. I'll close for the weekend."

"I'm not sure where the case will take me by tomorrow. I'll let you know later where we'll be staying. I can't wait to see you, Babe."

Emily gasped. "I have it. The name of the owner of the Land Rover is Lawrence Winchester. It's an address near the south rail yards, sounds like a fake. Joseph, he has a criminal record for assault and kidnapping."

"Can you text me his photo?"

"Sure . . . should be getting it right now."

"Emily, check hotel registrations in London for Scott during the last week. I know that's far-fetched and he may have an assumed name. He prefers five star hotels."

"I'll give it a good shot but no promises."

Emily phoned back in twenty minutes.

"Joseph, he was at The Marylebone Hotel three days ago. Also, I matched the photos of the second thug; the man with the scarred eye is Manny Leach . . ."

"What is it, Em? I sense there's something else to tell me."

"Not really, Joseph. I had a phone call with a silent caller, but I know the person listened to my voice longer than a missed number. I'm sure there was nothing to it."

Joseph thought about it.

Was it Daniel? I'll get to the bottom of this.

Joseph wasn't ready to tell her that he'd spotted Daniel.

Within half an hour, Joseph was at The Marylebone Hotel on Welbeck inquiring after Scott Marchand. He offered the photograph to the desk.

"It is highly irregular to give out such information. With privacy laws these days we could get ourselves into hot water." Joseph was satisfied to hear a justification rather than a blatant negative response.

"I understand your situation, Sir, but it is urgent." Joseph dug through his wallet for the familiar twenty pounds that usually bought an answer.

"Thank you, Mr. Harkness. Room 507."

"If Room 507 is vacant, I'd like to book it for one night, please."

"Let me see. The room is unoccupied so I'll make the reservation. It will take an hour to prepare the room."

"Fine. I'll be in the lounge."

Sliding the plastic key card into the door slot, Joseph was relieved to see a desk in the corner by the window. He removed the center drawer, hoping for a paper clue.

Roar of Lions over the Colne at Uxbridge.

Returning to the front desk, he asked if guest couriers and drop-off mail would be logged in.

"Did we lose something, Mr. Harkness? I'm sure nothing was delivered for you today."

"My apologies, Sir. I didn't clarify my reason for asking. A friend of mine, Scott Marchand, stayed here a few days ago. During his stay a parcel or envelope would have been delivered. I was hoping to find out."

The clerk removed the log. "I'll look at your friend's room activity for a delivery. No . . . nothing to his room. The concierge did receive an envelope and found Mr. Marchand in the lounge the day before he left."

Joseph handed him a twenty.

"No, Mr. Harkness, we do not accept tips for our service. It was my pleasure to assist you."

EIGHT

In spite of the obstacles, Scott was convinced he was on the right track heading toward Uxbridge. He quickened his pace along the sidewalk with the tube stairwell only meters ahead.

A parked rusty Audi was in view of Scott's window, watching for his departure. Two men, a tall man in a business suit puffing on a cigar and a Metcalf recruit sat in wait.

This was Metcalf's first appearance in his dirty tricks escapade. He'd received a telephone call early this morning from Reggio Calabria. The Italian was abrupt demanding a $300,000 US dollar payment within seventy-two hours.

"This is the only time I will speak to you. It is up to you whether you live or die. You understood the terms of our agreement." The line went dead.

Metcalf had never been to the mob headquarters nestled on the coast of the Mediterranean. His contact had always been a Brit with a suspicious accent. In the past, the man had barged into his home in the evenings with threats and inflicting bruises.

It was the anniversary of Metcalf's first face to face meeting with Switch, known for his choice of weapons. Winston had met him in a seedy bar for a $150,000 loan to repay a bad investment.

The first time he missed a payment, Winston's garage was engulfed in fire. With their interest and penalties his balance grew to over $300,000.

Metcalf's eyes were on Marchand. It was within his reach to seize the South African diamonds to appease his mob contact.

In his morning call, the voice from the Mediterranean was both convincing and threatening. The man repeated the word to him, 'KABOOM'.

His first thought was a car bomb and decided on driving his son's old Audi for his own tail on Scott.

Scott was disturbed by the presence of the Audi following at a snail's pace.

Sometimes I can't tell between good shadows and evil ones. I'll stick to my Scout motto and be prepared.

Early morning rush hour would be a bustling time for commuters on the rail lines, but Scott thought it would be the best time to blend into a crowd.

Walking briskly toward the Marylebone tube, he had an umbrella in hand. The rain deafened the sound, but his second sense focused on the Audi.

He crossed the street to a mailbox and dropped an envelope. A quick glance over his shoulder warned him the passenger was out of the Audi and walking too close behind him.

Turning abruptly, Scott slammed into the tail. The startled pursuer was facing him, and in the instant Scott injected his prey with an emergency vial of a paralyzer to the man's neck.

The stalker's eyes grew wide and his face stiffened as he fell forward onto Scott. Easing him to the sidewalk, Scott splashed a dash of whiskey from the tail's flask onto the man's face.

Without hesitation, he pilfered the man's breast pocket wallet and cell phone. A pair of Bobbies were patrolling near the corner and he whistled to attract their attention to the fallen man.

Metcalf exited the parked car and keeping a safe distance followed Scott, leaving Dillon to suffer. He was focused on Scott.

By the time the patrollers caught up to the seemingly inebriated Dillon, Scott had disappeared down the stairwell into the tube. The incoming train had just released its doors, and passengers poured onto the platform making it easier to blend in.

Scott tipped his hat down over his eyes, and his hand over the brim so his identity wouldn't be visible on security cameras. The transit doors closed on a flood of commuters, obstructing the lone police officer's pursuit of him.

Metcalf was irate that he had missed his opportunity to find out where Scott had gone with his clue. Fuming at being bypassed by the American, he vowed to overtake the mission. If he could intercept the clues, the diamonds would be his and the racketeers would be abated.

Winston smiled smugly with an evil glint in his eye and gave a solid kick to the newspaper box.

Scott, old boy, don't think you're out of my range. Wherever you go. I can track that micro-chip.

At the Windsor station, Scott bought a prepaid fare for a commuter train to Uxbridge. Carefully looking over the wickets and turnstiles, he purchased a newspaper and joined the boarding queue.

The train ride would be twenty minutes with frequent stops. He stuffed the receipt in his wallet for later relevance.

Station No. 9638—that's the only permanent identification on the ticket. The boarding platforms and the times are variables, so no-one could predict which platform or car number I'd take.

Settled into his train car, he pulled the assailant's wallet from his coat. The driver's license said Robert Dillon, with the photo similar to one of the nuns in the Land Rover. Scott recognized the address, an area in a seedy tenement with boarding houses along the Thames. Confiscating the license and cash, he tossed the wallet under the seat.

No need to waste good cash!

He again rehashed the scene.

Who is it? If someone wanted the clues, wouldn't they wait until I had all of them? I don't understand why these fools are attempting to intercept them. And who is the man in the Audi?

The conductor's announcement broke his train of thought. The next stop would be Uxbridge.

Scott returned his papers to a Velcro pocket in his lining and pushed toward the folding doors. Looking back, he surveyed the car and was relieved no-one was joining him.

Patting his revolver, he barged past departing commuters into the terminal. He had a choice of exit, east or west. The consensus of the crowd made the decision; it would be east, and the momentum pushed him to street level.

The clue quit at the door.

Standing on the sidewalk, a bus stand billboard advertised the Red Lion Hotel in Hillingdon. The picture showed a quaint village inn with character.

Could the answer really be that simple? The red LION? The River Colne can't be far.

He waved his hand and a taxi pulled out from a queue.

"The Red Lion." Scott demanded.

Entering the black double doors into the hotel lobby, Scott wasn't sure of his next move. He tentatively approached the desk clerk, standing behind a large counter with many coats of glossy black paint.

Scott interrupted. "Hello, do you have a room available?"

"Well, Mister . . ." The woman wore a brown tweed skirt and green hand-knitted sweater. She hesitated hoping Scott would offer his name.

"I'm sorry, Madam, please pardon my manners. I'm Scott Marchand."

"Oh, it's you, Mr. Marchand," she said. "We've been expecting you. A reservation was made by a friend of yours. I understand you'll be staying one night, is that correct?"

Scott was taken aback by the pre-booked arrangements but hid the confusion and fell into the pace of the conversation.

"Yes, one night. Do you remember the name of my friend? I don't want to thank the wrong person."

"I'm sorry, Mr. Marchand. He was abrupt and in a hurry, paying the bill in cash. He wore a brown leather jacket, ruddy complexion with one of those day old beards and had an awful pipe. Scott flashed back to the brown leather jacket sitting on the bar stool.

My faithful messenger.

"He arranged for you to go to the Black Park Adventure tomorrow. Your ticket is here, prepaid by the same man."

"This is a surprise. But what is the Black Park Adventure?"

She opened a brochure. "You start on a zip line and make your way Tarzan style, swinging from trees, then on ropes and grapevines."

Scott wasn't sure about this twist.

"Well, I admit I'm not exactly equipped but I see you have t-shirts and hoodies in your display case."

She opened the glass doors. "Of course, Mr. Marchand. We have jogging pants too." She looked up and he was laughing at the thought.

"Men's size large, please."

"Shall I add them to your room account?"

Scott placed a short stack of bills on the counter. "Is a hundred pounds enough?"

"That's more than enough. If it's okay I'll credit the difference to your room. Your room is on the second floor at the end of the hall with a view of the park. Room 203."

She placed a large brass key on the counter.

"Where can I get a good meal for dinner within walking distance?"

"You only need to walk as far as our Pub at the other end of the hall. We also have room service up to eleven."

He was about to leave when a second thought came to him. He turned on his heels. "By chance, does this Adventure thing go near the Colne River?"

"Why yes it does."

Scott smirked as he took the corridor to the stairwell. He thought he'd been transported into the past, a time when crooks and robbers didn't exist and you could leave your door unlocked at night.

Daniel sat in the pub, his instructions delivered. He tapped his pipe and fussed over a tourist map. A micro receiver in his pocket buzzed and he placed his ear to a connecting device to listen in on a telephone conversation in the office of Winston Metcalf.

"Adnan Mugabe, please put him on the phone." Winston's voice was agitated.

"Mr. Mugabe is in a meeting. May I take a message?"

"Tell him again who I am. I must speak with him now—you fix that up!"

A tedious silence ensued before the secretary returned.

"Hold a moment, please."

"Winston, I'm surprised to hear from you. Our meeting isn't for another few days."

"I've been instructed to collect an advance from you before we meet in London. You need to wire $100,000 to me right away to show your good faith."

"This is highly unusual. I can bring a check with me."

"Adnan, I need it today." Daniel could hear panic in Winston's voice.

"Very well, my secretary will make the arrangements. Give her your banking instructions." Mugabe hung up without pleasantries.

Winston was about to acknowledge the conversation with Mugabe when an incoming call beeped.

"Winston Metcalf here."

"Mets old boy, we'll be meeting in 'The Digs' at 6 p.m. Bring your payment or else."

"I can bring $100,000 this afternoon." Winston hoped for a sound of satisfaction from the caller.

"Metcalf, how's your son doing at university? Will he be home on the weekend?"

The receiver went silent.

Daniel decided to return to London when Scott returned from the Black Park to deal with Metcalf.

Marchand should be back from the Black Park soon and I'll be at The Digs before 6 p.m. I'll have to intercept Metcalf's $100,000 he plans to steal from the company.

NINE

Emily waited at the office for his call. She had counted the days since Joseph left and knew it would be just two more days.

"Joseph, I'm so glad you called," Emily said. "I've been thinking we need time together."

"Em, you're right. Our London rendezvous will be a start. I'll be at The Marylebone Hotel, and I'll meet you at Heathrow Friday morning."

"Can't wait to see you," Emily beamed.

Joseph asked, "Have you had any luck with the last message, Scott's clue?"

Emily suggested, "The next destination is Uxbridge, on the tube line west of London. The directions say to take the Windsor train and there's nothing until Uxbridge. The Red Lion Inn is the main reason tourists travel there."

Joseph hesitated.

"But Scott will already have collected the clue so I don't see the value in following in his steps on this leg. What if we rent a car to Uxbridge and take in the countryside while I have you for the weekend."

"I could see if we could round up a Vespa?" Emily teased reflecting on their Rouen adventure.

"I'll stick with the car rental." Joseph chided.

Emily said, "You didn't ask me for an update on the Webster case. The photographs from my first stake-out did the trick and Mrs. Webster's lawyer is confident it's solid evidence. I'll be called to testify on the infidelity, but it will be quick. She was happy to spend her husband's money and gave us another 2,500 euros for expenses. Not a bad haul for a slam dunk case.

"Are you keeping track of expenses in London?"

"My pockets are full of receipts. Can't wait to see you, Babe!"

Locking the agency, Emily took the staircase to the lobby. Before reaching the landing, the front door flew open and a man stomped in, tall and obese, and confident of his authority. Emily recognized him from the recent photos she'd taken.

"Where's the Harkness dame? You her?" The intruder's face was crimson red and his manner belligerent. Emily thought he might be drunk.

He yelled a tirade into her face and slammed the front door to create a powerful impression.

"I'm afraid the detective agency is closed for the day."

"Miss, it is about to re-open!"

The angry man poked her, his finger digging into her shoulder. She took a step backward to maintain her balance. He held a tight grip on her wrist, shooting pain up her arm as he twisted it. The stench of his breath on her face made her recoil, and she was correct in her initial assumption that he had been drinking.

Emily's eyes flashed to the other office doors, hoping for the chance of assistance. The other offices had closed except for a light in the print shop at the end of the hall.

My best bet is to hold my position. Returning upstairs to the agency would put me back on uneven ground and close an escape route.

"Who are you? If you touch me again, I'll call the police and charge you with assault."

"You aren't going to do that, you nosy dame. You had no business prying into my personal life. Nobody just walks away from me, not my wife, and definitely not you. You have no idea who you're dealing with!"

"I presume you are Mr. Webster."

Emily decided to face the music and try to subdue the conversation until she could recruit help. She slipped her hand into her coat and pressed the speed-dial for emergency.

"What is it you want from me, Mr. Webster?"

"I want the negatives and for you to testify you were mistaken."

His face reddened even more and his eyes bulged.

"Mr. Webster, I find you and your concubine uninteresting and I don't have any relationship with you. Any further discussion with you would be a breach of trust and an invasion of my client's privacy. If you feel you have reason to talk with me, please contact my lawyer." Emily kept her voice calm but firm.

"I ought to belt you good." Webster raised his hand spitting vile through his yellowed teeth; then heard an approaching police siren.

"You fool, did you set off an alarm? It's my word against yours, and yours won't count for much. I have acquaintances in the police department."

He pushed her again gloating about his connections.

"I have every right to protect myself. If you are still standing there when the police open the front door, I will lay assault charges and uttering threats. You have five seconds."

Two officers rushed the door. The first one cuffed the intruder while the second asked Emily if she was alright.

Webster resisted and continued ranting about his inside connections. Before he was pulled away, he spat at Emily.

From a distance, he looked like a buffoon to her, but his anger scared her and touched a raw nerve. From the police wagon he shouted back, "Watch yourself! I'll get even!"

"Officer, I'd like to lay charges against Mr. Webster for assault. I assisted his wife in a divorce case and I need a restraining order while the case is ongoing."

She pulled up her coat sleeve to reveal red and blue bruising.

"He has threatened me and sprained my wrist with intent to harm me."

Emily needed some understanding and compassion. Reading the policeman's badge, she looked up with her blue eyes. "Thank you, Officer Watson."

"We'll take this report to the courthouse and they'll issue the restraining order. Get some photos of that wrist, you might need it later."

Emily was shaken from the encounter. She took the bus to the St. Pierre museum depot and began the slow walk uphill to rue des Saules.

A wave of anguish overcame her as she quickened her pace up the final steps. She loved this life in Europe, but a premonition flashed before her not to risk her life to this extent, or Joseph's life. She needed to shake the reality that Joseph faced the same dangers.

Here I am alone without him, and he's focused on tracking a stranger. But this is our life right now.

Before entering the loft, she tapped on the door of her landlord's flower shop below, just to talk and receive some consolation from her friend. But Marie and her bloodhound Toby had gone for the day.

She poured a hot bubble bath, lit a few candles and absorbed herself in a tattered 'Agatha Christie' mystery.

By the time she slipped between the crisp cotton sheets her dreams came quickly. Dreams of Joseph.

TEN

Scott awoke at 6:00 a.m. hungry. He hung out his laundry bag for housekeeping, then took the staircase down to the restaurant at The Red Lion.

The full breakfast was poached eggs, smoked back bacon, porridge, whole meal toast and marmalade. He was ravenous.

In his new t-shirt and hoodie, Scott waited at the lobby to watch for the shuttle to the Black Park adventure site. The words 'viaduct over the Colne' from the park brochure was etched to his mind.

The lights of a mini-bus pulled up, and the guide called Scott's name from the door. He looked at Scott's shoes and put his hand in the air. "Those won't do, mate, but come with me." The guide dug out a duffle bag from the back seat of the bus.

"Leave your shoes here and we'll loan you footwear. Those shiny soled shoes won't work; they wouldn't be safe."

He waited for Scott to change, and brought the street shoes back to the desk clerk in a bag.

Repelled by the sensation of wearing someone else's shoes, Scott knew he didn't have a choice.

"Thanks, man. I'm all set now."

The group amounted to a dozen adventurers. Scott was introverted by nature, and found the piercing laughter and high-pitched chatter to be abrasive so early in the morning.

Those not in pairs were matched up with other lone participants. Scott slipped out of the group for his personal scavenger hunt. Assessing the options, he determined that when he was out of sight, he could deviate toward the viaduct of the Colne.

Scott studied the brochure and map. Passage through the five hundred acre sanctuary would be on guy wires, floating bridges, platforms, grapevines and ropes.

He was energized by the zip line, invigorated as he traversed over the height of the forest. In good physical shape from working out near his Paris home, he felt his muscles were being tested.

A tree ahead posted colored flags with a choice in direction; the red flag line a three hour route, yellow across an open field, and the blue flag over the Colne River.

Blue was the obvious one. He struggled across the rope bridge over the river, thankful for the loaned shoes. He wrapped his legs around the rope and heaved his body forward.

Looking down, the swirling current was magnetic, teasing Scott into a hypnotic trance. Alone above the sound of the cascading water, with nobody in sight from behind and no one to follow, he froze to meditate his next move.

Without warning, an overhead zip line reeled toward his head. The sound whistled closer and he ducked as the looming weight flew at him. Tied to the weight was a plastic card the size of a luggage tag.

It unnerved him that someone must be watching, setting the zip line in motion to knock him off balance into the gorge. His knuckles were raw but he gripped the swaying rope railing with one hand. With the other hand he yanked the tag free.

His breathing accelerated as he inched toward the platform with spasms in his shoulder muscles.

Easing his body to a standing position, Scott took deep breaths and opened his water bottle. Stooping over with his hands on his knees, he panted for air.

The tree platform had a panoramic view, a perfect vantage point. Scott pulled his zoom lens from its case. Toward the yellow route, he watched as one of the patrons rested on a platform high above the tree line. A bright glint of sunlight from the spot raised his interest and he focused his lens on the man.

He has binoculars! The man is watching me!

With his eyes fixed on the spy, he searched for anything that would help. He focused on the baseball cap, bright indigo blue with white lettering LA, not a typical hat style or logo for Londoners.

A Dodgers fan. Why the fantastic ruse?

Examining his opponent's platform, he searched for a coordinating zip line that could have fired the package.

Is the man alone? Someone from another platform could have used a different line. The caper still makes no sense.

Grasping the zip line, he advanced to the pickup zone. Returning to the Red Lion, he claimed his shoes and took the stairs to his room.

The cargo style card tag had three printed numbers:

6 2 5

Standing outside his sedan in the lot, Daniel puffed his pipe. The code was delivered and he was satisfied.

The teenager tourist wearing a Dodgers cap was delighted to fire the pouch for a few pounds.

This is going like clockwork. It will be one more day before Joseph catches up to the pace. I'll be back in Hillingdon tonight, but I have Metcalf to deal with first.

Daniel drove back to Charing Cross in London's west end theater district. He opened a portfolio case from the front seat and removed a single sheet of ivory note paper and a matching envelope. In a backhand scrawl he wrote:

AC lives forever at Major's Monkswell Manor.

Pulling up curbside at the Uxbridge train station, Daniel paid an attendant to stay with his car. He proceeded to the depot counter asking for red cap special services.

"Sir, I have an important task I need you to do. Are you able to deliver a message to one of your passengers on the next train into Windsor?"

"That's like a needle in a haystack, mate. How do you suggest that I find your man?"

"It will be easy. When you are boarded, make an announcement for Scott Marchand.

"Yes, that would work."

"When you've delivered the envelope, call me on this number. It's critical that he receive the message."

Daniel handed him a blank business card with a phone number and a fifty pound note.

ELEVEN

The return train to Windsor was half empty. Scott chose a window seat at the far end, separated by several rows of passengers. He hadn't received instructions about his next location and opted to return to London.

An automated message announced the departure, then an actual voice on the P.A. system. "Would passenger Scott Marchand please identify himself to the conductor?"

A warm flush reddened his face and as the conductor walked through asking for proof of tickets, Scott identified himself.

"You're Scott Marchand? Can I see some ID please?"

He rifled in his jacket for his passport.

"Have a nice day." The conductor produced an ivory envelope from his coat.

At the last stop before Windsor, Scott went to the lavatory to open the envelope in private.

He folded and placed the clue with the others in the lining of his coat.

What the devil is Monkswell Manor?

Leaving the Windsor station, he hailed a taxi back to the Victoria Suites Hotel. Ripping his jacket seam open, he spread all the clues on the bed, then headed down to the lobby computer.

A web search wasn't fruitful for either 'Monkswell Manor' or the initials A.C. He flipped through a magazine 'Entertainment in London' and took it back to his room.

Scott prided himself that his best thinking was in a hot shower. Coming out of the bathroom with a plush towel around his waist, he went to the entertainment guide.

There it was on the second page, Agatha Christie's Mousetrap. In fine print, 'Monkswell Manor'.

I've missed today's 7 p.m. curtain up. It'll have to be tomorrow. I wonder if they'll make me watch the whole thing. Might be irksome.

A white envelope with the hotel insignia slipped under his door. He picked it up quickly and looked through the privacy peephole, but the person had gone.

TWELVE

E mily's Air France flight was overdue. Joseph looked at his watch every few minutes and checked the Arrivals board.

He knew Emily would travel light, and he parked the rented Renault in the terminal's short-term lot. They could be out of Heathrow quickly.

Emily came down the escalator wearing Versace jeans, a pink cashmere sweater, a beige and white twist scarf and a brown leather jacket.

Her hair was pulled up in a fashionable bronze clip. Wispy strands cradled her face, emphasizing her sparkling blue eyes. Joseph thought she'd never looked more beautiful.

Elbowing through the throng, he embraced her with a heightened passion. He couldn't deny it and remembered his pledge.

Reaching to take Emily's valise, Joseph noticed her bruised wrist. Gently reaching for her hand, she tried to hide it but he saw her tugging on her coat sleeve and wincing in pain.

"What happened, Babe?" Joseph took Emily's wrist to his lips and kissed her.

Emily was startled how the touch of his lips sent a tingling shiver throughout her body. She wanted to cling to him but it would have to wait.

"Oh that, it's not important. I'll tell you later. For now I want to know what we're up to today. I'm starved, Joseph. How about a bit of breakfast?" Her blue eyes were locked into his.

"Sure, let's head to Trafalgar Square. There are lots of cafés and bistros in that area."

Joseph phoned ahead for a room at the Red Lion in Hillingdon. It was time to close in on Scott. They set out in the rented Renault, and at the first petro station, he pulled off for a fill. He brought a coffee back for Emily.

Buckled for the drive, she waited for him to turn the key, but instead he reached under the seat for a small box. With her hand over her mouth, she gasped on opening it, a diamond encrusted sapphire ring.

The card said, 'I love you forever'.

She stretched across the seat to kiss him, but a car honked at their pump to bring them back to reality.

It was a long weekend and the hotel was fully booked by Londoners seeking relaxation. Emily's arm slipped between Joseph's elbow and his ribs as they walked to reception. He was reminded how spontaneous she could be and looked at her with longing—a definite distraction.

Joseph directed his questions to a frumpy woman behind the check-in counter.

"Hello, we're trying to catch up with a friend of ours. He had a great time here and said we should try it. Do you remember Scott Marchand?"

The clerk wore a hand-knit sweater. Emily looked up and the woman's eyes were searching the ceiling for an answer.

"Oh yes, Mr. Marchand. He was such a nice man. He was here but seemed surprised and unprepared for the Adventure Park trip. The circumstances of his arrival were odd, a mystery really."

The desk clerk was eager to spill the information.

"What do you mean, a mystery?" Joseph prodded.

"A man stopped here the day before his arrival and made the reservation and booked the Black Park. Mr. Marchand was surprised about both reservations."

"What's Black Park? Emily persisted, not letting go of Joseph's arm.

"Here, this is the brochure."

"Do you mind checking which room Mr. Marchand used? I'd like the same one."

The clerk fiddled with the keyboard.

"Room 203 is assigned for a reservation but they haven't arrived yet. I could switch that. Yes, this will work."

Joseph laid twenty pounds on the counter and turned to leave.

"One more thing, do you remember what the man looked like who left the tickets?"

"Funny, Mr. Marchand asked me the same thing. He had a pipe. I'm allergic to smoke, and it stuck in my mind. Dark brown eyes and a ponytail."

Joseph's mind flashed to Daniel. But he wasn't ready yet to raise it with Emily. They took their key and enjoyed a pint of lager by the Tudor fireplace in the lounge. The next step wouldn't take place until morning and they could slow their pace.

Emily stayed in the lounge as Joseph collected her valise and his satchel from the trunk.

His head flung up at the whiff of tobacco and the hair on the back of his neck rose.

Daniel.

He stayed calm, not looking in that direction. Back at the lobby door, he glanced at a black sedan across the street. The driver's black fedora was over his brow.

Joseph picked up Emily and they headed to the second floor. The room was quaint with a private fireplace and a four-poster bed. Emily rubbed her hands together and raised her eyebrows at the sight.

"Charming. A perfect country getaway."

Joseph went directly to the room desk and searched the tray for a clue.

"Good old Scott."

He pulled out the strip of paper and laid it on the top of the desk.

"What does it say?" Emily asked. "We still have the third one to solve, but we must be closing in."

"I'll ask our talkative clerk if she knows where Scott went after the Red Lion. If she knows anything, she'll tell us."

Joseph went down alone to the lobby. He found a service exit from the stairs through the kitchen and stepped outside. The daylight struck his vision momentarily, as he watched the black sedan pull away.

What the dickens do you want from us, Daniel?

Emily was in a hot bubble bath when Joseph returned. Through the door he heard her singing his shower tune 'Que Sera Sera'. He chuckled and announced he was back.

Emily was wrapped in a white hotel robe and came out to sit on the bed.

Joseph said, "Scott is leaving us blatant clues. The desk clerk says she booked him back at the Victoria Suites. He must be out of clothes."

"Should we save time and go there?"

"Let's lay out Scott's clues on the bed. There's an excess of numerical codes—there must be directions we're missing to bring it together. Then we'll get him."

"A Swiss Bank account?" Emily asked.

Joseph put his finger to her lips and pulled himself up against her. "Later."

THIRTEEN

Scott dropped another envelope in a postal box not far from the station. Eloise was competent, but he knew she'd overreact if his communication lapsed.

Eloise had been a tour guide in the Amazon when he met her. She was guiding a group of university students through unbroken bush and her basic survival skills were proven and put to the test.

She was able to improvise. He once teased her of being an actress as she adapted so well to change. Sometimes she was so impressive Scott wondered if she had a split personality. There was always a look of mischief in her eyes and a fleeting flash of evilness.

Randy was happy to see Scott back at the Victoria Suites, and immediately placed his luggage onto a baggage cart.

Before Scott could speak, Randy enlightened him about the man shadowing him. Randy's description was of a concerned friend wanting to ensure Scott's safety.

"He was a handsome man about thirty years old, six feet tall, well-built, with golden brown hair and brown eyes. I particularly remember his eyes, direct and intimidating."

"Randy, I appreciate this. Do you have his name?"

"I'll have to check the register. It was Harden, no Harkness. There was also another man. He didn't leave his name but I recall his scarred face, one I wouldn't like to meet in an alley."

"Do you know why he was here?" Scott asked.

"He went to Westminster Abbey, just like you did."

Scott smiled with satisfaction that his clues were being collected.

Eloise put a fly in the ointment by hiring those Paris detectives but it won't amount to anything. The London boss is the only one aware of my mission. Who's this other gent appearing in disguise, he's always one step ahead of me.

After dinner in the hotel, Scott planned on an early evening of the news, with time to review the pieces.

He took the elevator up. His hallway was empty other than a couple having trouble with their room key across from his door. The young woman appeared distressed as she struggled with her luggage.

"Sir, do you mind helping us with our key?"

Scott didn't like contact with strangers and hesitated uncomfortably.

"I have my phone; why don't I call down to the Desk for you?"

He reached for his phone.

"Please, Sir."

The woman moved closer to him. Alarm bells went off in his head and he retreated with his own key in his hand.

The woman was right in his face.

"Open the door, Mr. Marchand!"

Her hot breath and the aroma of her sweet perfume repelled him. He felt a jab in his side and looked down. It was a French Lefaucheux double-barreled revolver; he recognized the model from his training in Pennsylvania.

The man inched around behind and relieved Scott of his room key and cell.

"Let's go into your room." He unlocked the door and propelled Scott through the doorway.

"Who are you? What do you want?" Scott said.

The pair didn't look at him or answer. Instead, the woman made a phone call while the man sat Scott in the desk chair. He tied Scott's hands, securing his feet to the chair leg and forced a gag into his mouth.

Up to this point, other than the bungled kidnapping, his attackers had been placid in their maneuvers, tailing him and watching his movements.

These people are seasoned. They know exactly what they are doing.

For an hour, the couple ransacked his room. They shouted at him as they searched, and finally returned to remove his gag. Leaning into his face, the woman gritted her teeth and screamed, "Who is the package?"

The words meant nothing to him, and without an answer, the man attempted to pistol-whip him, knocking the chair on its side to the floor.

They're going to kill me. Who are they?

His cheek was bleeding and the man gave him a single fist to the jaw and he fell unconscious. The last words he heard were hard to make out.

"Not so hard, Peter, we're not supposed to kill him."

In the morning, the room was silent, with no sign of the pair. He was on his side still bound to the chair, but relieved. As he struggled with his bonds, he heard the dreaded sound of the key in the lock.

"Mr. Marchand, you're awake!"

The man entered the room alone. He yanked the gag from Scott's mouth and grabbed his hair from the back.

He roared in Scott's face. "Tell me the numbers and you can live."

"I don't know what you want. I don't have any numbers." Scott pleaded. "You have the wrong person." The man laid his boot hard against Scott's face, and blood flooded his mouth.

What torture could be next? Pull it together, you've danced with danger before. The only restriction is the rope that binds you. Clear your head and get out of this!

The telephone in Scott's room rang.

"Who's calling you, Mr. Marchand?"

Scott made his best gamble. "My wife expects to hear from me every night. If I don't answer, she'll call the Front Desk and have someone sent up."

The man shouted. "Answer it!"

He stretched the phone line toward Scott but it didn't reach. He slashed the bonds and lifted Scott from the chair.

Scott reached for the receiver, and cracked it on the man's forehead. With a better footing, he elbowed the attacker in the face, knocking him to the ground. He heard a bone snap and was satisfied as blood oozed from the man's mouth.

Scott dragged him to the door. Grasping his collar, he thrust the man solidly with a boot out into the hall. The phone receiver was still engaged and Scott yelled for help. He held a gun on the man.

Two security men arrived in minutes, finding the stunned man propped in the hall.

"This man invaded my room and tied me up, and as you see I have been assaulted. Have him arrested and send a bellman for my luggage to transfer me to another floor."

"You are bleeding, Mr. Marchand. Please permit us to send medical help—you need stitches."

I'll find out who they are and give them back some of their own. No-one but the London boss knows of my mission.

FOURTEEN

Joseph paid the room bill and the Renault was out of the parking lot before 10:00 a.m. en route to Victoria Suites. Engrossed with case details, he didn't see Daniel's black sedan.

Emily said, "We're closing in on Scott, Joseph. What are we going to do when we finally meet?"

"I don't really know, Emily."

He glanced at the mirror and continued. "Eloise paints Scott as a victim doing his job, however the type of work itself speaks to his character. He is a man accustomed to danger."

Emily defended her client. "No, Eloise wouldn't marry a ruthless man."

"Behind us! It's the same car that was parked outside The Red Lion. I'll take a detour to see if he sticks with us."

Daniel dropped back, but never out of Joseph's site. He said, "We should swing by the address you found for Lawrence Winchester, by the south rail yards."

Emily didn't respond.

Joseph tried again. "Remember? The guy with the Land Rover; he supposedly kidnapped Scott?"

Emily laughed and poked him. "Of course I remember. I'll bet it's another wild goose chase."

She unfolded an unwieldy London city map.

"It looks like about a half hour from here, Joseph."

They drove into an industrial area where skeletons of old factories stood in shame. Rundown limestone buildings and dilapidated wooden structures were spaced along the train tracks between a variety of operating c-class businesses and storage facilities. It was difficult to discern an actual address for any of the warehouses.

"Joseph, look!"

He slammed the brakes and made a U-turn toward the back parking lot of an abandoned factory.

He sped toward the parked Rover. "Does the plate match?"

Emily checked her notebook.

"Yup, that's it."

Joseph pulled the Renault into the adjacent lot behind a parked truck. They inched along the outside wall of the suspect building. Looking both ways, Joseph expected to see Daniel's sedan, but it wasn't in his sight.

He whispered. "I don't see security cameras but these days the digital ones are so minute, we can't take chances."

They mounted a set of rickety wooden steps to a back entrance. Joseph held his hand up, to listen for any sound of inside activity. He looked at Emily and nodded.

The door handle gave immediately. Joseph eased it slowly and they wedged themselves through the doorway.

"Have your revolver, Joseph?" Emily mouthed the words softly.

He didn't reply but patted his holster.

Their eyes adjusted to the darkness, and from the floor above, they heard muffled voices in a heated discussion.

"Two of them," Joseph whispered, fingers in the air.

He led the way along the hall, creeping close to the wall so the weight of their feet wouldn't creak the floorboards.

Joseph was mistaken, there weren't two men—there were three.

The third had been alerted to their presence and skulked up behind Emily. Joseph raised his hands over his head in surrender not wanting to place her in danger.

The third man was Robert Dillon, who had a nasty encounter with Scott on the streets of London. Recovered from the injection and an overnight in the drunk tank, he landed at the warehouse as Joseph and Emily squeezed through the back door.

He held Emily's upper arm and shoved her up the stairs with a gun to her head. Joseph walked in front, his hands still high.

"Look fellows! We have company."

The room was barren with only a few wooden chairs and a fold-out table. Garbage from decomposed take-out containers littered the floor with a rotting stench.

Joseph signaled with his head to Emily to try to back up and stay close to the door. She knew her man, already responding before the signal.

Sizing up the thugs, she assumed the only one with a gun was the man behind her. Emily swung her leg around in a flash, hitting her captor solidly on the neck, immobilizing him. His gun fell to the floor.

As they fled for the door, Joseph flung a wooden chair back toward the men.

The three musketeers scattered to take pursuit but Joseph and Emily were already outside. The dust left a trail as the Renault accelerated from the lot. Daniel's sedan eased out from behind a rail boxcar.

Robert Dillon rubbed his neck and dialed a London number to tattle on the pair.

"You sure whipped that poor chap at the warehouse. You must have a good teacher." Joseph was beaming at Emily's karate chop and spunk.

"Yep, trained by the best."

Randy was alone behind the desk at the Victoria Suites and raised his head in surprise.

"Good day, Mr. Harkness. I didn't know we were expecting you back today. Let me check your reservation."

"No need to check, Randy. Just book us in the last room Scott Marchand occupied." Joseph was insistent.

"Mr. Marchand returned a few days ago. He was in 409. Let me see if that room is available."

Emily spoke up. "Just one night."

Randy looked disapprovingly at her.

"Randy, this is my wife Emily. She flew in from Paris to spend a few days helping me to find Mr. Marchand.'"

"Of course, pleased to meet you Mrs. Harkness." Randy's demeanor softened.

Joseph pressed a twenty pound note on the counter.

"I need more information, Randy."

"Mr. Marchand is a fine gentleman and I don't wish to get him into any trouble."

Randy hesitated and leaned forward. "He tackled an intruder trying to break into his room and used the hotel's medical assistance. His face was badly bruised. Unfortunately, the muggers escaped, but the manager is still upset about the incident."

"Randy, don't you realize the man you described with the scarred eye kidnapped him?"

Joseph's impatience was thin and showing.

"Where did Mr. Marchand go and where is he now?"

"I was surprised to see him return, he needed his luggage."

Randy was reluctant to say more than needed and Joseph pushed harder.

"Randy, you're not telling me everything! What else?" His voice was firm and Emily was impressed with his style.

"He did ask the concierge about theater plays."

"When was that?"

Randy's voice wobbled.

"The day before yesterday. I was given an envelope to leave under his door."

Emily prodded, "Do you know where he went after that?"

"Mr. Marchand went to his room. I never saw him after that."

Joseph automatically picked up a complimentary copy of The London News tucking it under his arm; then tossed it on the bed when they arrived at their room.

Taking a second glance at the front page, Joseph called to Emily.

"Look, Babe. This article—there's something disturbing about it. It sounds like a deliberate attempt on someone's life. This has the mark of a mobster."

CAR BOMB LEAVES KENSINGTON FAMILY DEVASTATED
Wesley, the son of Winston Metcalf a known financier in London's business district, was killed yesterday when he turned the ignition of his Audi. Wesley was a university

student returning home for the weekend. The car was parked curbside in front of the Metcalf home and appears to be a marked target. No-one else was at home at the time of the explosion. The family refused comment.

If anyone saw anything suspicious in front of the Metcalf's palatial home in Kensington, please call your local police department. A homicide investigation has extended to Italian sources.

Metcalf was livid when his cell phone rang. At this point, he couldn't avoid picking it up.

"Metcalf here."

"That's just the first bullet. Too bad you didn't pay up on time. You could have saved your son." The gruff voice waited for Metcalf's reaction, then laughed at his silence.

Metcalf's forehead was wet with perspiration.

"I don't know anything about your man being robbed coming out of The Digs; I gave him $100,000 in cash I swear. I'll get you the money again, I need a few more days. I will be coming into possession of a quantity of diamonds. The Amsterdam museum has declared them to be of the highest quality large stones. They'll clear my debt."

"Friday, bring the diamonds."

Metcalf put his hand on his aching head. "I'll meet with you at 'The Digs' at 4:00 p.m."

FIFTEEN

Scott unlocked his tablet and tapped in the numerical groupings: 173 from the Abbey; 69 from the Adventure Park.

An idea hit him and he dug for the Windsor station ticket.

I knew it had to mean something. Do they think I'm an idiot?

He was dressed in a fine charcoal grey suit with a blue and gold striped tie, and had purchased a tube of concealer at the pharmacy to shield his bruises.

He told the driver to stop the taxi in front of the queue at St. Martin's Theater. Standing outside, Scott noticed people with message boards near the box office.

A taxi driver held an orange placard 'Marchand'. He was surprised but approached the man.

The driver pulled a reserved ticket from his pocket.

"Who gave you this?" Scott demanded.

"I don't ask questions when I am paid to be quiet. He was a gentlemen, that's all I can tell you." The cabbie turned and walked away.

Curtain call was 7:00 p.m. and Scott gambled he'd have time for a flute of champagne. The mezzanine was full of chic gowns and the occasional tuxedo, airing an old fashioned opulence for public viewing.

Most of the crowd came in pairs or quads. Inevitably, they rallied in front of the serving bar and didn't budge.

"If only they could see themselves, they all look like peacocks," Scott muttered.

The ten minute curtain announcement came before he got his champagne. He pursed his lips; he'd get it at intermission.

Taking the carpeted staircase to the second balcony, he met with an usher waiting at the door who took him to his seat, second from the aisle in the first row. The aisle seat remained empty through the first half and it occurred to him the owner might have been late and prohibited from entering until intermission. The play caught his imagination and he engrossed himself in trying to identify the murderer. Intermission came quickly.

Scott lined up for a flute of champagne and a dish of ice cream. A tall man in a dark business suit and round gold-rimmed glasses approached him for subtle conversation.

"Enjoying he play?" the stranger asked. Metcalf was over-confident knowing Scott had never met him face to face.

"Yes, exhilarating." Scott was succinct not wanting to be pulled in by the stranger.

"Ah, here's your champagne, Sir. Please allow me to pay. I insist." Metcalf reached over to the bartender and deposited enough to pay for both orders. As he pulled back he took Scott's champagne flute by the stem and with his other hand he tapped in a white substance.

"Thank you, Sir. The bell has rung for the end of intermission." Scott avoided giving his name. The first sip was bitter and he left his glass on one of the cocktail tables before returning to his seat. Metcalf departed down the staircase to a waiting vehicle.

As the lights lowered, a gentleman appeared, with a silk top hat and a houndstooth coat over his arm. He looked at Scott and eased into the aisle seat.

Scott was polite. "Hello. Too bad you missed the first half. It really is an excellent play." His vision was becoming fuzzy, and his senses incoherent.

Turning to face Scott, the man spoke slowly in a low voice. "I'm glad you are enjoying the play."

His eyes burrowed into Scott as he spoke. Scott didn't speak but shifted in his seat.

The man continued, "Remember we must all pay the consequences of our actions!"

As the intermission doors closed, the gentleman stood and placed an envelope onto Scott's lap. A sliver of light disappeared as the exit door closed quietly behind him.

The sequence slammed Scott but he was too limp to react.

I'm like a mark; have I just been played?

The second half began, but Scott was oblivious to Monkswell Manor. The dark eyes of the stranger had invoked fear and intimidation that Scott couldn't shake. He fought hard to overcome his disorientation.

Scott's fist clenched the sealed envelope without yielding to temptation, and sweat formed over his brow.

Daniel straightened his top hat as he returned to the street alarmed at the extent of Scott's bruising.

At his hotel, Scott opened the program letting the envelope fall on the bed. He read the clue twice, then the second slip's number sequence.

Flawless clarity; Van Gogh's diamond museum

13 03 17 21 01 09 04

The highest number is lucky twenty-one. The entire number is too long for a lottery ticket or a vault number. I'll download a code breaker and see what I get.

He searched the web for any correlation between Van Gogh's works to a diamond museum. The Netherlands came up on top, at the Hermitage in Amsterdam, the location of the Van Gogh Museum. Then Van Gogh's 'Starry Night' in the Diamond Museum, between the Rijksmuseum and the Van Gogh.

He jotted notes about the diamond industry in South Africa. Gold and diamond mines in the 1800's had eventually fallen under the management of the Netherlands and European magnates, with regulations enforced to control distribution within and outside South Africa.

He booked a morning flight to Amsterdam.

Two men arrived at his hotel at 5:00 a.m. They stood outside watching for him, both smoking like rabbits.

At 6:15 a.m., Scott's taxi picked him up for Heathrow. Metcalf's men followed in their rental.

SIXTEEN

Emily was barely in bed when her phone buzzed with Joseph texting her Scott's latest clue. She pulled the comforter to her chin, but couldn't close her eyes as she entertained the possibilities of the words.

'Monkswell Manor' reverberated in her thoughts as she mouthed the words.

She sat up and turned on the lamp, then the iPad.

"I knew it was familiar—Agatha Christie's famous play Mousetrap."

She started to dial Joseph in London, but chose to let him have a night's rest instead.

When his cell rang at 6:30 a.m., Joseph kept his eyes closed as he fumbled on the night stand. Moments later Emily called. She was alert and laughed at his voice.

"Sleepyhead, wake up! I figured out the last clue."

He rolled over. "Well, spill it then, Babe."

"It's Agatha Christie's whodunit, Mousetrap at Monkswell Manor. It's playing at St. Martins Theater. That's where he got the last clue."

"Funny Randy didn't tell us about that."

"Did you get the final clue from his room?"

"Em, it was taped on Scott's drawer. We can go straight to Amsterdam."

Joseph read out the number sequence and the final puzzle piece for Emily to research.

Walking into the detective agency at 8 a.m., Emily collected the envelopes pushed through the mail slot, pulling out one that looked more important. It was on the letterhead of a Paris law firm. She slit it open.

> To Whom It May Concern,
>
> We have been instructed by the estate of Benjamin Tessier to locate his grandson, the said Mathias Tessier, heir to a modest fortune. The beneficiary of the estate, Mr. Tessier, was last seen in Paris approximately one year ago.
>
> If your firm is interested, please call at your earliest convenience to discuss fees and relevant information.
>
> Yours truly,
> Vincent Baynes
> Chartrand & Baynes, Barristers

Emily dialed the number and asked for Mr. Baynes. The receptionist was expecting her call and put it through directly.

"Hello, Mr. Baynes. My name is Emily Harkness, I'm a partner at the Harkness Detective Agency." She hoped her nervousness didn't reflect in her voice.

"Yes, Yes. Thank you for getting back to us."

"You forwarded a request for our services to locate Mr. Mathias Tessier. We are interested in the case."

"There is a time factor involved in locating the heir. If you are able to visit at our offices at the earliest, I can give you a dossier."

"Certainly, Mr. Baynes, I can meet at your convenience."

"Tomorrow morning at 10 a.m.? Will that suit you? I'll prepare a check for the initial deposit against your retainer of 3,000 euros. Will that be agreeable with you?"

"That will be fine. I'll bring a service contract with me. I look forward to meeting with you." Emily was polite and gracious.

Confident about Scott's impending return to Paris, Eloise had a skip in her step. The sun was shining on rue Euler and the spring tulips were pushing through the flower beds and window boxes.

At the corner of rue de Bassano and rue Euler, the smell of an aromatic coffee bar enticed Eloise in for two French vanilla bean lattes. Her hands were full with the take out cups, but she managed a tap on the agency door with her knuckle.

She called out. "Hello, Emily. How are you today?"

"It's so nice to see you, Eloise."

Emily rose and extended her hand, and Eloise leaned to an awkward embrace.

"Thank you for the coffee; that will hit the spot."

"I owe you one for the first day when I came in and you were so nice to me." They both laughed stiffly and Eloise felt she had cleaned the slate.

Emily motioned to the chair. "Have a seat, please."

"I got another letter from Scott. I need you to look at it.'

Emily opened the envelope.

"You'll see the postmark is still London—two days ago. There's no mention of his mission, just small talk about London. He says he'll return to Paris in a matter of days.

"This is good news, Eloise. Joseph is only a day behind Scott; they should meet up soon."

"That will be such a relief."

Eloise pulled her handbag onto her lap bringing out her checkbook.

"I know you have been accumulating expenses, so I have another payment for you. Will 2,500 euros be sufficient for now?"

"That is fine, Eloise. I'll write up a receipt for you." Emily took a leather bound ledger from her drawer.

Is it the tone of Eloise's voice? Is she too specific about the letter and its postmark?

Eloise left the office, satisfied with their brief visit, and Emily phoned Joseph to advise him of the developments.

"Joseph, I'm not sure where to start with my research." He pulled out his notebook.

"Go ahead, Em."

"There is a museum housing a loan of Van Gogh's works including 'Starry Starry Night'; it's close to the Diamond Museum in Amsterdam."

He laughed. "I'll get a flight as soon as possible."

"I'm a step ahead. There's a flight at 1:00 p.m. Heathrow to Amsterdam; if it's okay I'll book it. Also, Eloise brought in another letter from Scott sent two days ago from London."

"Good, that means I'm closing the gap."

"One more thing, Joseph. We received a letter requesting our services in locating an estate beneficiary. I'll meet with the lawyer tomorrow morning. They will pay us a retainer. I won't know until I have read the file, but we should be able to sew it up fairly quickly."

"You are amazing! Sorry I'm not there to help you."

Entering the downtown executive suite of Winston Metcalf, Robert Dillon was remorseful for allowing Scott to achieve the upper hand on the way to the Windsor tube.

Winston was enraged and tense at the sight of Dillon. "I can't afford mistakes; you can't allow Marchand to estimate your moves!"

"Yes, Sir. Marchand won't outsmart me again. I paid off a valet at the Victoria Suites about where he was headed. It's to Amsterdam, and I'll take one of the guys with me. I understand the stakes are extreme and time is a restraint."

Dillon rose from his chair and hesitated. "Sir, my condolences about your son. I can't imagine losing a son."

Metcalf was taken off guard by Dillon's empathy and regrouped his emotions. He softened, then stiffened up again quickly.

"Just take care of business!"

SEVENTEEN

Scott's taxi picked him up three hours before the Heathrow departure to Amsterdam.

From the cab, he booked the Renaissance Hotel on Kattingat One in the Centrum district. It was close to the Amstel Canal that wends its way through the city, near the Anne Frank House.

Scott googled for tourist suggestions, flipping past the art festivals, parades, galleries and museums. He slowed to glance at local discotheques, and moved on to the Van Gogh exhibit.

At ten past noon he arrived at the elegant hotel lobby buzzing with business traffic. He scanned each corner on his way to reception; his check-in was efficient.

Scott deflected the bellman, preferring to take his own luggage. His attention was drawn to a brochure at the Concierge Desk, featuring the diamond museum.

Scott hung up his suit and called down to arrange laundry and pressing. Changing into jeans, a grey T and a leather bomber jacket, topped with a British charcoal tweed flat cap. He opened the map on his phone and left to find the street Paulus Potterstraat.

The admission desk was near the door. He observed the lobby ceiling, the doors, security guards and the meandering tourists. A guard was posted at the doorway to each floor hallway, and he knew security cameras would monitor his steps. Momentarily it became claustrophobic.

Taking the staircase to the second floor, Scott strolled between the glass display cases. Stopping at each one to admire the clarity of yellow, pink and sparkling white diamonds, he contemplated their various shapes and sizes.

The museum walls were painted a stark bleached white, a contrast to Van Gogh's brilliant paints.

Japanese tourists clustered behind a museum guide in an area cordoned off with stanchions at the end of the hall. In the center of the melee, a cutter worked at a diamond cutting table, dressed in crisp white overalls and protective goggles. A clear glass case surrounded his workspace.

The demonstration was about to begin, revealing the intricate techniques to sever the larger coarse gem. A second security guard zeroed into position close to the gemologist while he worked on his precision cutting.

Scott inched in for a closer view. He was transfixed by the procedure. No-one had spoken when Scott's voice broke the silence with a simple question.

"If I understand correctly, will each of these diamond chips be graded for clarity?" he asked.

The tour guide looked disgusted that he would interrupt the demonstration.

However, the cutter stopped and pulled his goggles down to take a look at Scott. He pulled out a tray from under the desk, then nodded to a man standing by the window with his arms crossed over his chest.

The man stepped forward and tapped Scott on the elbow.

"Mr. Marchand, I presume?"

Scott was startled to hear his name.

"Yes."

"Stay until the cutting session is complete. And don't make any sudden movements."

Scott felt new eyes on him and turned to look. The man was tall with dark brown eyes, shoulder length hair and a brown fedora.

The cutter's talk was winding to a close. Scott was perspiring in the heat of the lamps and the shadow of the stranger. He took off his bomber jacket, contemplating a move.

"I'm about to hand you a briefcase, Mr. Marchand," Daniel said from behind Scott. "When you leave, take it with you; your instruction will be inside. Your wisdom will tell you not to turn around. You need to put your jacket on now."

Scott heard a click and felt the pressure of a handcuff, attaching his wrist to the briefcase, as the handle was forced into his fingers. Long seconds passed and he silently waited for further instruction.

Where is the key to unlock me?

"Leave through the front entrance right after the Japanese tourists."

Joseph's flight from Heathrow arrived in Amsterdam at 11:30 a.m., too early for check-in. From the airport queue, he took a cab to the Paulus Potterstraat, opposite the Diamond Museum. A café was open, with a view of the museum.

Sitting by the window, Joseph watched the tourist traffic. He didn't know what to expect; likely Scott had already been there and taken the last clue. It was Scott he needed to follow, not the clue.

He carried his coffee to the café door and stepped outside to survey the street. A dark BMW was parked down the street, and Joseph focused on the two men in the front. The windows were rolled down, evicting curls of cigarette smoke. For an hour, the men didn't move.

They must have followed Scott from the airport. He must be in the museum.

A dozen Japanese tourists exited the front entrance to board a tour bus, following a large bearded man with a placard in Japanese Kanji and Kana script. The guide barked orders for his guests to hurry.

Minutes later, Joseph's mission took a new life as Scott Marchand left the building. As if in slow motion, Scott took each step methodically, like he was controlled or monitored. He carried the briefcase, with the handcuff hidden under his sleeve.

The two men in the BMW stiffened as Scott approached the street. Joseph swung his head to see their next move.

The passenger in the front jumped out without slamming the door and pulled a revolver from his belt. Joseph recognized the third man from the abandoned warehouse.

A yellow taxi was letting passengers out on the curb, and Joseph intercepted it. The driver spoke first in Dutch, but soon realized the fear and urgency of his fare.

"Please sir, wait a minute for my friend. I'll pay you generously," Joseph said.

Joseph tossed his satchel in the back seat and sprinted across the street. He drew the glance of the BMW passenger approaching Scott, then caught Scott's attention.

The assailant lengthened his strides and reached Scott first, forcing the gun into his side.

Arriving at the two men, Joseph was now committed. He bullied his way between them and gripped the collar of Scott's leather jacket. With his left hand, he slammed one of the men with a hard chop under his chin with his fist.

"Scott Marchand, I've been hired by your wife. Get in that taxi over there."

Scott looked at Joseph, unsure whether to trust him. Considering the other man had a gun, in the fleeting moment he relied on Joseph with reluctance. It happened fast and the gunman was stunned, unable to defend his prey.

With a swift kick, Joseph sent the assailant's gun flying and the culprit lost his balance. Simultaneously, a pair of armed guards from the museum entered the fray forcing the man to the ground.

The BMW driver jumped from the car to join the foot chase. A gunshot rang out over Scott's head, and another fired from the BMW. Scott flinched with pain in the arm, but got to the waiting taxi. Joseph was right behind.

"Driver, get us out of here as fast as you can! Make sure the BMW doesn't keep up." The driver took a sharp glance at Joseph, smiled and put his foot to the pedal.

"If Eloise has sent you—who are you?" Scott needed quick answers.

"My name is Joseph Harkness, I've been following you and collecting the desk clues you left behind. I'm a private detective from Paris. My wife, Emily, has been keeping in touch with Eloise.

"Your attention to detail is commendable, Scott. I've been collecting your clues since the Abbey. Where are you staying in Amsterdam?"

"I'm already in at the Renaissance Inn."

"We can't go there until we're sure those felons are off our tail. Does anyone know where you're staying?"

Joseph saw the BMW a distance behind and gaining in relentless pursuit. Another black sedan was behind that.

Daniel's there too. Is he helping us?

Joseph cursed under his breath.

Daniel, this is no time to hang in the background. If you're going to muck things up, you owe me a little help.

Joseph said, "Are you armed, Scott?"

"Yes, I keep a revolver in the back of my belt. But it's difficult now that I'm carrying an extra limb." He nodded at the handcuffed briefcase.

"Do you have any idea who tried to intercept you?"

"It's complicated. My courier assignments are anonymous, always with only a minimum of contact. I wouldn't recognize my own boss. I've been fumbling from clue to clue. They never tell me anything in advance."

Scott hesitated and added, "I'm not sure why I should put total faith in a stranger who grabbed me off the streets of Amsterdam."

Joseph ignored the concern.

"The men in the Land Rover at Westminster—did they seem familiar?"

"The man with the scarred eye, yes! I saw him the day before they took me. It was in the hotel lobby; obviously, he was casing me."

Joseph said, "The one man was Lawrence Winchester but I can't find anything on him. We watched the security tapes showing you being shoved into the car, and the license plate gave us the owner."

"Joseph, I appreciate your concern but I'm trained to look after myself."

A thunderous crash hit the back of the taxi, shifting the car. Neither Scott nor Joseph had buckled the taxi seatbelts and the powerful jolt threw them both to the floor.

It was the menacing BMW. The passenger leaned out, firing a hail of gunfire into the back seat. Glass from the back window showered over them, but the bullets appeared to be wayward.

The taxi slowed and slammed into a red phone booth. Joseph realized the bullet had gone right through the back of the front seat striking the driver in the neck.

Crouching below their sight line, Joseph crawled to the driver's window.

"Too late for the cabbie." He muttered with regret. "Ten o'clock!" Joseph screamed to Scott.

They abandoned the cab and took off on foot to a shopping street. The driver of the chase vehicle came after them with his gun raised.

Joseph took a dive at Scott to put him on the ground, and began firing at the stalker.

"You okay, Scott?"

"What's your escape plan, detective?"

Joseph pulled Scott by the arm. "Over there, that canal boat. Fast, because it's about to pass. Can you jump aboard?"

Scott nodded. The two men took off running and landed squarely on the rear end of the cruise boat before it disappeared under the bridge. A final bullet whizzed overhead.

The century old saloon boat had ten cruise passengers, and in spite of the unexpected invasion, the tourists laughed and applauded. The captain at the front continued his script, describing the riverbank sights into a megaphone.

The BMW retreated from the scene, unaware of Daniel's presence.

Daniel stopped and raised his binoculars, observing Scott cradling the briefcase in his arms.

He nodded as he opened the computer app.

The briefcase GPS tracker is secure.

At the Renaissance, Joseph obtained an adjoining room, but joined Scott to discuss their combined strategy.

A manila envelope was taped to the outer side of the briefcase. Scott opened it to remove the letter, and a small key fell to the floor.

Briefcase combination '1 5 9'
"These diamonds are to be delivered to the Swiss Bank to the box identified in the numerical code you have collected."

"How do we know if this is the real thing?" Scott looked at Joseph. He opened the case, and they both stared at the brilliant diamonds.

Joseph asked, "Is there a message about what we do with them?"

Scott was silent. Letting the pebbles run through his fingers, his eyes were crazed in delight. He couldn't take his gaze away from them.

"Come on, Scott. Don't even think about it. Surely the diamonds have been weighed. We don't know for sure if they are genuine."

Joseph reached for the business card in the case. It had an embossed crest on one side, and words on the back:

The key is the solution; he is 'propped' in a dungeon.

Scott smirked, "I guess you'd better wake Emily."

Joseph laughed, a hint that they could become friends.

Scott asked, "Did you intercept the code at the last desk? A long series of numbers?"

He pulled a slip from his pocket. '13 03 17 21 01 09 04.'

"Yes, I got it. Where did that come from?"

"A stranger! A tall dark man at the theater. He came and sat for a few seconds and dropped an envelope in my lap; it's the same number from Scott's desk. He disappeared as quickly as he came. Scared the heck out of me."

Joseph knew it would be Daniel, but kept it to himself.

He said, "I had military training a number of years ago that included code breaking. This looks like a simple one."

"You amaze me, Joseph."

Joseph pulled a pad from the desk and started scratching.

"Let's see. They are all low numeric value. First we exclude all the zeros. The alpha method is the most obvious."

Joseph listed the numbers one to twenty-six, and beside them the letters A to Z.

"Look here, Scott.

"M C Q U A I D." Scott said. "What does that mean?"

They were both silent. "Scott, is the name familiar at all?"

"What if it's the name of the man with the key? If you recall from my first note in the Branly desk, he is 'the solution'."

"Sure. Could be that."

Scott stopped. "By the way, who do you work for?"

"I told you, your wife hired me. Surely you must understand her reasons better than I do."

Scott huffed and turned his attention back to the clues on the bed.

"I haven't thanked you properly for saving my life back at the museum."

"That's my job, Scott. Eloise took care of the retainer fees. When we get back to Paris, that is when my services end and not before. I never quit on a job."

Joseph made eye contact with Scott reaffirming his commitment. His cell phone beeped an incoming text.

"I told you, Scott, my wife is good with puzzles." Joseph handed him the phone to read the message.

"There is a local theatrical attraction called The Amsterdam Dungeon. I'll look up the address."

Scott nodded. "Can we go there today?"

"It's already dark and we have our rooms for tonight. Let's get a decent night's sleep and head there after breakfast."

After Joseph left the room, Scott called for a first aid kit. Removing his jacket in the washroom, he unbuttoned his shirt, partially soaked in blood on his side. A bullet had nicked him when he fled at the diamond museum, but his pride kept him from telling Joseph. Holding a cold compress concocted from the ice machine against his right side, he called reception.

In minutes, a bellman knocked at Scott's room, carrying an unlocked metal case with a red cross on the top.

"Your room has a sample kit with a few bandages, but I've brought you the hotel's emergency medical pack with antiseptic supplies. Leave it outside your door and I'll come by later to collect it."

"Thank you." Scott tipped the boy.

Convincing himself it was a minor flesh wound, he cleaned the gap with stinging antiseptic and removed a particle of shrapnel. He sealed it with antibiotic tape and wrapped a roll of gauze around his chest to secure the dressings.

He took a pain reliever and stayed awake to consider his possible fate.

EIGHTEEN

Metcalf stared out of his office window deep in thought. The mission had fallen behind schedule, creating intense anxiety. His men had lost their marker in Amsterdam, leaving a taxi driver dying on the street. The clean-up crew didn't arrive in time to eradicate clues left by his thugs.

Witness testimony confirmed that the fatal shot was fired from the BMW. The weapons and bullet casings recovered as evidence were secured in custody with the driver and his accomplice. Two male tourists from the taxi fled the scene, but Metcalf had no doubts about who they were.

If Metcalf's recruits could retrieve the package first, he'd feed Scott to the lions. He resented that he'd been kept out of the loop in the diamond scheme.

Metcalf tried not to focus on the pressure and threats from the loan shark.

I'm walking a thin line taking Mugabe's money.

NINETEEN

Joseph eased the Renault through the crooked lane behind the theater on Rokin. At 10:00 a.m., he pulled to a stop behind a dumpster when Scott got out to check the numbers on the row of metal doors against the brick walls.

Scott walked past a few buildings and stopped at the sign, 'The Amsterdam Dungeon'. He signaled to Joseph.

The street was clear, and Joseph joined him at the staff entrance. Scott turned the knob quietly easing the door open. Focused on the door, neither noticed a garbage truck idling near the dumpster at the end of the lane.

Once they disappeared into the Dungeon, Dillon alit from the stolen truck and crept up to the Renault with a square metal box under his arm. He laid it on the ground and removed a device and plastics to affix the unit to the undercarriage.

Inside the back of the theater were racks of costumes and stacks of prop paneling, and behind was a row of vacant dressing rooms. The hall was dark, with only a glimmer of light reflecting from the stage where the cast was rehearsing. To the left, a staircase opened to a hydraulic platform and an overhead catwalk.

Joseph gestured. "My bet is that McQuaid is confined in the basement."

The cellar was a maze of dusty props, shelves of paint, ladders and trunks. Joseph zoned in on a curtained area with filtered light from a grated window.

"Scott, I'll take the curtain—you want the doors?"

Joseph approached the far side of the room, stopping at the sign of a motionless body.

My instincts were right. That must be McQuaid.

On a metal cot, his hands and feet were tied loosely and he looked unshaven for at least three days. Empty pizza boxes and pop cans littered the floor.

"McQuaid!" Joseph whispered as he knelt beside the sleeping victim.

The man's eyes fluttered and opened with a start.

"Who are you?" he faltered.

"My name is Joseph Harkness. My friend and I have come to rescue you. Where are your captors?"

"I haven't seen them today. They are Dutch; a man and a woman."

Scott joined the conversation. "I know who you're talking about. That same pair pistol whipped me for no reason."

The kidnap victim blinked a response. He was weak and slightly incoherent.

"Mr. McQuaid, drink this." Scott held a bottle of water up to his lips.

"My name is Eli."

Scott's mind reverted to the first clue 173, that Joseph had turned upside down, mumbling 'ELI'.

His eyes opened wide with wonderment, puzzled by the arrival of two rescuers.

From the rehearsal area, a voice called out through the curtains of the stage staircase. "Anybody there?"

Scott helped McQuaid toward the exit staircase without drawing attention from the stage. Background music was playing for the actors, and Joseph dragged a costume trunk across the access, as a barrier in event of a chase.

Scott and McQuaid got to the top step when an actor called from the bottom.

"Hold it there, fellas. I can't let you take the old man." Scott looked down and saw the man had raised a gun.

Scott said, "He was being held against his will. Who are you?"

The actor started up, leaping a rung of three steps.

"Go Scott!" Joseph yelled upward. He turned and leaped from midway on the stairs pouncing onto the actor, plummeting them together to the cellar floor. A second man ran from the stage and landed a tackle on Joseph.

"Okay, I give up." Joseph raised his hands to surrender, and over his shoulder, Elijah McQuaid's feet disappeared from the top step.

Easing a few steps forward, Joseph swung his leg upward, knocking the gun from the assailant's hand.

Up the stairs like a jackrabbit, Joseph barred the door from the outside by pulling a dumpster against the edge of the metal door.

"Let's go, Scott! I can't hold them off for long." Joseph hit the remote starter from across the yard as he tossed the keys to Scott.

He heard an ominous thud when his thumb hit the 'start' button and froze.

I've heard that before!

"Scott, hit the ground! It's a BOMB!"

An inferno of heat blasted the theater door shut and the three men on the ground covered with debris. Shards of metal and glass threatened them. The thundering crush of the explosion paralyzed them momentarily.

"Scott, McQuaid, you okay?" Joseph yelled frantically looking through the dust. He'd been spared by the dumpster and heard them coughing from behind a parked Daimler.

Scott hoisted McQuaid to an upright position and together they got to their feet. "These cars are built to withstand a bomb. Just glad we were behind it or we'd both be dead."

Joseph was distracted by the garbage truck waiting at the end of the alley. He recognized one of Metcalf's men from the warehouse. The man watched the scene, but avoided coming to their aid. When Joseph made eye contact, the driver stepped up into the cab and accelerated to the street.

"We need to get out of here before the police arrive. There! That parked Peugeot taxi. Get in!" Joseph scrambled to the hackney. Relieved the door was unlocked, he hotwired under the dashboard.

McQuaid, bleeding from the head, was able to walk to the car with Scott's help, then they covered him in the back for the ride back into Amsterdam. The drone of sirens were closing in around the theater and Joseph maneuvered to the next street.

Scott shouted, "Who did this? We could have been killed!"

Joseph was calm. "You're forgetting, Scott! Metcalf's men are likely to be after you. Not me!"

Scott's adrenaline was high and his volume boomed.

"We need to take McQuaid back to London."

Joseph purported, "But Mr. McQuaid can't travel now. We'll get a room for the three of us and get him fed and watered. We'll ditch the hackney.

Scott was calculating a plan of his own, but nodded. "There's a Hilton and a Sheraton ahead, whichever has room will be fine."

Joseph checked into a suite with two queen beds and a sofa bed. Scott ordered steaks, spring water, juices and coffee from room service.

Elijah was put in a hot shower to bring some life back to him. Although Scott was heavier in build than Elijah, he had clean clothes in his suitcase that would do.

Joseph removed Elijah's bonds, and was puzzled by the lax restraints.

These bonds look like a ruse; perhaps Elijah is in on the scheme.

Sitting on the pullout, McQuaid spoke up, his knowledge returning with surprising speed.

He said to Scott, "I presume you deciphered the safety deposit access code. I never knew what it was, however I do have the key to the box."

Scott stiffened up again. "What do you know about a diamond shipment?"

McQuaid thought for a moment before speaking. "How do I know you are the good guys?"

"My name is Scott Marchand. In this business I don't carry identification. I work for an international courier firm, and was hired to follow these clues to the diamonds."

A knock at the door interrupted them, and they were silent as the server laid out their settings. Joseph and Elijah went ahead with the food, but Scott excused himself.

He took a clean shirt to the bathroom, with his leather jacket still on. He applied fresh dressings to his wound and wrapped his blood-soaked shirt in a towel, then stuffed the plastic bag into his suitcase.

When Scott returned, Elijah started up again. "You'd find out sooner or later, so I might as well tell you. I worked for a consolidated South African diamond mine owner, one of the world's largest producers. I helped myself to some uncut diamonds and replaced them with superb fakes. I didn't think they'd miss a few."

"Do you know where the genuine diamonds are?" Scott demanded.

Elijah looked down. "In the vault."

Scott knew he was losing control and shouted across the table. "I've been chasing puzzles and clues for ten days all leading to the diamonds in the safety deposit box. In *your* name!"

Elijah couldn't tell the truth without implicating himself. He wouldn't look Scott in the eye and his twitch was visible to the others.

"I made it to the diamond cutter here in Amsterdam before they were on to me. Mugabe's will kill me once he gets the diamonds back."

"What happens now that we have located you?" Scott persisted.

"My little key is all I have to save myself."

Elijah paused in thought, then fumbled in his pocket instinctively feeling for the key. "Now that you have both the key and the code, you can go to the Swiss Bank in downtown Amsterdam without me."

Joseph snickered.

Scott's cell vibrated. It was Christine, Metcalf's executive assistant. He opened his notebook to write his new instructions.

She said, "Bring McQuaid to London for three o'clock tomorrow. Metcalf's office."

The call was over in seconds, and Scott looked up at McQuaid's pale face. "There isn't much 'later' for you. We're instructed to have you in London tomorrow afternoon."

Elijah's eyes bulged in fear.

"No, I can't go to London. They'll kill me."

"The South African diamond mine owner has a merciless reputation to get even when he's been wronged. It's suicide for me to go."

Scott said, "Look here McQuaid, we've put our lives on the line to save you. We are all in the same pickle and you will be going to London with us."

Joseph asked, "When we found you, your bonds were plenty loose. You could have slipped out. Were we set up?"

"No . . ." Elijah stared at the carpet.

Joseph added, "Say your prayers if you need to. God will forgive you for your sins, but I doubt the South African will."

McQuaid stood to use the washroom, but instead thrust himself toward Scott's pistol holster on the bed. Joseph's knee-jerk reaction had Elijah by the ankles, sprawling him on his face.

"Answers, McQuaid!" Joseph gripped Elijah's shirt by the collar with both hands. He slapped Elijah on the back of the head, and threw him to the back of his chair.

"You're not a gracious guest, Mr. McQuaid. We've extended our hospitality and saved your life."

Joseph yanked him to his feet and handcuffed him to the leg of a heavy TV console. "And this is the thanks we get?"

"Please, I beg of you. Let me go."

With every word that McQuaid spoke, Joseph's anger grew.

"You are a selfish and greedy man. Do you expect us to sacrifice ourselves on your behalf?"

"No." McQuaid fell sullen, but still wriggled to try to escape the cuffs.

"Marchand, you were always part of the mad scheme. I hired your organization to set the clues."

Scott scowled at the outburst.

"It was all done over the phone and I'm sure Metcalf sold me out." Elijah insisted.

Scott's forehead pulsed. "Did you have to drag me all over London and then to Amsterdam?"

"It had to be that way. Several times the South African people were getting close and I had to throw them off. The only person who'd know the code for the bank would be the courier after collecting the clues.

"At the diamond museum, the kidnappers found me. I suspected it was a stake-out." Elijah stopped.

"We've got the key, ELI." Joseph tried the name from the code and received the predicted flick of his head.

Yes, I'm sure that is it. Not 173. Too soon to rule that out yet.

Scott said, "Elijah, we're *all* going to the Swiss Bank in downtown Amsterdam. We have to get there before closing if we want to get to London for the meeting tomorrow."

"C'mon pal, let's go for a ride." Joseph took Elijah by the elbow, with Scott following close behind. The concierge had arranged their car rental to be at the door.

TWENTY

Elijah, Joseph and Scott stood in the shadow, facing the ominous fortress of the Swiss Bank. The rental was parked close by.

Scott gripped the briefcase. "I'm ready."

Joseph nodded.

Entering through grand double brass doors into the sanctuary, they were greeted by fifteen foot ceilings, marble floors and mahogany counters. Security cameras followed them through the foyer.

Instinctively Joseph looked back to survey the street and reflections in the glass. There it was, the black sedan.

Daniel's like a hawk watching our actions.

The trio approached Customer Service in the center of the floor, and Scott asked, "Where's the safety deposit room?"

The woman motioned to the right. "Follow over to the desk in the far corner and someone there will assist you."

Scott thanked her and looked back at her over his shoulder. She turned her head to avoid him when he took a second glance.

Is that the Dutch woman who was in my room? There's a similarity. This doesn't feel right.

Scott shook it off and signed the ledger, then entered his electronic pass code on a hand held unit.

He punched in '6983', the first four numbers of the McQuaid code to engage the green light and sighed in relief. It was roulette choosing the correct variation.

The attendant led them into the vault. The bank's key and Elijah's key were inserted into the end of a long box No. 173.

Left alone in privacy, Joseph knew they'd be watched on security monitors. Checking the two cameras in the corner of the ceiling, the lens eye moved at his slightest motion.

Scott slid out the tray, released the lock and raised the lid. Four black velvet pouches with gold braid were laid alongside a sealed envelope. Joseph leaned over the tray to inhibit viewers.

Scott and Elijah each opened two pouches and tapped out the contents into four separate piles, shielded from the cameras by the empty box. The magnificent display of white, blue and pink polished diamonds was breathtaking.

"Who do they belong to?" Scott marveled.

"That doesn't really concern us; we follow the instructions to deposit the briefcase diamonds. Look, there's another key inside." Joseph said.

Elijah picked it up and held it close to his eyes.

"The number of another box." He knelt on one knee. "It's right below."

He fidgeted with the key while Joseph pulled a pickpocket pouch from his jeans. Poking a long wire through the key lock until the key inserted. The tray was wider, deeper and heavier.

Elijah drew it out and placed it beside the one on the table. He removed the first bag, a large black leather pouch of US currency in hundred dollar bills, placing two large fistfuls of bound bills on the table. Daniel had been discreet in recovering Metcalf's payments in the back lot of The Digs.

"Looks like hundreds of thousands of dollars." Scott said.

Elijah then lifted a locked zippered pouch that felt like diamonds.

"Here, Scott, you should open the envelope. It's addressed to you."

Scott took the ivory envelope and broke the wax seal with his pen. He read the message silently.

The polished diamonds will pay for your soul; place the diamonds from the briefcase in the lower box. Take the diamonds from the upper box and place them in the black pouch. Both keys will be given to the shoe-shine man. You will leave the bank empty-handed.

Scott made the exchange, placing the sparkling diamonds Daniel had provided in the briefcase, into the lower box. Another batch of fake diamonds went into the upper box for Mugabe.

Taking custody of the money bag, Scott, unnoticed, slipped ten diamonds into his pocket and placed the keys in another.

Elijah warned them, "Gentlemen, this isn't over! You're not the only people wanting the diamonds." His voice shook. "That kind of greed has few morals. We are the black ball in a billiard game."

Scott looked at them both. "Joseph and Elijah, I must ask the obvious question. Aren't you tempted to keep a few diamonds for yourself? We'll never see the likes of this again."

Joseph answered for himself. "None whatsoever. Whatever has gone on with stolen diamonds has drawn out a group of sinister characters. I don't wish to play games with those people. If we gave them any cause to be suspicious, it would take only one shot. I don't want a few pretty stones to pay for my soul."

Scott said, "I guess I've been in the underworld too long. I admit I'm facing tremendous temptation. Good thing I have you along to keep me on the straight and narrow."

Although Scott verbally relinquished defeat, he lingered behind momentarily.

"It's time to get out of here." Joseph warned.

"Do you have an escape plan, Joseph?"

"The car isn't parked far from the front door." Joseph answered, "But we're not finished with the clue."

A homeless man sat inside the front door holding a shoe-shine box. A worn hat was over his face leaving a tell-tale beard; he had dark eyes that could burrow into a man's confessions.

At his sight, Joseph knew it was part of the clue and stopped abruptly. "Excuse me, Sir. What's the cost of a shine?"

Elijah McQuaid saw his opportunity to shuffle away, but the strong arm of Scott yanked him back.

The shoe-shine man had a magnetic presence. He sat up with his arms over his lap, purposely showing a revolver to the men.

"The black pouch and the keys!"

He reached up and pulled Joseph's collar down so he could whisper in his ear.

"Joseph, get yourself out of this cavorting with thieves; you are complicating matters. Scotland Yard is co-operating with this undercover situation and won't be far behind."

Joseph was aghast and tried not to show his alarm to his comrades. He stared into the face of a ghost.

Turning to Scott, he demanded. "Give him the pouch. It is our instruction . . . people in the bank are beginning to stare. The last thing you need now are security guards."

Joseph couldn't shake the feeling of deception and the haunting of the face. The disguise was clever but he knew.

Daniel! Ha, my faithful guardian.

Scott gave the pouch to the man. At the same time, he smugly patted his left coat pocket. It was out of the sight of his partners, but Daniel saw it.

Daniel stood up and cautioned them, "I'll be leaving now. Stay in the bank until I'm gone. Daniel's sedan was parked across the street. He got up and gathered his office and shuffled outside, through the traffic and to his car.

As Daniel buckled to leave, a silver Mercedes caught his eye, parked two cars ahead. The driver's binoculars were trained on the door, and his accomplice leaned on the wall of the bank smoking a cigarette.

Daniel muttered out loud, "They must be Metcalf's men. I'll have to wait this out."

The man with the cigarette walked quickly toward the entrance.

Still inside, Joseph motioned to the others. The trio fell in behind a pair of businessmen striding toward the revolving doors, crowding close for cover. As they emerged from the revolving door, Joseph bolted for the driver's side of the rental, with Scott close behind dragging Elijah upright.

Within a few feet, Scott was jostled as one of the indignant businessmen was shoved by the cigarette man, waving a pistol in the air. Two security officers at the door rushed to apprehend the gunman as Scott and Elijah pushed through the crowd.

Joseph's entourage sprinted to the car, and as they ran, Scott shouted, "Joseph, it's the two men from the diamond museum."

Joseph said, "We are not as careful as we thought. Maybe they're tracking one of us."

He squealed onto the street, and the Mercedes U-turned in pursuit. As they passed the bank, Scott focused on the commotion.

Someone posted bail for these men. Someone with pull and money.

The Mercedes closed in on them, now inches behind. The driver held his gun outside the window waiting for the right shot.

With a single car break in traffic, Joseph yanked the wheel to the left and spun his rental across the other lane. An oncoming car hit his rear bumper, but Joseph raced on down toward the canal. The Mercedes turned left at the next corner and cruised the streets, but Joseph eluded him.

Joseph made sure they didn't have a tail, before returning back to the Renaissance.

At the hotel, with Elijah cuffed to the TV console, Joseph signaled Scott to come and talk out of earshot.

Joseph said, "I don't trust him, so we'll take turns watching him tonight. Tomorrow will be another challenge. He won't yield; any chance he sees, he could make a break."

"Once we get to London, Joseph, you're free to go your way and stay out of danger. It's my mission and I should take the heat."

"Scott, I promised Eloise I'd bring you home. That means shadowing you wherever you go. Sorry, pal, you're stuck with me."

"Have it your way. Why don't you get some shuteye and I'll watch the thief during the first watch. I'll wake you when it's your turn."

Scott poured nightcaps from the minibar for Joseph and himself while they watched the late news.

"I could do with one over here." McQuaid quipped.

"Sorry, Elijah you haven't been a good boy."

In minutes, Joseph's eyes became exhausted and heavy. He crawled into bed leaving Scott up watching TV and Elijah laying on the floor anchored securely.

Joseph attempted to sort his thoughts for the morning flight but his head started swimming. It was too late when he realized what had happened, and the last thing he saw was a hazy vision of Scott looking into his face.

Scott was satisfied Joseph was unconscious on the bed. He felt a pang of guilt but not enough to have stopped him.

"McQuaid, if you want your freedom, you'll do exactly as I say. Don't expect for one minute you can escape.

"We're being watched by people willing to kill you. It's not over yet. Understand?" Elijah traded threats.

"We'll return to London as planned, on the 7:45 a.m. BA flight to Heathrow. An hour of travel time and one hour time change. I have your passport; it was in the safety deposit box in Amsterdam."

Elijah asked, "Do you have a spare jacket? It's been chilly and grey since yesterday."

Scott rifled into his case. He had no choice other than the bomber jacket with the bullet hole.

"This will fit you, but if anyone asks about the hole in the side, don't say anything."

"Are you going to tell *me* about it?" McQuaid asked.

"There's no reason you should know."

Scott was used to working solo, without responsibility for a partner or cargo. Today was going to be a stretch of planning and patience.

"Okay, let's go."

As they waited outside the hotel in the dark for a taxi to Schiphol airport, McQuaid's eyes yearned for an opportunity to make a break. Scott knew what he was dealing with.

"Elijah, to remind you, I'm not your friend; simply a courier. My instructions are to escort you to London. My leg holster with a pistol is just an arm's length reach. Dead or alive, I will still get paid."

Elijah's rolled his eyes, the elongated warning didn't register or carry any weight.

Scott knew McQuaid was not sharp enough to figure out that the pistol would have to go through checked luggage or security alarms would come down on him like a tiger's cage.

"I get it," McQuaid huffed, pleased with his deception.

At 6:00 a.m. the alarm rang and Joseph forced his eyes open, challenging consciousness. Looking across the room with one eye, he realized the worst. Scott had drugged his nightcap. The other bed hadn't been slept in, and they were both gone.

They have at least six hours head start.

Joseph jumped up to dress and phoned Emily to explain the conspiracy of events. She was concerned for his safety but didn't want to alarm him more with her own fear.

"Emily, book me at 8:00 a.m. out of Amsterdam to Heathrow. Is there any way to check if Scott made reservations for two? They will have to use their real names to match their passports."

"I'll text you with a confirmation on your flight. But the reservation for Scott might be impossible with privacy policies. I'll see what I can do."

"If anyone can perform magic, it's you, Babe. Love you."

"I'll be awfully glad when this is over, Joseph."

The morning traffic slowed him down, but he was still at Schiphol in thirty minutes. Scouring the gates, he didn't see Scott or McQuaid. He called Emily again for any news.

"Hey, Babe," she said. "Are you feeling better? You just missed Scott and McQuaid; they took a flight out of Amsterdam forty-five minutes ago, so you're not far behind."

"Thanks, Em. When I catch up with Scott, he has a lot of explaining to do. I thought we had a trust relationship. Thanks for packing the Tylenol. How are things in Paris?"

"I'm glad you asked. It's been a struggle. I was presumptive to think this case would be a cinch."

"One or two days in London at the outside, Babe. Can't wait to see you." Joseph said.

"I can hear your boarding announcement in the background. Better get going. Love you."

Joseph's eight o'clock departure was on time. At the Heathrow rental counter, he asked for directions to Metcalf's tower. The clerk marked the route on his map.

Morning rush hour was over and he made good time in the rented Range Rover. There weren't spots to park on the street and he circled the block. The second time past, a Porsche edged out of a space on the opposite curb, and Joseph squealed up behind.

Scott had remained at Elijah's elbow from Schiphol's entrance, through security screening and to the departure lounge. At Heathrow, he opted for a car rental.

It will be best for a quick departure.

The two men drove in silence into London. Parking was at a premium in the area, leaving no alternative but to park underground. Driving down two levels, he chose a spot close to the elevator.

McQuaid was starting to show panic, fearing his consequences. He'd need to account for the theft of the diamonds and make restitution to the South African mine owner. The three of them had been too trusting, and Joseph second-guessed their judgment in giving a bag of cash and diamonds to the shoe-shine man.

"Elijah, is there anything I should know before we go to the meeting? The quickest way to get into trouble is to start telling lies. Anything to say for yourself?"

"I abused a position of trust and stole the diamonds replacing them with fakes. The genuine gems were cut and polished at the Amsterdam diamond factory.

"I hoped the return of the diamonds would bargain my freedom. But here we are. I don't know what more you want from me, Mr. Marchand."

Scott didn't reply to McQuaid. He had a dreaded sensation himself since learning of the reputation of Mr. Mugabe. He hadn't told Joseph of the ten five-carat diamonds he'd taken in the Amsterdam vault, the ones sewn into his jacket.

If the shortfall were discovered and they bothered to weigh or count the gems, reasonable suspicion would fall on McQuaid, the original thief. Certainly, a man of Mugabe's reputation will not be lax in his accounts.

TWENTY-ONE

Emily arrived at the offices of Chartrand & Baynes near the Champs-Élysées. The morning was clear and she enjoyed the few blocks of fresh air to the lawyer's building.

Stepping off the elevator, she stopped at the glass wall etched with the impressive etching of the firm's logo.

The heavy door yielded and the plush carpet slowed her step toward the counter's three receptionists. Emily reached her business card to the first one.

"Hello, I am Emily Harkness. I have an appointment with Vincent Baynes."

The woman reached for Emily's card and left her desk without speaking. She disappeared into an office and was back quickly.

Her voice was stern. "Have a seat."

Emily hoped Mr. Baynes would be more pleasant. Her first impression of the law firm was disconcerting. Fifteen minutes later, an apologetic Baynes entered the foyer.

"I'm so sorry, Ms. Harkness . . . I was on a long-distance call. I hope my staff made you comfortable."

He led her down a corridor to his corner office suite, adorned with elegant furnishings and walls of glass. It reeked of success and reminded her of the law firms back in Albany.

Emily took a chair at a round boardroom table at one end. Vincent Baynes laid out the papers and a file for review.

"Thank you for coming, Emily. We don't normally take on such cases due to the amount of leg work. In spite of having our own research staff, we don't have detectives on board."

"We appreciate being considered, Mr. Baynes."

"Well then, to the business at hand. As I stated in the letter, we need to locate a beneficiary by the name of Mathias Tessier."

He removed an eight by ten glossy from the file.

"Here is a photograph taken a few years ago. You're welcome to contact a family representative who is willing to answer your questions. We didn't query Mathias's occupation, finances, friends and habits—that will be for you. Here is the business card of the aunt."

Emily examined the picture of Mathias; he wasn't familiar. She was concerned about the broad scope and wrote notes as Baynes spoke.

"I assume the missing beneficiary is a resident of Paris, or at least France?"

"As far as we know, yes. Of course, if any travel is required, we'll reimburse your expenses. There is a time urgency clause in the Will. If Mathias can't be located in thirty days, the provision in the Will defers the property and possessions to one of the cousins."

Baynes passed her a copy of Benjamin Tessier's Will.

"Is the cousin, by chance, related to the aunt you mentioned?"

Vincent Baynes suddenly looked like a fool.

"Well, I hadn't thought about that. I guess this makes the case more complicated."

"It looks that way, Mr. Baynes."

"I'll give you the rest of the file to mull through. Mark whatever you'd like copied and my assistant will take care of it. I have another meeting, so take your time. I'll expect to hear from you in a few days."

Baynes stood and went to gather papers on his desk to prepare for his next appointment, continuing to talk from across the room.

"My assistant has a check for the retainer we discussed."

"Thank you for your time, Mr. Baynes."

She was half out of her chair with the intention of offering a handshake but he was quickly out the door. She thought about his behavior, that he'd been coy in not answering about the cousin's relationship to the aunt.

Emily remained at the table perusing the information. In spite of the poor quality of the data, she tagged numerous pages, then left to the outer office where a clerk was waiting to make copies.

Ten minutes later, Vincent Baynes returned to his office. Picking up the phone he called a private number in London, to Winston Metcalf.

"It's been set in motion. I'll keep my thumb on the Harkness woman."

Metcalf said, "You're aware I have a personal and financial interest in defending Verona Charbonneau."

Vincent was still listening when the line went dead.

Winston's greed and revenge against the Italian mob was paramount in his thoughts. Considering all sources of financial assistance, he counted on Verona's portion of the inheritance to pay the loan sharks.

Metcalf picked up the phone to make an appointment with his loan banker.

Keeping his options open, Winston Metcalf was also aware of Joseph's tail on Scott Marchand. If necessary, he could deter Joseph by using Emily Harkness; alive or dead, it didn't matter to him, he had suffered enough.

He looked down at a framed family photo on his credenza, engraving his son's face into his anger.

TWENTY-TWO

Emily invited Eloise for dinner at the Montmartre loft. She waited at the Abbesses Metro and they walked together uphill to rue des Saules.

It was a chance to use new cooking skills from her Cordon Bleu training in Paris the year before. She picked through her favorite recipes, hoping to impress Eloise.

She wasn't sure yet whether there was a basis for a good friendship, but thought this social time together could only test the waters. Emily didn't rush the pace and Eloise's reaction was more than she hoped for. They ended the gourmet meal with a chocolate tartlet and fresh raspberries.

Eloise took a third glass of Chardonnay and for the first time in Emily's company, she began to let her guard down.

Commiserating over absent husbands and the high price of Parisian fashions, they kicked off their shoes and watched an old movie from Emily's cabinet. At midnight, Eloise left in a taxi for Branly Quai.

After a quick cleanup, Emily opened her laptop.

She entered 'Benjamin Tessier'. It was on her mind all evening.

A number of ancestry files came up for a Benjamin Tessier born in Perche, France two hundred years before.

It's easier to find people from that era than our own generation.

It was peculiar to Emily that the file from Mr. Baynes said Benjamin Tessier died in France barely one week prior.

Must be an obituary online. Something local; a funeral home?

Several social media sites had the name Mathias Tessier but the photo didn't match up.

Why would Vincent Baynes deliberately stonewall me? This might not be the slam dunk I thought it was.

TWENTY-THREE

Winston Metcalf sat back down in his padded leather desk chair and dialed a South African number.

"Hello, Winston Metcalf for Mr. Mugabe."

"Thank you, Mr. Metcalf. I'll locate him right away."

Winston stood and paced at his desk, irritated by the wait while the phone clicked into a sound void.

A gruff voice with a heavy accent barked into the phone.

"Hello, Winston. I trust you've been successful."

"Yes, Sir. What is your intention for the 'package'?"

Mugabe grunted, "The courier will bring him to London tomorrow. I'll arrive early."

"Yes, Sir."

"Everything has been taken care of, I assure you," Metcalf vowed.

Mugabe said, "I hope so!" He hung up.

Winston walked to his window. He spoke out loud as he paced. "Scott Marchand is becoming a liability."

He sent a text to both Manny Leach and Lawrence Winchester, ordering a pick-up on Marchand, but to bring him alive—he needed answers.

Time to bring in the loose diamonds.

He opened his top desk drawer and fondled his revolver.

TWENTY-FOUR

The overnight temperature dropped below freezing, with frost clinging to the trees creating an instant winter wonderland. Emily buttoned up and took her tablet outside to capture the rare delight that had befallen Montmartre. She knew that in a few hours the sun would make the magical frost disappear, inhaled back into the sky.

She'd been up early, troubled by the Tessier file and determined to find clues. After breakfast, she picked up the card for the aunt of Mathias Tessier.

I assume she is the blood sister of Benjamin Tessier, so has a biased interest. Or maybe removed through marriage? Or married to a brother?

"Mrs. Charbonneau, my name is Emily Harkness. I've been hired by the law firm Chartrand & Baynes in charge of disposing of the estate of Benjamin Tessier. Mr. Baynes suggested I contact you to discuss Mathias Tessier. Would I be able to meet you for a cup of coffee sometime today?"

"I was aware you might be calling me. I'm well acquainted with Vincent. I'm working in a boutique on the Champs-Élysées and I need to be at the store by 10 a.m. I could meet you soon, or else at noon."

"My office is not far from the Champs-Élysées and I can leave my apartment directly. Would 9:30 a.m. be alright?"

"That works. There's a Starbucks near the Louis Vuitton store; I'll meet you there."

Mrs. Charbonneau was gracious. "Well I do look forward to meeting you."

With time to spare, Emily went to the detective agency to prepare a list of questions from the Tessier file, and at 9:15 a.m. she left for Starbucks.

The coffee shop bustled with patrons getting their caffeine boosts before work. Two women abandoned a corner table, and Emily eased her way through the crowd, intent on claiming it. She laid her portfolio on the table and sat to watch the door for Mrs. Charbonneau.

A flamboyant woman caught Emily's attention, wearing a wide brimmed slant hat with a leopard print that flattered her round face. With heavy makeup, Emily guessed her at over sixty, spry and bouncy on her feet. The woman found Emily with a 'yoo hoo'. She waved one leather glove as she gushed across the floor.

"Hello, Emily."

Mrs. Charbonneau extended her remaining gloved hand in a gesture of greeting. "Shall I get some coffee for us?"

"Thank you. I saw the vacant table and thought I should grab it, but I insist on paying for the coffee." Emily tried to pass a twenty to Mrs. Charbonneau but was met with objection.

"Absolutely no, Emily. How do you take your coffee?"

"Au lait, please, Mrs. Charbonneau."

"It's Verona," she replied.

"Oh, it doesn't matter which roast, but Verona will do nicely."

Mrs. Charbonneau burst into laughter. "No, no, my dear. My first name is Verona."

Emily's face flooded with embarrassment until the comedy of it left her in stitches. Verona was still smiling when she returned.

"My first husband used to call me Vera but I prefer my proper name. Now I have a funny story to tell when people are puzzled by my name."

"I'm glad to amuse you, Verona. Thanks for the coffee."

The two women removed their winter coats draping them over their bistro chairs. Emily withdrew papers from the portfolio.

"Please tell me, Verona, how are you related to Benjamin and Mathias." The inquisition had begun.

"I was married to Benjamin's younger brother, Truman; William married a woman the family disapproved of. She wasn't Catholic and that was a sensitive bone of contention. Formalities at Christmas and special occasions were strained. I didn't follow Mathias' growing up."

"I would be interested in knowing where Benjamin, William and Mathias last lived."

"I'm not sure we have enough time for all of that Emily, but I'll try. Benjamin married Sophia and they lived in a fishing town on the coast of Normandy. They kept a pleasure farm and were able to eke out a living from the farming and fishing. He still lived there in some sort of old person's villa when he passed away. The farm had been rented out providing a nice pension.

"William moved away to attend university in Paris where he studied economy and finances. He went on to hold a higher position in a bank in Paris. While he was at school, he met a pretty young girl; her name was Charlotte or Charlemagne. Mathias was born when they were both still in university."

"When did you or Benjamin last hear from William or Mathias?"

"I brought along the last Christmas cards with their envelopes. From the postmark and the scratchy address, you might find where they lived."

Verona looked twice at her watch.

"This will be helpful. I see, Verona, that we're out of time and I don't want to make you late for work."

"Thank you Emily. Call me anytime. I'd like to hear if you find Mathias. He is my grand-nephew."

"By the way, who is the cousin that will inherit the estate if we don't find Mathias?"

Verona's face flushed red and tense. Emily knew Verona was about to perjure herself.

Emily returned to the detective agency and spent the morning online, gathering information from the university archives listing graduates in finance programs in Paris.

Establishing a time frame, Emily worked backward from Verona, estimating William's university term between 1980 and 1985. She then searched annual reports for the larger banks in Paris, hoping to find William Tessier.

She wished Joseph were there for support. After brewing a second pot of coffee, Emily's perseverance paid off.

William Tessier, a bank executive, with University of Paris credentials was listed in one of the downtown banking institutions. The record was five years old, but her heart skipped a beat with a sense of accomplishment.

A professional first impression would be mandatory and she contemplated how to break through the bank's front line to reach a senior manager.

The truth would be her best tool.

She tried to make a telephone introduction to Mr. Tessier at the bank. After numerous telephone options by recordings, Emily pressed '0' for a live voice.

Proclaiming a sensitive and personal matter to be discussed with William Tessier, she was screened by the first operator, then transferred to his Executive Assistant.

"Hello, Ms. Harkness. Any personal business matters for Mr. Tessier can be relayed through myself. I'm sure you can understand and respect that Mr. Tessier is a busy man. We cannot fit you into his schedule for at least two weeks."

The woman's voice was curt, bordering on rude.

"I'm bound by client privilege not to divulge the details with anyone other than Mr. Tessier. Please take my phone number and ask Mr. Tessier to call me at his convenience." Emily was equally as abrupt.

Emily went to the bank an hour later. She loitered in the lobby searching a section of the wall featuring photos of the management and directors.

While examining the photo of William Tessier, she looked into the glass reflection. Emily was sure it was the same man standing behind her at the railing behind on the second floor.

Emily turned and nodded to him.

TWENTY-FIVE

In front of the office tower, an elegant Daimler DS420 Limousine pulled curbside for concierge service.

The uniformed driver stepped around in perfect posture and opened the left side passenger door. A man got out and stood beside the driver. They both looked toward someone still inside.

Joseph remained in the Range Rover to watch.

A man emerged from the Daimler with fanfare. He wore an ethnic hip-length silk tunic with gold braid, a snug pill box hat and silk trousers. His complexion was dark, accenting a perfected goatee beard. His dominant presence exuded respect, and the driver nodded a bow.

With ten minutes to spare, Joseph pulled a transmitter bug from his coat and scurried across the road to join up with the two men. They wouldn't have a reason to recognize Joseph so he rushed to get on the same elevator.

"Hold it, please!" Joseph stuck his arm in, forcing the doors open. They pressed ten and Joseph pressed twelve.

He looked into the steely black eyes of Mugabe. The moment was awkward, but he offered a greeting. "Welcome to London, Sir!"

He straightened to attention and attempted a handshake but the other man stepped between to protect his boss, dismissing Joseph.

"Please sir. My guest is a foreign dignitary. Handshakes from the public are not permitted."

"Of course. My apologies." Joseph moved back past Mugabe's aide, slipping the bug into his pocket.

The two men got off on the tenth floor, while Joseph remained on the elevator. A visual of the tenth lobby area was impressive, an open concept with marble reception and visitors exposed by glass walls.

A tall man with flawless grooming was at the elevator to receive his guest. His hair was dark with silver temples, and he wore round gold-rimmed glasses over a thin pointed nose.

Returning to the building mezzanine, Joseph was hopeful he could intercept Scott and McQuaid. This was not a situation they could bluff their way through.

Marchand and McQuaid entered from the Parkade stairs. Scott was astounded to see Joseph waiting for them.

"Are you happy to see me, Scott?" Joseph said with sardonic sarcasm.

"It was for your own good."

"I'm a big boy. I can make my own decisions."

Scott said, "Well I'm glad to see you've recovered so quickly. I didn't mean to harm you, Joseph. I'm taking care of my own missions and responsibility for the safety of others is not my forte."

"There's no time to belabor the point. Mugabe has already arrived. What's your plan, Scott?"

"Well, I have to take McQuaid up there. If I don't, I'll spark the wrath of the African."

"That's a given. I placed a bug on Mugabe's aide, so I'll be able to hear conversations while you're in the boardroom.

Joseph said, "Eli, I suggest you sit out the consequences. Scott, I'll create a distraction for your escape. In spite of your supreme abilities to manage dangerous situations on your own, please heed my cue."

Scott's eyes rolled. "That seems to be our only plan so let's get on with it."

McQuaid pleaded, "Please let me go now." He looked toward the daylight.

Scott nudged him toward the elevator. "You are the reason for this meeting. Come on."

Joseph placed a second bug into Scott's jacket. Experience forewarned him not to put his confidence in Scott.

"I assume you have a car rental as you came from the Parkade," Joseph said. "I have a green Range Rover across the street, so we have options."

The door opened on the tenth. Mugabe, his aide and the businessman were no longer in sight. A few feet from the door, Joseph spotted the two thugs, Winchester and Leach.

Leach's right hand was in his jacket on his revolver, while Winchester nervously jiggled his keys.

Joseph pulled back out of view.

I didn't count on them.

The elevator closed on Joseph. Scott and Elijah waited at reception.

Mugabe paced in the inner sanctum. "Winston, you understand that the diamonds are not enough. In my culture such a theft crime is reprehensible and requires payment of another kind."

Adnan scowled using theatrics to thrust his fist high. "You had the audacity to send a shoe-shine man to me with the key and the entry code to secure my own goods. What an affront."

"What are you suggesting Adnan?"

Mugabe's voice raised more. "You might find this distasteful but I have a modest request for a pound of flesh. Mr. McQuaid must pay for his sins."

He leaned closer and Metcalf backed away.

"Sir, have you ruled out the justice system in England? You have enough incriminating evidence to put McQuaid away for the rest of his life. Why not give him to the mercy of Scotland Yard?"

"I deal with things in my own way, Winston."

"And what is to happen to my man—Marchand?" Metcalf asked.

"He has followed the instructions and shown good faith in recovering Elijah. However, we have another consideration to resolve."

"What is that?"

"The diamond weight is short. I talked to the diamond cutter and he swears there were twenty diamonds in each of the bags your men retrieved."

Mugabe's eyes flamed as he spoke. "Ten five-carat diamonds are missing. The cutter is one hundred percent trustworthy, leaving us with a choice of thieves: your Dutch accomplices, your own tails, Scott Marchand or even Elijah McQuaid.

"Neither of the two men can be dismissed today until a confession is made."

Metcalf resented not having control and called one of his own armed assistants to join him. He liked even numbers, and the vulgar intimations Mugabe proposed disgusted him.

Winston Metcalf used his desk intercom to ask the receptionist to bring the guests into the boardroom. Christine, his secretary, held Scott's arm and Elijah followed.

Christine was five foot two with shoulder length brown hair, framing a square jaw. Her strong will showed in her insistence on picking the table seating for the guests.

Adnan Mugabe's aide sat at one end of the long table, with Scott and Elijah at the other. Winston Metcalf was mid-point on the window side with Winchester on point.

Scott instantly recognized the man from St. Martin's Theatre and the bitter taste of the champagne. Metcalf appeared to avoid his gaze.

Everything is not as it seems.

Mugabe stood up to take charge.

"First, I would like to address Mr. McQuaid. The surveillance tapes, at the mine, identify your theft from my diamond shipment. You switched my diamonds with your own fakes. You were gracious to me in accepting my hospitality, and then left the country with a fortune of my gems. What do have to you say?"

"My sincere apologies, Adnan. If I could turn the clock back, I wouldn't have behaved with such disrespect of my good friend. It was a shameful and weak lack of judgment. I did take the diamonds to Amsterdam, I acknowledge that and humbly beg forgiveness."

Mugabe pounded his fist, shaking the table.

"Don't refer to me as your friend and don't talk about respect. You are vile vermin." He spit the words.

"My diamonds were returned to me by another hand. Did you truly expect I wouldn't notice the miscalculation in weight? There are still fifty carats missing, ten five-carat stones. You not only stole from me once, but twice."

Elijah McQuaid's face went white with shock.

"No, no, I didn't."

Winston Metcalf watched their faces and saw the flash of guilt on Scott.

The only people who know of the ten stones are Scott and likely Joseph Harkness. Later, I'll play the two against each other.

He would deal with Scott in his own way. Greed was foremost in Winston's mind, calculating an opportunity to seize the fifty carats for himself before Mugabe. The mob pressure was ticking loudly in his head.

I must have money before 4 p.m. or my meet at 'The Digs' will go badly. The bank agreed on remortgaging my house but it only gives me $200,000. I'm still short funds for the Italian.

Winston said, "I assure you I'll look into the matter."

"No, no, no . . . Winston. You don't understand. Whoever stole the fifty carats from my shipment has to pay for his guilt. It is half a million dollars missing, gentlemen. I want to wash my hands of this matter."

Their voices had escalated and portions of the conversation could be heard outside the boardroom. Christine, at reception, couldn't help hearing the meeting, and made a call on her cell phone. It was answered on the first ring by an American accent assuring her the situation was under surveillance.

"Thanks, Christine, it's coming through loud and clear." The voice on the other end of the line said.

Making a sweep of her surroundings, she returned the phone to a pouch in the lining of her suit.

Joseph picked up her words on his Qphone frequency. He focused on the voice at the other end.

Daniel is in this deeper than I thought. I'm sure that was him.

Inside the boardroom, Scott rose to speak edging toward the door.

Mugabe burst in laughter. "Sit down!"

He motioned to a place beside him at the table. "McQuaid come here." Mugabe's assistant laid out a slate board and a case.

Elijah McQuaid, with Soloman's guidance, grimaced as he shuffled to the chair.

"Mr. Marchand, I invite you to do the honors."

"What are you talking about?"

"I have deemed the price Mr. McQuaid is required to pay to make restitution for his gross disrespect is a pound of flesh. This knife will be swift and clean."

He opened the case and laid down a scalpel.

McQuaid gasped in horror and looked to Scott for rescue. Scott's throat seized with fear. He couldn't talk and his body locked in fear.

Metcalf buzzed the intercom for Leach to join them. Christine found him in the stairwell smoking.

Joseph couldn't wait longer. He pulled the fire alarm handle by the elevator, and briskly strode past Christine. She stood to block him but he pushed through.

Barging into the boardroom, Joseph raved. "There's a bomb in the elevator. Evacuate immediately!"

It was enough of a distraction to grab Scott. Winchester jumped up in pursuit. Joseph slammed the boardroom door and threw a ceramic pot at the door.

Metcalf was on his phone and didn't join the chase. As the stairwell door closed behind Joseph, a curdling shriek came from the boardroom.

Elijah!

Joseph jammed a bar in the door, and the two men ran for their lives.

"All the way to the bottom, Scott. To the green Range Rover across the street." Scott was still trembling.

Metcalf opened the stairwell security images on his computer and smiled to himself.

You can run, but you can't hide. Security will have you in moments.

McQuaid remained in his chair, whimpering and quivering, with a towel around his hand. Mugabe was temporarily appeased with the punishment he'd dispensed.

Knowing the floors would be monitored, Joseph sprayed black aerosol over the lens. He took an extra floor, slipping to the basement unnoticed and out an emergency exit to the street.

Joseph opened the car on the run using the remote, with Scott on his heels. Metcalf's men burst through the front doors. A vehicle on the street was waiting, the same Bentley that had been parked near the office. With a screech of tires, the Bentley charged toward them.

A horrific crunch startled Joseph when the driver clipped the Range Rover. Scott wasn't yet inside and the Bentley's front end slammed into his thigh.

Whipping around, he slung Scott over his left shoulder placing him into the back seat.

He spun the Range Rover mounting the sidewalk, with tires burning. Safely away from the scene, he looked in the backseat at Scott. The silence alarmed him.

Scott needed attention, convulsing in pain with a contusion visible through his clothing on his upper thigh.

Policemen at two o'clock.

He stepped on the gas and careened up onto the curb to a pair of London Bobbies on foot patrol. Jumping from the car, he yelled with all his might.

"Ambulance, call an ambulance! He's really injured. It was a hit and run downtown. I don't know where to take him."

The first officer leaned into the back to take Scott's vitals. His breathing was labored and he was losing blood.

The second officer reached EMS. "Tommy, what's his pulse. The doctor needs to know?"

"I only counted 38. His skin is grey and cold. He's semiconscious."

"Can you perform mouth-to-mouth? We can't move him until the medics come."

Joseph interrupted. "Stand back fellows, I'll do it."

He was regaining his control.

Joseph leaned in and propped Scott's neck, breathing air into his lungs. Without losing a beat, he slipped his hand into Scott's pocket and removed the bug; then he ripped the ten diamonds from Scott's lining.

The sirens wailed toward them, and curious bystanders closed in for a better look at Scott's suffering.

Joseph found Scott's cell, then turned to the crowd. "Move back! Let the medics do their work!"

Three paramedics hovered over the back seat with both side doors open. One had an oxygen mask over Scott's face and held an intravenous line. The other two attempted to extract him to a waiting gurney. It was agonizing for Joseph, watching the team negotiate every inch to bring him out.

In hindsight, Joseph knew he shouldn't have tried to help Scott up after he'd been struck.

I should have called an ambulance in the first place. But the Bentley wouldn't want Scott taken alive.

One of the policemen wanted a statement from Joseph.

"Just a moment," Joseph said. A half block away was the black Bentley, its front headlight missing. Joseph watched as the two men leaned against the car, watching his chaos.

Scanning the other block, he shook his head. It was Daniel in his black sedan, watching through binoculars.

This can't wait.

He raised his palm to the policeman and darted to the street through the emergency vehicles. Hitting the pavement running hard, he closed in on Daniel as his sedan peeled out from its spot.

When I get a hold of you, Daniel . . .

He kicked the gravel by the curb and returned to the Range Rover.

"Officer, see the black Bentley down the street? Those are the men that ran my friend down. They have the audacity to show up here with Scott's blood still on their headlights. Arrest them! They still don't know we've tagged them."

The bobby signaled to his partner and whispered instructions. The officer employed a ruse to speak with the photographer across the street, but ducked to an alley and emerged behind the Bentley.

A backup sharpshooter took a stance at the end of the alley, surprising the two men.

Joseph continued with the officer, providing the address of the accident scene at the high-rise office tower.

"Security cameras from the lobby will show the accident."

He excused himself.

"Hi, Babe. We're in kind of a mess here in London. Scott has been hit by a car. It looks like internal bleeding and broken bones too. An ambulance took him to Windsor Hospital. He'll be going into surgery. Eloise should be told, but it wouldn't be safe for her to come to London. Scott was hit deliberately and we don't need another target."

"I understand. I should tell her Scott has a broken leg and needs to stay in London for a few days. We'll get him back home as quick as we can. She'll want to go to him, but I'll do my best to deter her."

"I hope it's just a few days."

TWENTY-SIX

Metcalf remained in his office with Adnan Mugabe. His aide, Solomon, returned to the boardroom with news of the accident.

Winston Metcalf said, "With Scott out of commission, we can't assume anything. I'll send men to the Windsor Hospital to keep watch. Solomon, get this cleaned up right away. I find this repulsive." Elijah McQuaid was on the floor with a tourniquet around his left hand. His face was ashen white from the throbbing pain surging up his arm.

"McQuaid, shut up! Be thankful I didn't kill you. Now tell me where the other ten diamonds are. Some of my friends say I am fastidious in regard to detail, yet others who are not my friends might say I'm ruthless. Do you have an opinion Mr. McQuaid?"

Solomon gently lifted McQuaid to his feet as Mugabe ranted.

"Mr. Mugabe, Sir. I beg your forgiveness from the bottom of my heart. I swear I don't know what happened to your missing diamonds. I wouldn't dare lie to you after what has happened?"

McQuaid stammered, unable to catch his breath.

Mugabe's dark eyes penetrated into the soul of his prisoner, as if he were trying to put him into a trance. Then he turned sharply toward Winston Metcalf.

"Winston, this man is not the one who has skimmed my diamonds. This is becoming tiresome. It is either one of your men or your agent, along with his accomplice. Yes, I won't forget those names."

Winston stiffened up. He was now a suspect too and had failed to get the diamonds for his meeting with the mafia hoodlum.

"Winston, you have seventy-two hours to comply. I don't wish to bring disgrace upon a loyal servant."

"Solomon, have my car readied immediately."

Adnan Mugabe stepped forward to shake the hand of Winston Metcalf, but stopped short knowing full well Metcalf seethed with disdain.

"It has been interesting doing business with you, Winston. I'll hear from you Thursday morning."

Mugabe dropped a thick envelope of cash on Metcalf's desk, then marched out like a General in command of invisible troops.

Winston watched until the elevator doors closed and returned to his secretary, barking orders to her.

"Christine, instruct the janitors to take care of my office immediately. Call security and have McQuaid escorted out of this building. Then get the security tapes for the main lobby since 11:30 a.m." She didn't move as she listened.

"Pronto!" Winston yelled. He cursed under his breath in front of her desk.

I'm afraid I have sold my soul to the devil either way.

Christine stood up smartly and walked into Metcalf's boardroom. She bent beside Mr. McQuaid and helped him gently to his feet.

She whispered, "Come with me, Elijah. You'll be alright, just gather your strength. Make sure you keep the towel tightly over your hand until you are away from this building."

Taking him by the elbow, she gave him a warm smile and a wink.

Metcalf picked up the envelope and counted out $75,000 leaving him with a sickly feeling; he was supposed to have $300,000 for the payout. Without a conscience, he decided to borrow the deposit from the organization and try it as a payment at 'The Digs' along with his mortgage funds.

In the outer office Christine picked up her cell and made a call to Daniel.

"He has his mortgage funds and Mugabe's deposit."

TWENTY-SEVEN

Joseph stared into the darkness from the Windsor Hospital waiting room window. Time had no measurement in this crisis, and the anxiety dragged as he waited for Scott's return from surgery. Joseph's character would drive him to make things right.

Neither of us are out of the woods until the diamonds were returned.

Joseph was replaying the boardroom voices in his head when he heard his name.

"Mr. Harkness!" A doctor was walking toward him.

"Yes, Doctor. How is Scott?"

"Are you his next of kin, Mr. Harkness?"

"I am representing, his wife, Eloise Marchand in Paris. I can get her on the phone if you wish."

"I'll talk to her tomorrow when we have a better recovery picture. Surgery took longer than anticipated. Mr. Marchand had internal bleeding and skeletal injuries. His spleen ruptured beyond repair so we had to remove that organ, but he'll recover well. He needs medication and rest for several weeks.

"His hip bone was bruised but not fractured, and his thigh bone has a compound fracture requiring a splint. We used pins to secure it. For now he is resting comfortably in Recovery. The nurse will get you after he's been admitted to the floor.

"Before he was put under he was calling your name."

The doctor finished his summation and left Joseph in awe absorbing the consequences. Thirty minutes later, the nurse directed him to Room 915.

The fluorescent lights on the bed were set low to allow rest but with enough light for the nurses. Joseph came around to the side of Scott's bed by the window.

Scott raised his hand and opened his sunken eyes. His skin was sallow and ghostly pale. Joseph had a sinking feeling at Scott's sight.

Again, Scott reached out his hand. "Joseph."

His words were slow. "Thanks for saving my life and for taking care of things; you know what I mean. I'm sorry I got you into this mess."

They were both silent sharing this desperation.

"The good news is that the doctor assured me you'll recover from these injuries. How is your pain?"

"I'm pretty numb right now. They have me on a lot of drugs."

"We need to look at it from a different perspective. Both Mugabe and Metcalf will be coming for you and the diamonds. You're still in danger. Stay alert and keep your senses sharp."

Joseph hesitated and then reinforced his fear. "Suspect everyone, Scott. Everyone!"

Scott's eyes were closed. "I see what you're getting at."

"Emily will soften the news of your injuries to Eloise. She needs to know, but it would be dangerous for her to come to London. Another kidnapping is a definite risk."

Scott nodded. "Yes, you are right."

"Just listen to me for a while Scott. Listen only; there's no need for you to talk until later. Okay pal?"

His eyes fluttered. "I'm listening."

"I took your cell phone and the diamonds before the medics put you in the ambulance. It was Metcalf's men in the Bentley that clipped you.

"Also, Scott, have you seen a black sedan watching your movements? He never gets too close."

"Maybe." He drifted.

"This next part . . . and Scott, you have to listen. An opportunity presented itself and I took it. The medicine cabinet behind the nurse's station was left unlocked during rounds. The long and short . . . I helped myself to a few vials, a small dosage of propofol. There's enough to temporarily paralyze an assailant without lasting harm."

Scott chuckled in his semi-conscious state. "I didn't train you to do that."

"I'll hang out here as much as I can, but we can expect company. Someone is likely to be around to try to finish you off, Scott. Here are two vials of tranquilizers and half-size syringes. Stuff them into your pillow without the nurses finding them. If someone tries to suffocate you or adjust your intravenous, use these. You can't ask questions when you're dead."

"Who's coming?" An eye opened.

"The thugs chasing us appear to be on Metcalf's payroll; there's the Dutch pair, possibly others sent from the London organization; I don't know. The African Chief, if he's still in the country, won't forgive or forget the stones. I'll cart an overnight chair down here and this time I'll take the first watch."

Scott couldn't help releasing a painful chuckle.

Engulfed in his paper, Joseph's head raised at the sound of a woman outside the door speaking to the nurse. He put the paper down and stood in the darkness for a glimpse. The woman wore a heavy coat and a woolen hat.

She looked quickly at Scott's door. Her forehead was tight and her eyes raised. A tall man in a doctor's coat, with hair tied back, stopped to reassure her. He gave her a comforting pat on the back.

I'm sure he handed her an envelope. That's odd.

TWENTY-EIGHT

William Tessier searched the telephone reverse directory for the number Emily had given to his Assistant.

Harkness Detective Agency. I wonder what this is about.

He googled the agency and its principals; it popped up on the first page, a new detective shop on rue Euler. He decided to leave the bank a half hour early and drop in on Emily Harkness.

Tessier walked briskly from his bank at the Champs-Élysées to rue Euler. Declaring a private business meeting out of the office, he left his car in the underground parkade.

At four o'clock, William arrived. Emily was at Joseph's desk engrossed in the computer, and an instant flash of recognition passed between them. Emily matched the man to the picture she'd seen at the bank earlier.

It was unquestionably William Tessier, father of Mathias Tessier, the beneficiary to Benjamin's estate.

"Ms. Harkness, I presume." He was congenial and forced a pleasant smile as he offered his card.

"Mr. Tessier, how nice of you to come. I've been looking forward to meeting you."

Emily invited him to take the visitor's chair.

William was a tall broad-shouldered man with thinning hair and dark eyebrows, handsome she thought. He wore a dark blue expensive bespoke silk suit and tie, exuding a distinguished attitude.

She smiled. *He'd be easy to identify in a lineup as a banker.*

"No doubt you're wondering about the reason for my visit to your bank earlier," she said.

"Well, there's the expression about curiosity that killed the cat." William relaxed and smiled. He was struck by her beauty and gentleness.

"There is indeed. It's a profound feeling."

"It would seem you have some questions for me."

"Yes I do, Mr. Tessier. I have been retained by a local lawyer from the firm of Chartrand & Baynes. Do you know a Vincent Baynes by chance?"

Emily noticed his slight change in body language, a timid eye movement.

William hesitated to buy time for a suitable answer.

"I believe I may have heard the name somewhere."

"Are you acquainted with Verona Charbonneau?

Emily didn't want to insult him by tripping him up so early in the interview, and continued before he answered.

"I met with her and she indicated her last contact with you was a Christmas card a year ago."

"Well if she got a Christmas card, she must be somewhere on my wife's list."

Emily continued, "I should tell you about Vincent Baynes before I ask questions. The Will of Benjamin Tessier, whom I presume was your late father, leaves the estate to his grandson, Mathias. If I don't locate your son within the next few weeks, the estate reverts to a cousin."

She broke from her summary to look up. William Tessier's face was flushed.

"Perhaps Ms. Charbonneau has her own agenda," she added.

William Tessier was shocked. "Ms. Harkness, you have taken me off guard. I didn't know my father had passed away. You see, he's been suffering dementia for a number of years and resides in a nursing home in the north of France. The staff would know how to contact me and you say Verona Charbonneau knew about all of this."

Emily could see William Tessier was genuinely astonished and angered by not being informed of the news earlier.

"I'm sorry for your loss, Mr. Tessier."

He nodded and pulled out his phone. "Do you have the number for this Vincent Baynes?"

Emily went to her own desk and located a business card from her drawer.

"If you will excuse me for a few minutes, I would like to call Mr. Baynes."

William was on his feet showing considerable agitation. Moving from the desks, he punched in the number.

"Vincent Baynes, here. How may I help you?"

"Baynes, this is William Tessier. I'm at the Harkness Detective Agency and I've just been informed about the passing of my father. I am distraught you didn't contact me. Don't you have any compassion or respect? If Ms. Harkness could find me readily, so could the people in your offices."

"My sincere apologies for your loss, Mr. Tessier. We are a major law firm normally dealing in high value estates. Ms. Charbonneau brought the Will to us. We were immediately unable to locate any further next-of-kin and deferred to the Harkness Agency to assist us."

"Courtesy is not the value of an estate; it is decency. When did this occur? Where is my father buried?" William's anger hadn't yet been appeased.

"Since the agency is under contract in this matter, I suggest you inquire of Ms. Harkness. I gave her the complete file. She has all the information we had."

William paused and looked at Emily in search of sympathy. She was embarrassed seeing the insensitivity shown by Baynes. Verona Charbonneau indicated a falling out between the father and son many years prior, but this was an enormous shun.

The call between William Tessier and Vincent Baynes ended abruptly. He returned to the guest chair, lowering himself with an exhausted huff.

"Would you like to see the file now, William?"

Emily opened the folder with a photo of Mathias on top.

William leaned forward with his elbows on the desk. Emily stayed motionless to give him the silence he needed. He rubbed his temples. Observing the anguish of a son discovering the loss of his father lent insight into a man reeling from the pain; of his relationship with his parents, of rejection yet immense love.

William leaned back in the chair and looked at Emily.

"Can I get you some water?"

"Yes, please." His voice had become soft and defeated.

Emily extracted two icy bottles from the office refrigerator.

"William, I'm afraid I don't have answers for all your questions. I need to revisit Ms. Charbonneau; she must know the circumstances of your father's passing. We've searched a number of resources for an obituary, but so far we're empty handed. I will follow up with her this afternoon."

"Of course. Here is the number and last address I have for my father's nursing home. Perhaps they can give you a direct answer. I last saw my son, Mathias, two years ago; he was majoring in architecture at a university in Paris. He never liked to tell me about his private life. I'd be pleased if you could find him for me too."

"We will do our best, William."

"Maybe check local architectural design firms to see if he is an employee."

"I appreciate your candor. You've given me enough to work with. I'll give you an update tomorrow."

"In spite of being under contract with Vincent Baynes, is it also possible to take me on as a client? I would like to see my son. Here's my direct line." He jotted on the back of his business card.

"Let me discuss this with my partner to see if we can come to a basic agreement."

"The fee is of no concern. Whatever you want."

TWENTY-NINE

Metcalf's accomplices, Winchester and Leach, got the call to meet at the Courthouse Café for instructions.

"Guys, tell me quickly about the bail on the hit and run. How'd you get out?"

Manny, the one with the wonky eye, answered. "You'll find out soon; a big legal bill is on the way. The bloke said he was a friend of yours from Italy."

Metcalf gritted his teeth and looked at them both with disdain.

They guaranteed me they would find ways to convince me.

"Scott Marchand is in intensive care at Windsor Hospital thanks to you, Winch. Harkness stays close to him. Find a way into the hospital, like an orderly's uniform. Assuming neither of you are guilty of stealing Mugabe's diamonds, Marchand will need to give them up.

"Not us, Mr. Metcalf. We'll take care of Marchand."

"Furthermore, Winchester, who is this shoe-shine man Mugabe mentioned?"

"I don't know anything about that, Mr. Metcalf.'"

Winston studied their faces for the slightest grimace.

"You're paid well to carry out instructions. Be creative. Do I have to dictate paint-by-number instructions? If that's the case, I've got the wrong men. There are others on my payroll ready and willing. Furthermore, make yourselves scarce around my office."

"Yes, Sir. We can handle the situation," Manny affirmed.

"Don't kill him until you find out where the diamonds are. I have an ace in my pocket to take care of the Harkness fellow later."

"Understood, Mr. Metcalf." Winchester squirmed.

Winston barked back, "I've told you repeatedly not to call me by my business name."

Lawrence retracted. "Yes, Chief, my apologies."

When the pair left the café, Metcalf phoned a number in London. He didn't know where it rang, but recognized the American accent.

"I'm returning your call, Sir. You wanted an update on the Mugabe diamonds."

"You're not in control, Winston. This Harkness fellow is a wild card; dissuade him, but don't harm him. It looks like you're pitted against Marchand.

"Don't fiddle around with hospital uniforms; you must be more astute. In two days, I make my update to New York. I expect to find everything in hand by then."

Winston grasped to please the boss.

"Sir, I'm not convinced that Harkness is an innocent tag, but we'll do our best to keep him on the perimeter. We're still focused on Scott Marchand for the wayward diamonds."

THIRTY

Emily braced herself and dialed Eloise. There wasn't an answer, and she allowed herself a sigh of relief that she could postpone the bad news.

Next, she phoned Verona Charbonneau to request another meeting but that call went to voicemail. She assumed Verona might still be at the boutique and decided to walk there before catching the metro home.

The streetlights were on and stores were closing for the day amid winter darkness. Her timing to intervene with Verona on the street was perfect.

Verona, dressed in a mid-length brown cashmere coat with a fox fur hat and matching muff, walked out the front door of the boutique in Emily's sight.

Surprised to see Emily waiting by the lamp post, a flash of anger waved over Verona's face, but she forced it into a pleasant greeting.

She mouthed the words. "Hello Emily, nice to see you."

"I'm sorry for arriving unannounced, but I have an urgent need for information. Could I take you for a quick coffee?"

Verona wasn't pleased with the interruption, but hid it. "Well, I suppose, but I do need to get home to my family."

"I see there is a café next door. Will that be alright?" Emily inquired.

Verona took the lead and found an unoccupied table while Emily went to the counter to order lattes.

"May I ask, Verona, how it came to be that you were notified of Benjamin Tessier's death? Unfortunately, William Tessier, your nephew, was unaware of the passing of his father. He has taken it rather badly."

Emily expected some emotion of sympathy, but Verona's voice bristled in defense, hiding her pleasure.

"I was the only family member to visit Benjamin at the nursing home during the last six years. If his son had taken the interest to keep in touch, he would've been the person they called."

"When did you last visit with Benjamin Tessier?"

"Are you suggesting I have been untoward in relation to my visits?" The bitterness in Verona's voice was growing. "Three months ago."

"What condition did you find Benjamin in? I understand he was suffering from dementia."

"He always recognized me."

"Did anyone else visit with him that you know of?"

"My nephew, Simon, was with me at my last visit."

"Is Simon the nephew who is next in line to the estate?"

Verona Charbonneau rose abruptly from her chair.

"You make it sound like something to be ashamed of. I'm sorry Emily but I really must be on my way."

"Thank you, Verona. I'm grateful for your help."

Emily smiled and offered a handshake. Verona ignored it and marched from the café with flamboyant flair without looking back.

At the Montmartre loft, Emily kicked off her shoes and dropped her coat on the sofa.

She picked up the phone to try Eloise again. This time it was a smooth quiet voice at the other end.

"Hello, Eloise. Are you alright?"

"Yes, Emily, I'm fine. It's nice to hear from you."

Emily detected an inflection of depression, or self-pity.

"I have some news for you. It's not good news but it's also not bad."

"Is Scott okay?" Eloise's voice deflected panic.

"Joseph and Scott were fleeing some thugs in London. Scott got clipped on his thigh, in a hit and run accident. Joseph is with him at the hospital. He had surgery and the doctor's prognosis is for a full recovery . . ."

"I need to go to him, Emily." Eloise interrupted.

"No, Eloise that's not a good idea. The men chasing Scott wouldn't think twice about kidnapping you." Emily was firm. "Scott doesn't want you to be in danger."

"But . . . he's my husband, Emily." Eloise sobbed hanging up the receiver with a flash of jealously.

Why should Emily be telling me the condition of my husband? Who does she think is running this show?

Eloise washed the tears from her face and looked up the emergency number Scott had given her. She was shocked when a gruff voice answered.

THIRTY-ONE

Through the night, the nurses checked Scott's dressings and refreshed the IV. One wall of his room was half glass and Scott was visible as far as the end of the hallway.

Joseph was sensitive to every movement and shadow, each stirring him back to the present. His eyes were heavy with sleep threatening him more every minute.

At 2:00 a.m., a flood of light from the hall fell on his face. Minutes before, the nurse had been in, and Joseph checked his watch. It was too soon for her to be returning.

A man in a surgical uniform crept close to the wall and watched through the glass, analyzing the pace of breathing in the room. Certain that Scott was in deep slumber, he turned his attention to Joseph in the night chair.

Joseph didn't flinch, but peered from the slits of his eyes, calculating every move. The man wore dirty Reeboks and was unfamiliar with the room, setting off alarm bells for Joseph.

The intruder worked his way to the IV pole. Pulling his hand from his pocket, he raised it to the dim light and prepped a syringe.

Estimating it would take three paces, Joseph jumped to his feet. Forcefully grabbing the right arm of the culprit, he yanked it around his back. The intruder yelped as his shoulder popped in a dislocation, but he raised his free arm around in an attempt to inject Joseph.

Joseph swung and thrust him to the floor, knocking the syringe to the other side of the room.

The head nurse ran into the room. "What is going on here? She looked at Scott, still asleep, and rushed to his bed.

Joseph said, "Margaret, call security! We've had an attempted murder."

The command in his voice put her in motion. At the nurse's station, security was alerted to the commotion in Room 915. It was enough time for Joseph to confiscate the syringes from Scott's pillow. She was back in seconds.

Maintaining his hold on the assailant's dislocated shoulder, Joseph squeezed tighter, satisfied to hear a new groan of pain.

"Mr. Harkness, what has taken place in here?"

Before he could answer, the disturbance awoke Scott in an incoherent stupor. Margaret turned the daytime lights on and leaned over Scott to check his condition.

In the light, Joseph recognized the man with the scarred eye as Manny.

It's likely that his partner, Winchester, is nearby.

"Nurse Margaret, if you check the syringe on the floor, I believe you'll find a lethal dose intended for Scott's intravenous."

Joseph was still holding Manny when two security officers barged in. "This man dislocated his shoulder. Remain with him in triage until the police arrive. This is an attempted murder. Understand?"

The guards grabbed Leach roughly, securing him with a plastic tie. Removing his wallet, the guard noted his ID as Manny Leach. With medical gloves, Margaret placed the syringe in an envelope.

It took the two security men to keep Manny under control down the hall. Two police officers came to their rescue at the elevator.

The nurse said, "You were expecting this, weren't you Mr. Harkness? That's the reason for the night chair. You might want to talk to the head of security to increase guard duty."

THIRTY-TWO

E mily left her office at 9 a.m. on the shuttle to Charles de Gaulle.

It would be a short flight to Dinard near the coast of Normandy. In the plane, she unfolded her map of France to plot the location of Saint-Germain-sur-Ay on the English Channel.

Standing outside the Dinard airport, Emily took a moment to breathe in the sea air and stretch her legs. Pondering her options to get to the village, she rented a compact with GPS, then referred to a local tourist map of the coastline.

Saint-Germain-Sur-Ay was between Barneville Carteret and Agon Coutainville, a few kilometers from the D-Day Normandy beaches of World War II. The country drive was awe-inspiring with sand cliffs, white beaches and lush flora. As an artist, she envisioned a palette of cerulean blues and brilliant leaf greens.

Stone cottages, orchards and resorts banked the narrow road to the village. She pulled over at a vineyard fruit stand for some sweet red grapes and to ask directions to the nursing home near Le Bertheliere.

Passing the tourist compound, Emily came to the Flower of the Sea. A wide terrace led to a magnificent stone house covered in vines, with windows encased in white shutters. A garden veranda with a stone floor was occupied by several senior residents lingering in wooden lounges. A trio of inhabited wheelchairs was lined in a row against the wall, and a pair of residents strolled in the garden collecting winter vegetables.

Emily parked and prepared her questions for the house matron.

She heard her name in the distance as she left her car. "Hello, Ms. Harkness."

The front screen door was opened and the house matron, a tall thin woman over fifty, came down the front steps.

Emily called out, "Hello, you must be Jeanne Marceau."

"Indeed, I am. I've been watching for you."

"Please call me Emily."

"I'll give you a tour of our home. We like to call it a Guest House rather than the drum reference to a nursing home. We have eight guests now; presently. We're licensed for ten but haven't yet filled the room Mr. Tessier vacated, and another room is being remodeled.

"We encourage our guests to enjoy the terraces and to wander in the gardens. They gather a few vegetables now and then, and are fulfilled by contributing to the kitchen in this small way. A local artist in the village comes weekly for painting classes and a fitness instructor is here three times a week."

Emily listened politely. She wanted to get to details of Benjamin Tessier, but decided it could wait.

"This is like a resort for our residents," Jeanne said. "The hill offers a wonderful view of the ocean and white beaches. Claude Monet visited this area years ago and painted lovely landscapes. You might find them in the galleries in Paris."

Jeanne opened the front door and led Emily to the great room, an expansive space with a center fieldstone fireplace. A palm shaped paddle fan circulated overhead, ventilating with sea air.

African mahogany couch frames were stuffed with ornate leather cushions and vivid tribal canvases with rectangular weaving. A petite woman curled under an afghan on the couch, and in the corner two gents pondered a game of checkers.

Jeanne didn't stop promoting. "There's constant activity, lawn croquet, yoga, even craft sessions. We're always open to new things. I'm applying to increase my guest capacity to twelve residents. We have plenty of room and the more the merrier.

"The only regimented aspects are three square meals and bedtime. By the way, I asked the cook to prepare an extra plate for lunch for you."

Jeanne adored her guests, but it was nice to have a younger person to talk to.

"That would be lovely. Jeanne, would you mind showing me Mr. Tessier's room, I'm curious to see his world."

"Certainly. He was a wonderful man. Everyone loved him" Jeanne lit up as she spoke. "His humor and kindness; we miss him very much."

She rounded the corner. "He was at the end of the west hall; we can go there right now if you like."

Benjamin Tessier's room faced the front terrace with a garden view and the ocean beyond. His window opened to allow the sea air to invade his space.

It had simple furnishings, a double bed with a wooden carved headboard and a cedar trunk at the foot. The corner had an antique Morris chair beside the dresser chest. His personal items had been removed, revealing darkened spots on the walls where pictures had hung.

They retreated to the dining room. The pine table could hold sixteen people with an assortment of chairs, and the eight residents were already there, crowded toward one end in their usual chairs.

Jeanne stood proudly and said a prayer for the food. It was simple but abundant in the residents' eyes: chopped vegetable salad, beef barley soup, salmon and tuna sandwiches, deviled eggs, and rice pudding.

Emily looked at her watch, conscious of time and that she hadn't achieved her objective.

"Jeanne, I have more questions about Benjamin Tessier. I'll need to leave before long to catch my flight to Paris."

"Yes, of course, let's talk in my office."

Emily was led to an airy office overlooking the backyard.

"What's the date of Mr. Tessier's death and who was the attending physician? His son in Paris wants to know where he was buried."

"Mr. Tessier passed away two weeks ago this past Sunday. We called Dr. Allier from the village and he was puzzled by Benjamin's sudden death. I remember the date because he had visitors in the morning. It was a relative from Paris, a fine lady with a grand presence, along with her nephew. They signed into the Guest Book."

"Was the guest Mrs. Verona Charbonneau?"

"Yes, that's right. She comes every now and then. Not a compassionate woman, she always pried into Mr. Tessier's business affairs."

"Is there a death certificate indicating the cause of death?"

"Yes, I have a copy here in my files. Dr. Allier said they were natural causes." She leaned and whispered. "But I don't think it was right. Mr. Tessier was foaming at the mouth which can mean arsenic poisoning. "I wouldn't put it past the Charbonneau woman to have doctored his tea."

"Did Mr. Tessier have a sizeable estate?"

"He lived simply but invested well. He had a farm on the coast, so I guess you could say it wasn't an amount to be sneezed at."

"Have his affairs been forwarded to Chartrand & Baynes in Paris? That is the law firm looking after the disposal of the estate."

"No, Mrs. Charbonneau took all those papers on that last morning." Jeanne said, feeling foolish for being tricked.

"Is there anything else you can think of?"

"He always told me the estate was for his grandson Matthew—no the name was Mathias. He thought the world of that boy and said his estate would make things right. The grandson was here at Christmas and they got on dandy. The son, William, was here for Benjamin's birthday two years ago but called on special occasions.

"You know, Emily, he wasn't senile—only on in years. I have a photo here in my desk that I took when Mathias was here. You can have it."

"Was there a funeral?"

"Of course, we had a nice service in the village at one of the chapels; then we invited folks in for tea. I didn't go to the burial, but it was at the cemetery about two kilometers east.

"I can't believe the blatant audacity of that woman. It would certainly seem her actions were premeditated."

Emily gathered her belongings. "Thank you, Jeanne, but I must get on my way. If you think of anything else, please call me."

Emily phoned Vincent Baynes with her Normandy update, but she was perceptive in hearing his pauses and quiet gasps at her news.

Baynes congratulated her on the progress in Normandy, but to Emily, they were hollow words; between the lines she crossed into his protected territory. She flashed back to feeling stonewalled the first day of her investigations into the Tessier family; today she had the same feeling. With new distrust toward Baynes, she felt uneasiness about Verona.

"Mr. Baynes, who provided the Will to your firm?"

The phone was silent as he hesitated. "I believe . . . it came from Verona Charbonneau. You will have noticed the Will was dated two years ago, but a special provision was added on the morning of his death. I didn't see anything suspect about it, Ms. Harkness."

Emily could tell from his formal reference to her that he wanted distance; he had called her 'Emily' since their first meeting.

She reinforced the informality. "Vincent, the house matron at the nursing home portrays a different picture of Benjamin Tessier's passing than I was given from Ms. Charbonneau. Am I free to press for the truth in this matter?"

His voice faltered. "Of course . . . the truth."

"Also, do you have an address for Verona's nephew Simon? I don't know his last name, or even if he is a blood relative."

"Ms. Harkness, these are questions to be deferred to the detective on the case. Do you understand how expensive my fees are for one hour? Call me back when you have made your conclusions!"

Emily was stunned by the sudden change of his tone.

After hanging up on Emily, Vincent Baynes dialed a private line in Central London. The call was answered on the second ring by a gruff voice.

"Vincent Baynes here. I'm afraid the detective is digging deeper than we anticipated. She knows about Verona's last visit and the Will."

"For Heaven's sake, Vincent, keep a leash on her. We can't have Verona exposed. I'm not ready to tighten the ropes yet so delay the investigation; do whatever you must. Albeit, Vera is a nuisance, but she has me by the nose. If Ms. Harkness comes up with any solid evidence let me know."

"Yes, Sir."

"She is disposable too you know."

THIRTY-THREE

T he morning after the attempt on Scott's life, he laid awake, conscious and concerned about his wife in Paris.

"Scott, that needle could have killed either of us. We'll get you out of here soon." Joseph stopped to listen to the medical discussion outside the door.

The doctor stepped inside. "Your splintered thigh is scheduled for a cast today confining you to a wheelchair. The therapist will determine if you're eligible for a walking cast. A physiotherapist will see you today. Good news is that your stabilized internal injuries are healing well."

The doctor said he'd see him again the next morning, but Scott had more on his mind.

Joseph closed the door. "Scott, it's time we talked about the diamonds. You know we won't have any peace until they are returned."

"Yes, I know. The line of work I'm in is lackluster, chasing villains, running from bad guys. No real accomplishment. I'm getting tired of the erratic pace of my life. The temptation of a few diamonds is enough to enable us to make a change."

"It doesn't matter what the excuse is."

"If I'd taken time to consider the consequences, I could've fought the enticement. You're right, they should be returned."

Joseph nodded. "I bugged the conversations in Metcalf's boardroom. I'm convinced he's the intermediary. It would be to your advantage, Scott, to deal directly with him. I'm also not out of the woods as I was shocked to hear Mugabe mention my name as a threat."

Scott looked troubled; he could not tell Joseph the truth. He had saved his life and deserved better.

"Scott, how will you know when you've successfully completed your task? What's happened in the past?" Joseph asked.

"I usually get a call. It's from a blocked number but I've figured out how to triangulate the location. I have a photographic memory, Joseph. I never forget the sound of a voice."

Joseph picked up Scott's cell and handed it to him. "Can you check for any new incoming calls?

"A call from an unknown number yesterday, but nothing else," Scott said.

Joseph looked into Scott's face and made him squirm. "Are you sure about that?"

Joseph took the phone back, and clicked for information on an unexplained call.

"Scott, come clean. There's an unidentified call on your phone lasting five minutes. Who was the caller and what was it about? I'm walking the tight rope too. I can't be in the dark."

"It was a private matter, not your concern. As far as Metcalf's people go, they seem to know where I am at all times, like Big Brother. They are waiting and watching,"

Scott silently pointed at Joseph, then to himself.

"I know there is a death warrant out for both of us," he said.

"The day after tomorrow, when you're in the wheelchair, I plan to get you on a flight to Paris. We'll make arrangements for extra leg room. We need to get the diamonds to Metcalf while we're in London. Do you think you'll be up to it?"

Scott wouldn't answer.

Joseph said. "We're running out of time, so it can't wait. I'll go to Metcalf's building, late this afternoon. You'll be safe here with the security guard. I'll borrow a chauffeur's uniform and Metcalf will have the diamonds in his hands before he knows what happened. He'll assume it was a courier delivery."

"That is brazen, Joseph!"

"Do you have a better idea? It will be dusk by 5 p.m. so I have time to get there and back before the night shift. You need to stay alert. I haven't seen any credentials from the security company, so I can't depend on how solid they are."

"Don't worry about me, Joseph. I've been trained to take care of myself."

"Remember the vials are under your pillow."

Back at his hotel, Joseph prepared a plan to return the diamonds. He dated the corner of a letterhead swiped from Metcalf's reception and laid it on top of the current London Gazette. Under a light, he spread out the ten stones on the letterhead and photographed them with precise detail to be unmistakable as evidence. He had learned the value of documentation, knowing it could absolve him.

Joseph took a head start to Metcalf's to beat rush hour. Employees were exiting the office tower in clusters heading toward bus stops and tube stations, and to the parkade. He parked onto a side street and blended into the five o'clock crowd.

Pulling a chauffeur's hat down over his brow, he churned through the revolving door with his head low to avoid cameras.

The elevators were on other floors. He looked at his image in the polished brass on the main level and was comfortable with the disguise.

On the way to the tenth, he was joined by another courier and two businessmen. The courier gave him a courtesy nod and exited on the ninth.

The tenth floor was quiet, emptied of staff and reception. There was a bell and notice to ring for service, but Joseph didn't stop at the desk.

He barged down the hall to Metcalf's office and opened the door unannounced. Metcalf was on the phone and looked up alarmed at the intrusion.

Joseph called out, "Courier, Sir! Nobody out front."

He laid the envelope on his desk and turned quickly toward the door. His movements were fast but put Metcalf on defense.

Metcalf reached into his top desk drawer. He yelled out, "Excuse, me. Who are you?" He slammed his phone and pulled the revolver out.

Joseph was already part way down the hall, pretending not to hear the recall. He heard Metcalf call for security, and picked up speed.

A gunshot whizzed by his head as he dove around the corner. He raced for the stairwell, leaping over the tenth floor banister. At the ninth floor, the other courier was walking toward the elevator.

Joseph intercepted him. "Hey, pal. It's the end of the day; you won't be needing your hat and jacket until tomorrow. Can I trade for 100 pounds? You can pick yours up with the parkade attendant in five minutes."

"Are you sure they'll be with the attendant?"

Joseph hurried him along, making a switch of the hats and tugged at his jacket sleeve.

"Here's the money. Thanks, buddy."

Joseph joined the courier on the elevator lobby but left on the second floor, running down to the parkade, then to the attendant.

"There's a courier coming for this in a few minutes." Joseph shoved it into the attendant's hands with 20 pounds.

He jaywalked to his car, oblivious to honking taxis, then sped from the business district back to the hospital. His mission was accomplished.

Metcalf re-ran the elevator tapes tracking the chauffeur's hat Joseph wore. Baffled by the basement activity, he flipped again to a shot of the courier van at the dock. He recognized Monarch Express Courier on the side of the truck. He froze on the frame of the courier employee speaking with the parking attendant.

"What the devil . . ."

He went back to the tape, this time frame by frame. The chauffeur's hat obstructed a clear view of the offender's face in the lobby and then again in the hallway and elevator.

The nagging image of the courier climbing into a Monarch vehicle flustered him.

Winston opened the envelope and let the ten diamonds drop one by one to the leather desktop. He leaned within inches for a quick inspection, then walked to his window to think out his strategy.

Scott!

The flash of guilt he'd seen on Scott Marchand's face in the Mugabe meeting came back to him.

This makes it easy. Scott can take the fall.

Winston's laugh had an evil resonance.

He barked at Christine to hold his calls, then locked his door and spread out the sparkling diamonds on a crisp white letterhead. With a magnifying glass, he admired the clarity and beauty of the jewels.

Daniel had gambled that it would be one of the genuine diamonds that would be inspected.

Winston remained at his desk. Looking into space, he wrestled with the immense pressure to inform Mugabe of the diamond recovery.

But no-one knows I have them. They can be mine.

THIRTY-FOUR

Emily closed the agency early and returned to the loft in Montmartre. In jeans and sweats, she went downstairs to find Toby and collect him for a walk. Her stress melted away when he saddled up for his hugs and rubs.

The two of them bounded up the long staircase, Toby's bloodhound ears flapping all the way to Artists Row.

She stopped for a café au lait on the hill before returning. From the loft, she called Joseph, mostly for support.

"Joseph, I hope you'll be coming home soon. I hate to confess it, but I've taken on more than I can chew. I miss you."

"Joseph, I've bad vibes about Baynes and the circumstance of the death of Benjamin Tessier are suspicious."

Over the phone, he imagined her grimacing.

"Then there's the calculating Verona Charbonneau. The challenges of my next interviews with either of them are not promising."

"Em, what can I do to help?"

"Well, I need your advice. Baynes hired our firm, but I don't trust him. Verona Charbonneau is misleading me. I need a person to tail her and monitor her calls."

"Have a look at the resumes in my office. What about this young fellow, Carter? He offered to do freelance work whenever we need him. Give him a try tailing the Charbonneau woman."

"That would work; I'll call him."

Joseph said, "Scott and I intend to fly home the day after tomorrow. Can you manage that long?"

She laughed. "Of course. I'll go back and talk further with William Tessier. I promised him an update. He wants to retain us to locate his son outside of our business with Baynes and I owe him an answer."

"That doesn't need to be a conflict. I'll research Mrs. Charbonneau, here. Sooner or later, liars trip themselves."

"Thanks, Babe. I love you, Joseph."

Emily turned to listen to the noise at the balcony window. *Tapping. I can't imagine what that could be.*

Dimming the table lamp, she tip-toed to the drape. As she slid her finger through the lace curtains, a large stone shattered through the glass to the floor. A note was tied to it.

Emily looked out from the dark room, and watched a figure disappear toward St. Pierre.

Sitting on the floor beside the stone, she untied the rope. Her face lost color as she read the message.

Get Joseph out of London.

Emily quivered at the thought of imminent danger for Joseph.

THIRTY-FIVE

Scott wasn't in his bed, Joseph looked to the door in a panic. The security guard was absent too.

He called out in panic. "Nurse, where is Scott?" As he ran from the room, Margaret appeared.

"Oh, it's okay. They took him down for x-rays about ten minutes ago. You can wait for him there or in his room."

"Where is x-ray?"

"Main floor. There are signs to Radiology."

Joseph trusted his instincts—something was wrong. It was too late in the day for x-rays for a non-emergency patient. With determined strides, he took the elevator to the main floor.

The check-in desk was lined up processing patients. As every minute counted, Joseph had to be aggressive. He stepped in front of a woman, and held his hand in the air to ignore her expletives.

"Excuse me, Ma'am. It's urgent that I locate Scott Marchand. Is he in x-ray?"

The receptionist looked at her charts.

"I'm sorry I don't have him on my list. If you have further questions, take a number and I'll serve you in order."

Joseph stepped back.

The fastest way to get Scott out would be the service elevator. They would need two people, a vehicle and a gurney.

Joseph raced to the loading dock and stopped behind a cart to get a look.

Lawrence Winchester was closing the back doors of a cube van marked 'Hospital Laundry'. As Winchester opened the driver's door, Joseph surprised him with a pistol against his face.

"Winch, old boy, I'll take those keys. Now help me unload Mr. Marchand. We can get him back to his room before Nurse Margaret figures out what you did. How's Manny?"

Winchester's face was drained. He was at the end of the line, too late to make a break from the van without risking a bullet. With no way around Joseph, he tried to feign his cooperation.

But Joseph had forgotten their third man could be there, Robert Dillon, with whom he'd had a previous encounter at the old railway warehouse.

As Joseph walked Winchester to the back of the van, the door flung open with a crash. Dillon loomed from inside with a long range assault rifle pointed at Joseph.

Winchester burst into laughter. Dillon scowled at him then turned back and raised the rifle higher.

"If you look around, Joseph, you'll see you're the one with the disadvantage. Back away and drop your revolver."

Winchester kicked the gun aside.

Joseph jeered, "Nice to see you Robert."

Robert stepped down from the truck.

Joseph continued his mocking. "Are you ranked the third man according to your abilities?"

Robert charged at Joseph, with his gun casing poised to butt him in the head. He stopped inches from Joseph.

"You don't challenge me!"

Satisfied he'd drawn Robert into striking range, Joseph dove for the legs. Robert turned on a dime waving the rifle. Joseph grabbed the butt and forced the gun toward Robert.

His hand reached for the trigger. "Back off or I'll shoot you in the face," Joseph said.

The tables had turned for Dillon. "Winchester! Get out here!"

Winchester stepped from the back of the truck and walked slowly toward his partner.

Joseph said, "Look you two. I don't have any bones with you—I am protecting the life of my friend. But I warn you, if I see you lurking around me or Marchand, I'll take the shot. Right now, bring the gurney back to the loading dock."

Joseph hesitated. "Gentlemen, tell Metcalf his diamonds were returned to him by courier this afternoon. I have evidence to confirm that."

Winchester raised his voice, "You gave him the diamonds back? He'll never confess that to Mugabe. You're not seeing the bigger picture—you're being deceived. Metcalf is just another puppet. You aren't free. Never; that's not how it works. The head honcho is a formidable American. You'll *never* be free."

With Scott on the loading dock, Joseph threw the van keys across the parking lot. He laughed now.

"Run or I'll shoot you both."

Scott was still groggy from the drugs. He fought to focus but Joseph and the others were a blur. He was on a merry-go-round, spinning as he tried to rally his balance.

Winchester's last words about freedom reverberated in Joseph's thoughts, just as an unmarked van rushed to the dock. The driver jumped out and yelled at him.

"Get out of the way! Now, Joseph! This is my second warning!"

The driver was back in his van before Joseph realized what had been said. The van peeled out of the parking bay. Both vans disappeared leaving Joseph with Scott's gurney on the loading dock.

Daniel.

THIRTY-SIX

Emily didn't hide the urgency in her voice. "Mr. William Tessier, please! This is Emily Harkness; he's expecting my call."

"May I ask the nature of your business?"

"That won't be necessary; Mr. Tessier is aware."

"Please wait."

Emily was left on hold for several minutes.

William Tessier's tone was genial. "Thanks for calling, Emily."

"I've got information to discuss with you, William. Could we meet? I don't like details over the phone."

"Yes, of course. My first meeting is at 10 a.m., and we might be more comfortable at the café on the next block. Are you at your office now? I can meet you if that works for you."

"I'll be there in fifteen. Thanks William."

Quickening her step along rue Euler, she found the café and looked inside to see if he was there. Fidgeting, she waited at a table by the window until he entered.

"Hello, Emily. I'll get some coffee for us."

"I take mine black, thank you." She smiled.

Emily removed her Normandy papers and placed the photo of Benjamin Tessier and Mathias on top.

William returned with the mugs, his eyes drawn to the picture of his father and son together.

He fell into his chair and picked it up, holding it for a long time. Bringing it closer to see the faces in greater detail, his eyes welled up.

"I can't tell you what this means."

"I understand. I'd like to tell you about my visit to your father's nursing home and the circumstances of his death. There are some unusual conditions."

"Go ahead. I want to hear every bit of what you found."

"Your father's guest house is a lovely ranch style estate not far from the ocean. Be assured he was happy and comfortable there.

"His room had a view over lush gardens and terraces. From there you can hear the ocean surf crashing into sea rocks. Here is a brochure the matron gave me."

William opened it and his eyes became glassy as he turned the pages quickly. He folded it for his inside pocket.

"Yes, it does look pleasant. He would want to be near the ocean."

"The house matron, Jeanne Marceau, gave me a tour of Benjamin's room and we talked about your father's affairs. He'd invested well and had a nice estate. What concerns me is that Ms. Verona Charbonneau was a frequent visitor. The nurses insist Benjamin was not suffering from dementia, but simple aging and forgetfulness."

"I see," he said. "Pardon me, but how is that relevant?"

Emily was careful in her words. "Verona paints a different picture, and I have some suspicions of a crime in his death.

"Your father's passing was two weeks ago this past Sunday. A death certificate was written by a village doctor who declared Benjamin died of natural causes. But privately he confessed he suspected the possibility of poisoning.

"Your father is buried in the cemetery a few kilometers from the guest house; it was a small ceremony with residents and staff. Ms. Marceau will be happy to talk to you if you have other questions."

"Didn't they do an autopsy?"

"I'm afraid not. He's a country doctor in a small village without access to forensic labs or testing equipment. In my opinion, you have reason for an exhumation."

William shook his head to comprehend it. His elbows were on his knees and he rubbed his temples.

"William, I have further news. It isn't good either.

"On the Sunday morning your father died, he had two visitors, Verona and her nephew, Simon. Verona spent considerable time going over your father's affairs. When she left, she removed a waft of his papers."

"This is outrageous! Just incredible, Emily. How dare that woman. We were never close, but nonetheless she was related by marriage. I'm shocked and disgusted by her interference."

"The nurses said that when Benjamin was found deceased, his mouth had been foaming; the nurses suspected arsenic. Apparently, Verona insisted on making him a special cup of tea before she left. She had motive and opportunity to slip saccharine and arsenic into his tea. That is my suspicion."

"Just appalling. Why didn't they call me? They have my number. I call every year at Christmas and on his birthday."

"Verona Charbonneau is strong and domineering. She controlled your father. I don't have evidence, but off the record, it appears she demonstrated calculated greed. I don't know if the nephew, Simon, was following her orders or was personally motivated.

"Verona has intentionally put us off track until the time period lapses. She gave instructions to the home to record her as the main contact and Ms. Marceau unwittingly complied."

William's ashen face was taut, the conversation taking a visible toll on him.

"I know it's been difficult, William, however Verona is no longer cooperating. She is deliberately misleading me. Do you know who Simon is?"

"Simon . . . yes. Verona married my father's younger brother, Truman, who passed away from a car accident years ago. Verona remarried and adopted her second husband's children. If you look into that lineage, you might find Simon."

"Thanks, that answers some questions. Here's the photograph; you keep that one, William."

William stood and shook her hand. "Thank you for the update. I do appreciate what you're doing for my family."

At the agency, Emily pulled grad and alumni lists for Paris universities offering architectural majors. Two schools fit the criteria, but the sites didn't show photos. She'd need a personal interview.

Removing her reading glasses, she knocked over her coffee.

Nerves! I have to tell Joseph about the message thrown through my window.

She unfolded the paper and read it again.

Feeling intense fear from the threat on Joseph's life, she reached with courage for her cell. With each ring, she hoped to hear his voice.

"Emily? Is something wrong?"

"Yes, Joseph, very wrong." Her nerves overtook and her voice failed her. She sobbed quietly.

"What is it, Babe?" It pained Joseph to hear her cry.

"Last night someone threw a rock through the patio with a warning."

She blurted out, "Come home Joseph, your life is in dire danger!"

"You know me, Em, I don't back away from danger. If I don't face my enemies upfront, I am a weak man. You didn't marry a weak man, did you?"

"No . . ." She laughed, wiping the tear from her cheek.

"Then we stay the course. Did you see who threw the rock?"

"By the time I got my wits about me, he was running down the street."

Emily took the Abbesses metro downtown and then to rue Bonapart on the south side.

At Ecole Nationales de Paris-Malaquais, she searched the archives for a possible match. In the second hour, she identified 'M. Tessier', a graduate from the previous year, and with a magnifying glass she found a match in the yearbook.

Searching appointments at Paris architectural firms, she tracked a possible link to one of the city's largest design companies. She sent a text to William Tessier.

Stepping outside for privacy, she called the architectural firm. "I'd like to speak with Mathias Tessier please."

"Mr. Tessier is in a client meeting until noon at least. Can I give you his voice mail?"

Emily replied. "No, it's a personal matter and I should speak in person."

She checked the transit routing online to Mathias's office. It would be an hour by metro and bus, but the trail was warm and the provisional time on the Will was decreasing fast.

The firm was in a renovated historic stone building with four floors. Emily presented herself at reception.

"I'm sorry, Mr. Tessier is in a meeting that should last throughout the morning."

Emily pleaded. "I only need a few minutes. Is it alright if I wait here? Perhaps the meeting will have a break in the middle of the session. I've come all the way from the 18th Arrondissement. I only need five minutes."

"Suit yourself. But I can't guarantee anything, you understand."

"Of course. Thank you."

Emily deferred to a pile of magazines on the coffee table and took a spot on the visitors' sofa. Her attention was drawn to a selection of photographs of employees receiving awards. She stood to look closer. Mathias was there.

An hour later, a handsome young man approached her and she recognized the likeness to his father.

"Ms. Harkness?" Mathias was proficiently courteous.

"Mr. Tessier, thank you for seeing me. I'm Emily Harkness of the Harkness Detective Agency."

"It's a pleasure to meet you. There is an interview room here by reception, but I only have ten minutes."

"I'll try to be quick. First, my condolences regarding the passing of your grandfather."

Emily watched his face intently to see if he was stunned by the news.

"Grandfather! I hadn't heard." He was visibly shaken.

Emily paused for a moment of grief before proceeding.

"I've been retained by a local law firm to locate you, since you are the sole beneficiary. There is a time provision to bring you before a judge and validate your identity. It is complicated. You see, your aunt Verona Charbonneau is attempting to contest it on behalf of Simon."

"This is ridiculous; Simon isn't even a blood relative. Verona cares about nobody but herself. How did my father take this news?"

"He was deeply saddened and asked me to locate you. He is anxious to see you."

Mathias seemed to soften.

"What do we do now?"

"I thought you'd like a copy of this photograph the nursing home gave to me."

She laid the picture on the table but Mathias didn't touch it. Instead, he wheeled his chair in the opposite direction to conceal his emotions from Emily. He was briefly transfixed by past memories of his grandfather.

"When can you come with me to file your claim at the courthouse?"

"I can book an out-of-office meeting anytime. Tomorrow at 9:00 a.m. would work for me." Emily could tell he had something else to say.

"Do you mind if I invite your father to join us?"

"I would like that." He took a sigh of relief.

"Just so we don't have interference from your aunt, I ask you not to speak of this. There are a number of distrustful people close to the matter."

THIRTY-SEVEN

Searching for names of prolific diamond mine owners in South Africa, Adnan Mugabe came to the top. Joseph located a number and placed a call to his office.

"Hello, I have highly confidential documents to send to Mr. Mugabe. Can you provide me with an address that is secure?"

A woman answered with a heavy foreign accent, possibly Dutch.

"Who is calling please?"

Joseph was on the spot to come up with a name—should he dare, he wondered. It would confirm he had the right man.

"Metcalf's office." He firmly announced.

The line was quiet at first.

"Mr. Metcalf's office has that information."

"I'm working out of office and it's after hours here, please oblige me. It's urgent to deliver these photos to Mr. Mugabe."

The clerk recited a London hotel address where Mr. Mugabe would be for a few days.

He prepared a courier envelope and inserted a copy of the photo of Mugabe's diamonds on Metcalf's letterhead. Satisfied the trap had been set for Metcalf, he returned to his hotel to make travel arrangements to Paris.

Metcalf anxiously paced around the mahogany desk; he knew Mugabe was known to take matters into his own hands for trespasses against him.

Why would I not have been party to those instructions delivered to Marchand? I could have controlled this better.

The intercom buzzed and his eyes rolled with annoyance.

"What is it, Christine?"

Christine queried in trepidation. "I have the New York office on the line. Do I say you're in?"

"I've got it," he grumped.

He was composed for a confrontation.

A gravelly voice spoke. "Winston, is that you?"

"Yes, Sir."

"Have you recovered the missing diamonds?"

The pause was obvious to both of them. Metcalf was sweating but tried to keep a steady voice.

"Not yet, Sir, but we can snatch Marchand and his friend anytime. My men are capable of whipping the truth out of them."

The purposeful silence lingered and Metcalf wiped his brow, causing him to lose his calm.

He's toying with me. That's all.

"Winston, I remind you that I have eyes and ears in many places. Do not cross the line of deception."

Jacques Simpson hung up and a new fear grew in Metcalf's throat. The American corporation was increasingly concerned about their point man.

What eyes and ears?

He rubbed a lump on the back of his neck.

The London mafia connection was cleverly chasing Metcalf's actions since their last meeting at 'The Digs'. The henchman had accepted the loan premium, but within minutes he was attacked on his way to the car. In disguise, Daniel unburdened the man of the cash. Winston was sweating with anxiety, fearing the next threat.

His line rang again and his heart pumped hard.

"You're walking a tight wire, Mets. My employers are impatient with your stalling. You've got two final days to come up with the full return. An additional $100,000 is added due to our inconveniences. We can hurt you in many ways."

"You have my word—48 hours." Winston swallowed hard knowing how difficult it would be to repay $400,000.

Alone in his hospital room, Scott watched out the window as the drizzle trickled in rivulets over the glass. Beyond the lights on the street, the grey sky had intermittent fog. He was anxious to leave this rainy city and its labyrinth of felons.

He was startled when his cell phone rang but recognized the number. "Hello." His voice was tense.

"We've been compromised, Mr. Marchand. You'll need to take care of loose ends."

Scott had never argued with his boss before.

"Considering my circumstances, Sir, I propose that could be best managed when I return to Paris."

"We want Harkness removed from the picture," Metcalf demanded.

"I've been able to orchestrate the mission without drawing his suspicion. We need him as a buffer for a few days."

"Mr. Marchand, do you know where the orders come from. I'll give you two days."

Across in the adjacent hospital wing, a man stood in the window watching Scott's room with a sound transmitter focused on his window. His conversation with Metcalf was complete.

One more nail in his coffin!

Emily walked to the courthouse to secure the documents. She wasn't in possession of the original Will, but the copy had an official registration seal. William and Mathias Tessier insisted it was a matter of principle to follow grandfather's wishes. Verona was not going to easily rob Mathias of his birthright.

The obstacles in establishing the value of the estate were the missing papers that Verona removed the morning of Benjamin's death.

Emily mumbled under her breath.

I'll get Jeanne's affidavit that they were removed.

William agreed to meet with Emily and Mathias outside the courthouse. Mathias's birth certificate had been recovered from a shoe box full of old records in William's attic. He brought along his own to validate the lineage between Mathias and Benjamin. Only one week remained before the provisional clause could be enforced. Time and acceptable documentation was important.

William Tessier was less interested in Mathias's right to his father's estate than seeing his son again. He no longer remembered the issues putting a rift between them. It was the burning passion of a father awaiting the impending arrival of his son's return after a long absence.

Emily prepared documents for the beneficiary claim and a request for the appointment of William Tessier as executor; it was followed by an application for probate.

Relying on her instincts, Emily concluded she wouldn't inform Vincent Baynes of the advances in the case. She surmised from their last meeting she'd need answers for every detail. Baynes would be looking for loopholes.

She called Joseph to relay her plan for the next day.

He was keen to hear the progress. "I couldn't be prouder of you, Em."

"I felt an obligation to both William and Mathias. It is difficult to determine what the job is—to win for the sake of your client or follow truth and justice. Our client, Chartrand & Baynes, won't be grateful for my initiative. I'm sure they'd prefer that I substantiate Verona's case."

Joseph said, "Well I have findings for you. I've been delving into the background of Mr. Baynes. He is a high priced lawyer, and it's out of character for him to take on a simple case to locate a beneficiary. It doesn't fit his profile."

"What's his motive then?" Emily asked.

"I don't know, but two years ago he was called before the Bar to defend charges of misrepresenting himself to a client. At the same time, he was accused of assaulting a witness. Then for undeclared reasons, the charges were dropped."

"I have a circle dance going on here too."

"Can you hold off talking to Baynes until I get back to Paris? We're booked on a morning flight. Could you pick us up at the airport? I'll text you the flight details."

"I'm afraid I have an early meeting with the Tessiers. I won't be available until after ten. Does that work?"

"I'll give you a call."

"Are you aware of thugs following you, Joseph? Take the threat against your life seriously."

"I keep my eyes open."

Joseph arrived at the London hospital as the doctor was signing Scott's discharge papers.

Finding a pair of blue jeans in Scott's suitcase, he cut the left leg at the hip to fit over the cast. It was still winter in January, and he covered Scott's exposed foot with the thickness of two socks.

They bade adieu to the nursing staff, and wheeled down to the emergency entrance to a waiting handi-cab.

Joseph studied the driver and relaxed.

No connection.

Joseph and Scott exchanged few words en route to Heathrow. Tension dissuaded any discussion and Scott was remembering the voice at the other end of the phone, resonating like demons. And now totally dependent on Joseph to get around, Scott stirred resentment.

I know, Winston, you're my boss and that it was you who drugged me. You don't have the guts to meet me face to face. I'll bide my time.

The flight was undersold and Joseph stretched out in a seat across the aisle from Scott. He texted Emily to see if she was meeting the flight, but there was still no answer when he turned off the phone.

Barely an hour out of London, the pre-landing announcement was made. Scott stared out into the clouds, inventing scenarios to overcome Joseph.

He's dragging me down from my mission. I need to find a situation where I can take the upper hand.

As they taxied to the gate, Joseph checked his messages. Emily's text was there, confirming a special taxi at Arrivals to take Joseph and Scott to Branly Quai.

Eloise stood by her parlor window and watched the taxi pull up. The time without Scott was long for her and in preparation, she rented a wheelchair. Anxious about the moment, she straightened the Queen Anne chair and fussed with the cushions.

She went back to the window. Seeing him in his weakened condition alarmed her. She knew him to be strong and valiant, always the leader and a fighter. This was a different man getting out of the taxi.

Joseph and Eloise gingerly maneuvered Scott and his cast down the stairwell and settled him in an adjustable easy chair. The taxi was still outside, and Joseph excused himself.

Scott called to Joseph who was at the door. "Thanks for what you've done, Joseph. When I get used to those crutches I'll come by your office and square things."

His phony pleasantries suffocated his evil thoughts.

THIRTY-EIGHT

Standing in the silhouette of the courthouse, Emily made a striking impression. She wore a fitted black suit with a crisp white blouse, and her hair gathered in a loose knot. William was the first to join her at the steps. He suggested she go ahead to the coffee shop and that he'd join her when Mathias arrived.

She understood his request, knowing he needed a private moment with his son.

"Good luck, William. You both deserve this."

"Thank you for making it possible, Emily."

As she walked to the café, she turned to look back as Mathias raced up two steps at a time to reach his father. She stopped in the glass reflection of the café and watched.

Their embrace showed Emily what was important in a family relationship. It had been two years since she had seen her own parents and it stirred pangs of envy. She removed a tear from her eye.

Emily was sipping coffee when the men arrived. "Well, gentlemen, let's get to business to ensure enough time to get these papers processed and notarized."

From her briefcase, Emily withdrew the 'Claim to the Estate' and the supporting documents.

"I spent some time in the courthouse yesterday. Mathias, you'll need to complete the claim document, and William the executorship application."

"Absolutely," said Mathias.

"Do either of you have any concerns before proceeding with the filing?"

William urged, "None from me, Emily. Please proceed."

"When the law firm is informed that your papers have been filed, there is still time for other parties to make a challenge."

William said, "Don't worry about repercussions Emily. All we want is to follow the wishes of my father. Shall we go in?"

The applications were routine, each stamped by the court. Departing the courthouse, Emily checked her watch. She was aware Joseph should be back in Paris by now, and her heart skipped a beat as she hurried toward the metro.

She heard a voice, and without stopping, scanned the space surrounding her while quickening her pace.

Must be my imagination. Then she noticed a shadow keeping pace with her. He wore a green Harvard sweatshirt.

Bounding to their second floor office, she listened with her head to the door, then put her hand on the door handle. It was unlocked, meaning Joseph was inside. Her heart leapt with relief and a giddiness overcame her.

Dropping her briefcase to the floor, she ran to Joseph's arms. He cupped her face and kissed her and they stood locked in a tight embrace.

"I really hope we don't have customers coming in this morning." Emily moaned.

"I have today booked solely for my wife. No thugs, criminals, kidnappers . . . just you."

She wanted to tell him about the tail, but couldn't taint the moment.

Her moment in paradise was jolted by the phone.

Joseph answered it.

"Jeanne Marceau here. May I speak with Emily?"

"Yes, she's right here."

"Jeanne, it's nice to hear from you. I've been meaning to call you to thank you for your help. I trust you are well."

"Emily, it's not me I'm calling about. It's Benjamin, may he rest in peace."

"Of course, Jeanne, what is it?"

"Since we had our talk about the Charbonneau woman, I've been troubled. Considering the time that's passed since Benjamin's death, it would be easy to say the evidence is cold. However, I went through every detail about that Sunday morning and I've found new incriminating evidence."

Emily reached for a pen and urged, "Any information is valuable. Please go ahead."

"We keep a waste carton to dispose of used syringes and medicine bottles that we return once a month to the medical lab. This morning I looked through the bin wearing plastic gloves and I found an unfamiliar brand of syringe and a vial labeled 'arsenic'."

"Lands sake, Jeanne!"

Joseph leaned in trying to decipher Emily's coup. She raised her eyebrows and nodded at him.

Jeanne said, "Emily, I'm relieved it may help; it makes me feel better. How can I get this to you without any damage?"

"Since the murder was in Saint-Germain-sur-Ay, it falls under local jurisdiction, so any charges would be laid in

Normandy. Can you text me the police chief's phone number and I'll call him. In the meantime, keep the evidence secure until I get back to you."

"I have a small refrigerator in my own room. It should be safe there."

"You are marvelous, Jeanne. If I were there I'd give you a hug. Put it in a clear plastic bag and keep it hidden. Be careful who you trust."

The phone flashed a call waiting, and Emily told Jeanne she'd call back with anything new. Joseph's hand was stretched out for the phone. "I'll take this one," he said.

"Vincent Baynes here. I'm calling for Emily Harkness?" His voice was abrupt with urgency.

"This is Joseph Harkness. Emily is away from her desk at the moment. Can I help you?"

The answer started with a painful silence then a series of huffs.

"Tell her to come by my office. It's urgent."

"What time do you suggest, Mr. Baynes?"

"One o'clock today."

"Very well, we'll be at your office at one o'clock."

Joseph detected that Vincent wasn't pleased Emily had reinforcements.

He turned back to Emily.

"Sorry, Babe. He's a paying client. What else could I do?"

Emily was back in his arms. "You're forgiven."

"I guess you need to bring me up to date on the Tessier case before we meet with Baynes."

She sighed and spread the documents across the desk.

"But first," she said, "Jeanne Marceau's call. You won't believe it."

Emily was expressive in her explanation, waving her arms in French excitement, at the revelation of the vial. She recounted her visits with Mathias and his father, and the interference of Verona.

Joseph nodded. "It appears everything is falling into place. It looks like there's enough to put the Charbonneau woman away for a long time."

Emily said, "I don't understand Baynes. He is demanding and he's hoping we fail. It doesn't make sense that he'd hire us, but then defend the lies of Verona. Our news for him today will come as an unpleasant shock. Joseph, I'm glad you're home for this meeting."

Joseph's face straightened up. "That's a lot of pressure."

Emily said, "I've accumulated some expenses: court costs, the trip to Saint-Germain-sur-Ay and taxis in Paris. I'll prepare a final bill if it seems the case is concluded."

Joseph and Emily took a detour to the Champs-Élysées metro, stopping at a Brasserie. In London, he had dined too often on fish and chips or steak and kidney pie, and had a renewed ravenous appetite for French fare.

The waitress brought him a Gruyere Onion soup and Beef Bourguignon, and Emily picked at a turkey and brie baguette. They discussed their script for Baynes, taking coffee to go.

With last gulps, they took the elevator to the law firm. Joseph introduced them to the receptionist. Twenty minutes later the assistant directed them to a client interview room.

Vincent arrived. His face was red, giving appearances he might explode at them.

Emily intervened, speaking quickly and resorting to the formality of Vincent's surname.

"Mr. Baynes, this is my detective partner, Joseph Harkness." Baynes muttered an acknowledgement and took his chair at the table. He slammed his file and glared at Emily.

"I hear you've taken matters into your own hands. Ms. Harkness, you've been to the courthouse without discussing your findings with me."

She wouldn't be intimidated. Emily straightened her back and raised her chin as she spoke.

"You hired me to locate Mathias Tessier, then you impressed on me the urgency to meet a provisional time limit. Those two things I did. The last time I saw you, it was strongly directed I should use my initiative to solve the puzzle."

Vincent knew he'd misled her. "Granted Ms. Harkness, but it was not within your scope to enforce legal matters."

"Mr. Baynes, I explained the situation about Verona Charbonneau. She deliberately tried to put me on the wrong track. She avoided direct answers and sent me on a goose chase hoping the time would expire.

"It was necessary for me to travel to Benjamin Tessier's nursing home in Normandy to ascertain the date and cause of death. I discovered Verona had been at the villa the morning of Benjamin's passing. The village doctor signed a death certificate stating natural causes, however he indicated to the staff that Benjamin's condition had symptoms of poisoning."

Emily looked up to get his reaction, but he wouldn't commit even a facial expression.

She continued. "Verona Charbonneau would personally benefit if I failed to locate Mathias Tessier. That would be an injustice, wouldn't it, Mr. Baynes? Simon, is not even a blood relative. He is a step-son from Verona's second marriage."

Baynes snapped back. "That's not for you to question. The legal strength abides with the Will. This is all conjecture. And you don't have any evidence to accuse Verona of tampering."

"But I do, Mr. Baynes. I have a sealed affidavit from the house matron declaring that Benjamin died under suspicious circumstances. His personal papers were removed by Verona on that Sunday. Members of the staff attest to delivering mail and bank statements to Mr. Tessier, but Mrs. Charbonneau denies their existence.

"The staff provided a list of the addresses from discarded envelopes. Witnesses state that those papers were among the ones taken by Ms. Charbonneau. The real clincher is a vial of arsenic with Verona's fingerprints, recovered from the trash."

Baynes color paled and his voice cracked. "Go on," he said.

"Further, the nurse who gave Mr. Tessier his last morning medications insists he was hale and hearty before the visit. Verona prepared a special cup of herbal tea for Benjamin before she left, and within an hour, he passed away from arsenic poisoning. The family is prepared for an exhumation."

Emily stopped there to watch Baynes. He was silent so she pushed harder.

"Surely you don't want to be implicated in a cover-up?"

"I don't have any knowledge of this situation. Of course, I don't have reason to defend Ms. Charbonneau. Verona will still expect the estate to be discharged in the interest of her step-son. She's got the guts and ferocity to challenge it."

Emily said, "I'm a detective because of my moral conscience. I've completed the mission you assigned. I'm not bound by any legal restraints to conceal information leading to a murder."

Vincent's tone changed during her recitation. The tables had turned and he didn't want to be vilified by Verona's greed. He was caught in a trap, but needed to worry about the direction from London more than his partners' grilling. He wanted this nightmare to end.

Metcalf will be irate! He's a dangerous man.

"I appreciate your forthright approach. Please send me the bill for your expenses. I'll deal with the ramifications."

"As a matter of fact, Mr. Baynes, I have it with me. I remind you, I'm a witness after-the-fact to the murder of

Benjamin Tessier. We didn't have a client attorney agreement in regard to murder."

Rising, Emily pulled a sealed envelope from her briefcase.

"I caution you in your actions, Ms. Harkness. I'm not at liberty to give you advice, however when you get close to people like Verona there's a price to pay."

He sounded genuinely concerned for Emily's safety. "There is another power at play. Be careful."

Joseph shook Vincent's hand.

"Thank you, Mr. Baynes. We will heed your warning." Joseph was proud of Emily's heroic conduct.

At 3:00 p.m. Joseph and Emily left Chartrand & Baynes. On the way to the tube, she spotted a man in a dark coat and fedora with his gaze on them.

"Joseph, hold up." She reached for his arm.

He saw the worried look on her face. "What is it?"

"Glance discreetly about forty feet behind us. The man in a long coat by the guardrail is watching us."

Joseph knew it was Daniel.

Returning to the Abbesses station near Montmartre, they were relieved the Tessier case was behind them.

Toby bounded downhill as they got close and Joseph shook the hound's jowls.

"Been a good dog, Ole Boy?" Joseph was prepared with a package of beef jerky in his pocket.

"He's been my companion a few evenings when I needed it. Amazing that a dog's magic will take the stress away.

"Joseph, prepare for a Cordon Bleu dinner tonight! I need to pick up a couple things first—want to come with me?"

"Actually, Em, I've been in London for so long there is some business I need to attend to. Can I take an hour?"

Joseph strode back to St. Pierre and hired a taxi to Champs-Élysées. On the drive from the airport he'd passed the shopping district, with exotic window displays by Ducati and BMW. While away, he'd been concerned about Emily's exposure on public transit.

This might be the opportunity to surprise her.

He paid the cabbie. "No need to wait."

Near the Arc de Triomphe, he entered the Renault showroom.

Every man dreams of a Masserati, but there's something about the Twizy. It'll fit behind the flower shop. Emily can zip around Paris and on weekends we can jaunt to the country.

"Can I be of assistance, Sir?"

"You had a red Twizy in the window earlier?"

A woman with a fox fur flounced through the front door, and the salesman called to another man at the counter.

"This man is interested in the Twizy; can you look after him?" His attention was already drawn to the fox and he turned his back on Joseph.

"Yes, Sir, you're interested in our sassy little Twizy. Such a fun car!"

An hour later Joseph bounced into the kitchen to the heavenly aromas. He came up behind Emily putting his arms around her kissing her on the cheek.

"I've got a surprise for you, Babe!" Emily could hear the excitement in his voice, he was almost giddy.

"Well, let's have it then!" She turned and planted a firm kiss on his lips.

He lifted her into his arms and took the staircase down. They went around behind the floral shop.

"Joseph! I can't believe it! Keys—give me the keys." She stroked the hood of the little red car. The pair sat in the car inspecting the bells and whistles, when Emily remembered.

"There's dinner on the stove."

THIRTY-NINE

Scott had started taking limited walks in the neighborhood with his walking cast and cane. He told Eloise it was for exercise, but he needed to escape her suffocating pampering.

He was a block from the house when his cell rang. It was Metcalf's boss at the international courier firm. The New York contact; he remembered the number.

Scott imagined what the man looked like. The voice was an American, and triangulation told him the call was routed from somewhere in London.

"Scott, do you know anything about a photograph of the missing diamonds?" The voice stopped waiting for a possible reply, then continued. "Sent to Mugabe?"

"A photograph . . . diamonds?"

Scott stammered, taken off guard. "Who could have done such a thing?"

"I have it from a reliable source that the ten missing diamonds were last in your possession."

"Preposterous? Where did you hear that?"

"I was expecting a denial. Your answers lead me to believe you're being defensive and stalling for time."

"Sir, to my knowledge, the diamonds are in the hands of Winston Metcalf in London."

"I would like to know about your knowledge. Are you blaming Metcalf for taking the diamonds?"

Scott was cornered; either way he had tripped himself up.

"A detective, Joseph Harkness, was hired by my wife to locate me in London. My mission was to follow clues to an old theater house in Amsterdam where I found the old man."

Scott gained confidence as he spoke. He found a bench to relieve the stress.

"I successfully recovered Elijah McQuaid and the safety deposit box with the diamonds. But the clue to check in with the shoe-shine man sounded implausible. The bum demanded the cash, the keys and a zippered case containing the diamonds."

"This man, Joseph Harkness, who your wife hired to find you—he is *not* part of our operation. Have his actions changed the course of your mission?"

"Yes, but he also saved my life more than once."

"Would Adnan Mugabe be pleased with your decision, Scott?"

Scott rambled in his response. "The safety deposit box code and key were delivered with McQuaid for Mr. Mugabe, at Metcalf's office. That's the last I saw of them. I'm not witness to Mugabe's access to the goods."

Scott gulped hard on his lie and heart palpitations made him dizzy.

"Did the detective have access to the diamonds?"

Scott toyed with the idea of making the lie even bigger by incriminating Joseph.

"Yes, he was with me at the vault." Scott confessed.

"Is there anything else I should know about Harkness?"

"He was never with the diamonds unsupervised."

"I notice you are reticent to give direct answers. You have several options, Scott. First, confront Joseph Harkness about the photograph at the center of the truth. Secondly, you can confess directly to Mugabe about the diamond skimming—he will be in London next week. Or finally, you can meet me face to face in Paris with the truth."

Scott mulled the choices and began to test his might.

"I'm afraid, Sir, I'm not aware of your authority over my mission. Are you a superior to Metcalf?" Scott had never spoken to the mastermind before.

"What a small mind. You're out of time Scott. I've made the decision for you. All three choices—start with Harkness. I'll call you again soon and I expect evidence."

The line went dead.

Scott hobbled home and to the bathroom to vacate his nervous stomach. The call with Metcalf's boss replayed over and over.

How would the American know about the photographs? There must be an inside connection reporting on activities in Winston's boardroom.

Scott dialed a London cell number.

Vincent Baynes dreaded making the call to Verona. He couldn't put it off, and expected she wouldn't take the news well. Each ring of the phone resonated in his ears.

"Verona, you should know that Mathias Tessier has been located in Paris. I know you hoped the provisional condition wouldn't be met and Simon would inherit the estate, but it is more complicated. We underestimated the determination of the detective.

"Your lack of cooperation led Harkness to visit the nursing home, where she uncovered sufficient evidence to open an inquiry into the death of Benjamin."

Verona screamed obscenities into the phone, and her voice sputtered as Vincent shouted her down.

"Wait and hear me out, Verona." he said. "The nurse delivering mail to the inmates claims Benjamin had financial statements and status reports of his investments. I believe they are reconstructing his affairs through those banks and institutions.

"Verona, you don't have a choice but to bring me the documents you removed. If you attempt to liquidate or alter any, you'll be charged with falsification and fraud. The affidavits from witnesses suggest you poisoned Benjamin's tea. Come forward right away or you are looking at jail!"

"Absolutely outrageous!" Verona blustered. "Squash them—I demand it. Do something about Emily Harkness!"

"It's too late. Mathias has filed claim to the estate with the court house in Paris. His father has applied to be executor."

"You're a lawyer, Vincent those are the things you are paid for. Do I need to remind you who my brother-in-law is?"

"No need to remind me. I regret I ever met you Verona and your brother-in-law, Metcalf. This is all your own doing."

Vincent let his disdain slip. He wanted to slam the phone in her ear but knew it would be a tragic mistake.

"Watch your mouth, Vincent. I won't tolerate this behavior from you. You'd better fix this!"

Winston Metcalf's sister-in-law was on the telephone.

Christine answered the call and rang it through right away to her boss.

"I'm afraid, Mr. Metcalf, she sounds upset and says it's urgent she speak with you."

"She gets herself worked up needlessly. Try to calm her; I have other pressing matters on my mind."

Christine tried to appease Verona without success.

She knocked on the door. "Sir, I'm sorry but she said she won't go jail and you should smooth things. But she was ranting so much I couldn't understand. She's on the line."

"Tell her I'm in a meeting, but I'll talk to Baynes as soon as I'm available."

Metcalf's slammed his file and paced to the window.

Scott tossed in bed, visualizing an outcome for each option. He didn't want to awaken Eloise or give her cause to worry.

Eloise had followed Scott's instructions to the 'T' by performing at the Harkness Detective Agency to recruit sympathy. In the past, he'd often hired a detective to follow him on a mission, and then set him up as the fall guy.

Scott formulated a new scheme. He would meet with Joseph on the pretense he'd come to square up expenses. After subtle inquiries about the diamonds, he planned to trick him with leading questions while recording the answers.

He chuckled quietly.

I can dupe him into a confession and I'll deliver it to Metcalf.

Convincing Joseph of a last trip to London would be a challenge. But he could serve him on a plate.

Scott was in the kitchen brewing coffee for Eloise when she sauntered from the bedroom in her robe.

"Why are you up so early? It's six o'clock." She wrapped her arms around him waiting for any tender reaction.

"I'm still a working man, my darling." He pulled from her grasp.

"You're not well enough to be thinking about work."

"As a matter of fact, I have business to take care of this morning. I'm going over to the Harkness place to pay my expenses. It isn't fair to keep them hanging."

"Do you want me to come along?" Eloise offered.

"That's not necessary. I'm pretty good with the cane now and the walking cast. I'll be back before lunch."

FORTY

Vincent Baynes hadn't slept. He arrived at the office with shattered nerves and bags under his eyes. The thought of dealing with Verona created heightened stress. He knew she'd be rash and unpredictable.

At nine o'clock, his private line rang. Fearing it was Verona, he felt a claw twist in his stomach. Confrontation was a power tool he used in business to achieve his own goals, but with Verona he felt trapped in a spider's web.

"Hello, Vincent Baynes here."

"Vinnie, I haven't had any good news from you."

It was the voice of Winston Metcalf in London.

Vincent cleared his throat, then took a sip of water to ease his sudden dry mouth.

"Winston, how are you doing?"

"I'm a busy man and don't have time for prattle. Verona called me. She's upset and tells me you need to straighten things out. Did the Harkness dame complete the task?"

"Well, as a matter of fact, I met with her yesterday. She had more gumption than expected. The beneficiary was located and proceeded to file at the court without coming to me. She definitely dropped an elephant into the mix." Vincent was finding strength in his new found anger.

Metcalf said, "You were supposed to follow the plan. You're obviously lacking in legal prowess. You were supposed to keep Emily under your thumb. I wanted her to be an Ace in my pocket to control Joseph Harkness."

"Winston, this is the direct doing of your sister-in-law. During the investigation, it has come to light that charges of murder may be filed against your girl. Verona got sticky fingers and drew the attention of staff at the nursing home. It appears she poisoned the poor man's last cup of tea with arsenic. Do you expect me to smooth *that* over?"

Metcalf said, "Are you having an attack of morals? Everything has a solution. Take care of it! Do whatever you have to do to put the Harkness woman out of the picture. We'll talk again."

Vincent drummed his fingers considering a solution. Pulling out his top drawer, he fidgeted to the back until he found a small notebook held together by an elastic.

Thumbing to the inside back cover he opened to a scratchy phone number. On his cell phone he sent a text, and the phone immediately beeped back a reply.

Affirmative, I'll take out Emily Harkness. Simon

The receptionist knocked on Mr. Baynes's closed office door to announce the arrival of Ms. Charbonneau. She was tense, yet on guard due to Verona's agitated state.

"Yes, of course, bring her in."

A heavy mink coat bolted through the doorway, shoving the receptionist out of the way. Her hair was in embarrassing disarray with mascara dripping down her cheeks and cherry red lipstick marking her teeth.

Vincent rose to greet her. "Verona, it's nice to see you."

She shouted, "Let's not do that Vincent. Have you come up with a plan to fix things? Does Mathias have to survive for thirty days? Couldn't he have an accident or something? Same goes for Emily Harkness. Winston has people who take care of things."

"Verona, there is no fix; it has gone too far. This is the end of it. Call your brother-in-law if you like; it won't change anything. I'm already taking care of the Harkness woman but that won't change anything. Yes, it's gone too far. I wash my hands of your meddling."

Her face flamed with rage. All her ugliness had rallied to assist her. "I won't have my integrity challenged. Do you really anticipate I could be charged with the murder of old Benjamin? I've spent the last few years planning this and you can't ruin it. You can't say 'no' to me!"

"I said no! Furthermore, Verona, I expect you will be apprehended soon. You should head for your country retreat in the north of France. Stay out of contact and cool down."

Leaning over his desk, she glowered. Her breathing slowed and she was calm for an instant before a grotesque sneer returned from behind the smeared lipstick. She reached into her coat.

The muscles in her face tensed and her eyelids blinked only once when she fired through the mink, startling herself.

The look of alarm in Vincent's eyes pleased her.

"That's for crossing me."

Verona continued to spit in his face and fired once more, striking him in the chest. In the slow motion of the moment, she experienced ultimate pleasure. She watched as the blood seeped through Vincent's shirt. Then his head fell forward.

Bayne's secretary rushed into the office and screamed. Verona barged past her out through the lobby ranting. She'd become a mad woman, chanting in childish delirium.

"Vincent, Emily, Mathias—three little ducks in a row. Ha!"

FORTY-ONE

Winston's mandate was to appease Mugabe and eradicate all witnesses. He needed to remedy his strategy in placing the guilt for the stolen gems on Scott.

He didn't know the boss was in Paris and had already contacted Scott about the photograph of the diamonds that were couriered to Mugabe's London hotel.

What's a man thousands of miles away in New York going to know of the whereabouts of the gems? He'll have to take my word for it.

Anticipating that Mugabe would take out the survivor, either Joseph or Scott, these rare blue diamonds would be his, a half million dollar profit. Tasting power, he wanted more, forgetting he was not at the top of the structure triangle.

Scott hobbled into the rue Euler office just after Emily and Joseph had opened. He pretended to be in good spirits.

"What a pleasant surprise," she said. "I'm Emily Harkness. I feel like I know you so well, yet we haven't formally met. You're Scott Marchand?"

He was startled by her beauty and her innocent blue eyes. "Indeed I am."

"Joseph will be along in a few minutes, please have a seat. How did you get here with a cane?"

"I confess I cheated and took a taxi. I'll admit staircases are challenging but I'm getting practice up and down in Branly." Scott chuckled, still mesmerized by the magnetic eyes.

The office door opened and Joseph came in with three coffees.

"Hey, Scott. I saw your coattail down the street and took a gamble on an extra coffee."

"You never miss a clue, do you Joseph?"

"I try not to."

Joseph invited him to take a seat.

"What brings you all the way down here?"

"I don't like loose ends; I want to clear my bill. I know Eloise has made some deposits. Would another 5,000 euros plus 5,000 to cover expenses be sufficient?"

"That's sounds about right. It isn't necessary for you to pay it all at once."

"Not a problem. Eloise doesn't know about the funds I have stashed away for a rainy day. As I said before, Joseph, I've been paid generously for my services."

Instead of writing a check, Scott pulled a thick envelope full of bundles of bills from his coat.

"It's all there in cash."

He shoved the envelope to Emily.

"I'll get you a receipt, Scott."

Emily moved to her own desk and delved into the stationary drawer for the receipt book. She didn't count the bills.

Scott leaned and whispered over Joseph's desk.

"Joseph, could I speak to you in private for a few minutes?"

"I don't keep anything from Emily. You can talk freely."

"Please, Joseph. It's important."

Joseph yielded to the persistence in Scott's voice.

"We have a utility room in the back. This way." He gave Emily a wink.

"Joseph, I need to know about the ten diamonds. The ones you took."

"I don't like the way you phrased that, Scott. I didn't take any diamonds. You did."

"I was referring to the delivery you made while I was in the hospital."

"That was quick and sweet. A clean getaway. Don't worry."

"I'm afraid that I do. Metcalf is denying he received the diamonds. Wait until Mugabe finds out."

Joseph was curious. "How do you know Metcalf is denying the diamonds?"

"I'm being followed. I've been ordered back to London."

"You have a choice, Scott, to go or *not* to go. Tell the truth—everything will be fine. They can't risk headlines."

Scott looked at Joseph. "I'd feel better if I had backup."

Joseph read between the lines; he was being asked to accompany him.

Why is he asking me to risk my life again? My job is over!

"I don't know, Scott. I just got back and Emily has a full load to deal with. I can't do that to her again so soon."

Scott was silent and crestfallen. He deliberately stumbled on his way back to the visitor's chair, to solicit sympathy.

"When are you to be in London?"

"Tomorrow morning."

"Tell you what. No promises, but leave it with me until I can talk to Emily. I'll call you later this afternoon."

"I'd appreciate that Joseph."

The elusive American, Jacques Simpson, fingered the engraved 'C' on his silver medallion. He paced, waiting for Winston Metcalf to answer the phone.

He resisted the temptation to unseal the dossier on his desk labeled 'Ducharme'. Trisha's effort had been rewarding.

"Is the meeting set now?" he challenged.

"Yes, everything is in order. The trap is set for the fox."

"After your years of service, Winston, I'd like to meet with you in person."

"Of course, Sir, at your convenience." Winston was buzzed at the flattery.

"I'll be in touch with you later. I'm booked in at the George V." The American ended the call.

This complicates my plan and I'll need some deviations. I'm sure he won't show his face, his anonymity is part of his power hold.

Simpson punched in a number from memory and a female voice answered.

"Who gets to be the winner?" she asked.

"You'll know when it's time. In the meantime, keep your man in line."

The woman walked to the hall bureau. At the back of the drawer wrapped in a Hermès scarf was a long double-barreled .45 caliber revolver. She stroked the pearl handle.

FORTY-TWO

With chardonnay on the nightstand, Emily propped up her pillows and reviewed her iPad files. Joseph was watching the evening news.

She called out, "Where does legal jurisdiction fall? The Will was written in Saint-Germain but probate will be in Paris.

"Two separate issues, Emily. The Will and the murder."

Emily nodded. "The murder charges will be laid in Normandy; all the witnesses live in the area. We might need to go back for the trial."

"Since I'm unbiased, should I make the call to the Police Chief, Em?"

"That would be great."

This was the first opportunity Emily and Joseph had for an in-depth conversation of the diamond theft.

"Emily, Scott has been untrustworthy. He drugged me at the Amsterdam hotel and swiped the diamonds from the safety deposit box. Then he sent me into Metcalf's den to return the stolen stones.

"Emily, it was barbaric—Mugabe's vengeance and blood thirsty quest, punishing McQuaid."

Emily was disgusted and squeamish even though Joseph had not given the details.

"Sorry, Em. I didn't need to tell you about that."

"Well, it gives me an honest picture of the situation."

"Scott wants me to go back to London to vouch for him one final time."

"I don't like it."

"Emily, I rely on my instincts and something is wrong. Wrong, I mean, between Scott, Metcalf and Mugabe. I'm the only witness to Metcalf snagging the diamonds. If anyone needed a scapegoat . . . I'm the odd man out."

Joseph hadn't shared his recent Daniel encounters with Emily. There had been an old silent bond between the three of them, but it again seemed complicated.

"Emily, you should know this. Twice I've crossed paths with a man in a disguise who gave me messages to abort Scott's mission. I've been hesitant to say the words, but it is Daniel . . . our Daniel, from Interpol. He told me Scotland Yard was involved in London."

Emily was stunned. "Daniel! Are you sure?" Her heart pounded.

He said, "Yes . . . I'm sure."

"Was it threatening or meant in goodwill?"

"I'd say goodwill."

Emily reflected back on her last meeting with Daniel at the farmhouse near Rouen.

Always something mysterious about him. Like a dark knight.

"If you go, how can you be prepared for the London meeting? I don't like it, Joseph. Sounds like a set-up!"

He said, "I need to make an insurance call."

She cautioned, "Mugabe sounds like a dangerous man. Be constantly on guard."

"He is dangerous, but truth and honesty are paramount. A man is nothing without his reputation and this is an arrogant man."

Emily asked, "What's your plan?"

"I'll state upfront that McQuaid and I accessed the vault. I'll avoid using Scott's name, but I'll vouch positively to the whereabouts of the diamonds."

"And you expect him to say thank you?"

"I'll deal with that and record the call for evidence."

"Metcalf will be irate when he discovers it was you who sent photographs. Two of the three men wish you would disappear."

"Emily, Scott might be our biggest threat. I've been skeptical since his visit this morning. His words were rehearsed and his motive is now clear. He's fabricating a confession for me."

Joseph's fighter instinct prevailed. "I'll go and face Scott and wrap this up."

"Can't it be a day trip?"

He kissed her forehead. "Yes, a quick in to London and out by the middle of the afternoon. We'll have dinner at Place du Tertre tonight with a view of the Eiffel Tower."

Joseph called Scott and agreed to meet for the morning flight. He'd book them, both returning late afternoon.

He then dialed Adnan Mugabe's South Africa cell number. Joseph was about to hang up when the heavy accent answered.

"Mr. Mugabe?"

"Yes. Who is this?"

"My name isn't important. Are you free to talk in confidence? I have some delicate information."

"I am alone. Go ahead."

"I'm a detective who assisted in the recovery of McQuaid's safety deposit box in Amsterdam."

"You have my attention, Mr. Harkness."

"I'd like assurances that what I am about to tell you is strictly off the record. I respect your ethics of valuing truth and honesty above all."

Mugabe considered the flattery a worthy compliment and smiled maliciously.

"You can trust me to be discerning."

"I wasn't in possession of the diamonds until I delivered an envelope to Winston Metcalf for a friend. I sent you the photograph in South Africa to respectfully show you evidence of the delivery.

"I don't have any involvement in relation to the theft from the safety deposit box. It seems a key player has been working both sides. The character of a man is in his soul, and the eyes are a window to the soul. Eyes tell the truth."

Mugabe was solemn. "I'll accept that."

"I've been asked to accompany Mr. Marchand to London. Metcalf may offer him as a sacrifice, accusing him of having the gems."

"I see you're a man of honor, Mr. Harkness. I'll consider your position."

Joseph said, "I'll accompany Scott to vouch for him and verify the delivery of the stones."

"I have no objection."

"Do you have any questions?" Joseph asked Mugabe.

"I do." His base voice boomed. "When were you first aware of someone having possession of my diamonds?"

"I won't be evasive with you. The truth is always written in the face of the criminal. I've seen enough guilty men, in my line of work, to know the difference, Mr. Mugabe."

"Thank you, Mr. Harkness. I'll rely on your advice."

On Eloise's insistence, Scott dressed in his finest for their dinner at Les Ombres at Branly Quai. He was glad of the distraction after the Metcalf call.

They walked from the padlocked garden suite and climbed the stairs to a waiting taxi. Scott had always avoided the neighbors, preferring a low profile at home.

With weeks of stored gossip, Eloise opened up to talk the ear off Scott. He nodded and added questions to keep it alive, and was satisfied she hadn't noticed his lack of interest.

The sommelier recommended some wines, but Scott was distracted and waved him off politely. "Please give us few minutes and come back."

Eloise pointed out the Chateaubriand with Béarnaise on the menu, and he raised a finger to the passing waiter. But his thoughts were not in Branly Quai.

The waiter returned again to stand at his side.

"Are you going to order a wine, Scott?" Eloise prompted him.

"Sure, whatever you'd like."

"Scott, you're neglecting me."

"Of course I am, darling."

Unaware of his slip, he leaned toward the wine steward to select her favorite.

Eloise made a toast.

"Scott, congratulations are in order. You are home safe and I have accomplished a deception on the home front."

"What do you mean, Eloise?"

"I led Emily to believe I was a helpless poor wife fretting over my missing husband."

"I don't like it, Eloise, when you start talking like that."

"Someone had to keep the Harkness people on track while you evaded them in England."

"I thought you enjoyed Emily's companionship. She has been so kind to you."

"I find ways to amuse myself, Scott. Emily is kind and trusting to a fault."

"I prefer the soft gentle wife you were pretending to be."

The romantic evening was off to a poor start. Scott didn't want to be there, and resented his wife's manipulation.

Before dessert was offered, he requested the check and ordered a taxi.

"Eloise, I have a lot of pain in my leg, we should go home."

"No, it's too soon," she pouted. "We have the whole evening ahead."

"Please, Eloise, we need to leave."

On the ride to the house, Eloise fidgeted and fretted, constantly checking her watch.

She tried again. "We really don't need to go home this early. We could go for a nightcap."

Pulling up at the garden suite, Scott saw a silhouette in the living room window. A van was in front.

His blood pressure rose. "We are being robbed, Eloise! We've caught them red-handed."

"Scott, they're probably armed." She put her hand on his arm to hold him back.

"I'll call the police then."

"Suit yourself."

Scott put the phone away and hoisted himself from the backseat, hobbling alone to the front door. The wrought iron gate was ajar and he checked the latch.

It's not forced. It doesn't unlock without a key. I remember locking it myself.

Easing the handle, he inched the door open. His crutches leaning against the inside crashed to the floor and Scott was grabbed from behind. He couldn't see the invader but a strong arm locked around his throat, choking his air.

"Where are the diamonds, Marchand?"

He was barely able to breathe.

"I don't have any diamonds."

The thief threw him to the floor and tore up the outer stairs. The van was gone before Scott got to his feet. Eloise stood at the door and called to check if he was okay.

Sporting fresh bruises, he went directly to the shower and then to bed without a word to Eloise.

It is incomprehensible and unthinkable.

He laid awake to replay it over and over.

Eloise planned the robbery. The burglars never touched her or pressed her for the gems. She's a greedy vixen. Is she in cahoots with Metcalf? Nah, too preposterous.

He couldn't recall if he'd mentioned the diamonds to her. He was normally rigid; it was his rule *never* to discuss his cases.

Joseph asked to speak to a detective at London's police headquarters. His call was transferred to a desk Sergeant who was intrigued by Joseph's story.

"Sir, may I have your permission to record our conversation?" The detective asked.

Joseph said, "Yes, of course. For the sake of our discussion, call me 'Tom'."

"Alright, Tom. It appears you've found yourself involved with some nasty men. Are you purely an observer, or a player?"

"Your questions should be relevant to the issue; I'm not on the witness stand. Don't you want to know about the courier operation?"

"My intention isn't to challenge you, Tom, I'm establishing my vantage point in this hearsay."

Joseph said, "You can decide for yourself. If I attend a future meeting with them, I'll wear a transmitter to record the conversation."

"Give me a name I can validate. You must understand, I need to confirm what you've told me."

"The man manipulating this scheme has powerful connections. Several of his thugs have committed offenses, yet they've come up with hefty bail. The thought of a corrupt connection to someone in authority has to be considered."

"You have to give me more, Tom."

"Very well, Winston Metcalf is the man at the crux."

"Slow down, Tom! Winston Metcalf is a highly regarded upstanding citizen of London. He's a known supporter to some significant politicians and contributes to projects and charities. I'll have difficulty in getting my superiors to buy in."

"Well then, I guess I'm on my own. If you don't mind, I'd like to keep your direct line handy in case I fall into a trap."

"Sure, Tom. Bring me something concrete and we can take a serious look."

"Thanks, Jones, for listening."

Joseph was pleased to set up the foundation of a future investigation.

With a detective's mind, Jones will search it to appease his curiosity.

FORTY-THREE

A stern face stood before Emily's desk as she finished her call. The man pulled an envelope from his suit.

"You've been summoned. Have a nice day." The man tipped his hat and left.

"What's that about, Babe?"

"It's my case for the divorcée, Webster?"

"Yes, I remember."

"I'm afraid I held back some details of the case. You were involved in some pretty heavy stuff at the time."

"Emily, you never need to worry about me. I'm supposed to protect you."

"It should have been simple. I took incriminating photos of the husband having an affair. His wife demanded an exorbitant settlement and that should have been the end of it. But a few days later, the husband came around to the agency and confronted me."

"Did he hurt you, Em?"

"The argument was heated and he grabbed and twisted my wrist. When the police arrived, I was angry enough to file assault charges. I went to the Prefecture of Police and applied for a restraining order. Remember the day you asked me about my wrist?"

"I do, but that's a nasty story."

Emily stretched the summons on the table. It was simply a witness testimony supporting the evidence of the photographs, not for the assault case.

"When is the hearing? I want to go with you."

"Wednesday, next week."

Scott was tired and gaunt. He loitered at the BA ticket counter at Charles de Gaulle. Joseph returned with their boarding cards.

"You look worn out, Scott. Still getting grief from the leg?" He gave him a friendly pat.

Scott brought his crutches, for security, but also for show and sympathy at the meeting. He struggled with his carryon until Joseph took it and threw the strap over his own shoulder.

"Here's your credit card and boarding pass. Thanks for paying."

"No problem," Scott said. "I did ask you to join me."

"Right."

After an awkward silence, Joseph said, "Scott, I need to know if you've had further contact with Metcalf."

Scott looked guilty and decided not to force a denial.

"I confirmed I'd be attending this morning."

The answer was too succinct and Joseph was more convinced of a setup.

I'll need to keep one foot holding the door open.

Scott avoided eye contact. Winston had promised him a share of the diamonds in return for swearing to Mugabe that Joseph was the pilferer. Scott counted on Winston siding with him now. The tension between the two men was growing.

He looked out over the wing at the clouds without speaking. Joseph, in the aisle seat read the Financial Times and wrote in his tablet.

Verona Charbonneau's townhouse in the affluent district of Paris sat on a quiet hill overlooking the distant Arc de Triomphe.

Inside the plush structure, Verona was out of control. Arriving by taxi from Baynes's office, she stamped into the empty house and slammed her closet. Throwing her coat on the sofa, she clutched the luxury Vuitton cushions and thrust them to the floor.

She felt no guilt over the Baynes shooting. In her drawn out inferno of rage, she swore and ranted about his disloyalty, then her husband's infidelity.

Barely audible, she said, "It's the Harkness woman. I should have killed her too."

Verona found a bottle of Jamieson's Whiskey and turned the lights out. An hour later, she sat in silence in the darkness, her hair matted and her clothes disheveled muttering curse words.

She had returned to the house to discover her husband was extending one of his usual prolonged trips. Collecting her phone messages, she concluded this was the climax of his unfaithfulness.

"You'll get yours too, my dearest!"

Compounded by the episode with Vincent, Verona's nerves went over the edge.

"Vincent, you stupid man. You could have fixed this." She spat into an empty space where she visualized Vincent was standing, mocking her.

"Clean up your shirt!" she shouted in the air.

Through the parlor curtains, the glow of blue and red lights pulsed. The silence in the room confused her, then a pounding at the front door. Unable to comprehend what was happening, she huddled on an over-stuffed armchair. She wrapped a throw around herself with her knees tucked up under her chin. The phone rang in the background.

Cupping her hands over her ears, she waited for the pounding to stop. With a crash, the front door splintered as two officers barged through with guns drawn.

Wild eyed, Verona looked up. "Are you here to pick up Benjamin?"

One demanded, "Are you Mrs. Verona Charbonneau?"

"Yes, I am."

"I'm afraid, Ms. Charbonneau, you're under arrest for the murder of Vincent Baynes. Do you understand the charge?"

"Vinnie, is he here too?" Her voice was childlike.

The phone was still ringing. The police Sergeant picked it up; it was her husband. Stunned by the developments, he assured the officer he'd be back in Paris that evening.

Since Verona couldn't comprehend the charges, the police ordered an ambulance. Within minutes, medics arrived and administered a sedative. They were gentle, helping her onto the stretcher for transport to the hospital's psychiatric ward.

She was limp and co-operative. "Don't forget to eat your dinner. And please tell Benjamin to finish his tea," she whispered.

"I'll remember that, Mrs. Charbonneau."

Yellow tape barred the door to Vincent's office. Emily's business card was on the floor. Mr. Chartrand picked it up.

FORTY-FOUR

Joseph rented a blue Renault at Heathrow. He manually slid the seat back to the maximum so Scott had more leg room. The weather had taken a turn, a pleasant change from the dreary rain to a mix of sun and cloud, bringing the green London landscape to life.

"Do you want a bite at one of the pubs before the meeting?" Joseph asked.

"Sure, a pint and a pie never hurt anyone."

Joseph watched the establishments along the boulevard and pulled over at a tavern, the Hogg & Duck. He found a parking spot in the same block and Scott hobbled along the walk with Joseph.

A lager with his hearty lunch relaxed Scott a bit, but he still avoided looking Joseph in the eye.

"We should get on our way." Scott said while shuffling in his pocket for some pound notes for the waitress, then pulled himself up with the crutches.

They returned in silence to the car at the back of the building. Joseph walked around to the driver's side, leaving Scott to get in on his own. He didn't.

Shuffling the crutches to his left hand, he dug into his jacket until he felt the cold steel of his gun. Out of Joseph's vision, he hobbled around to the driver's window.

"Hey pal, you get out here." The gun was in Joseph's face.
I didn't see this.

"Scott, there's no need for a gun. What do you want?"

"Give me the keys. Slowly get out and toss your pistol in the drain."

Scott calculated Joseph would try to slam him with the car door and stepped back out of range while holding the gun.

"Open the trunk, Joseph!" Scott stayed out of range of Joseph's potential karate chop, then sucked in confidence. "Keep your hands over your head and get in!"

"Scott . . ." The butt of Scott's revolver smashed on the back of Joseph's head and he slumped into the trunk.

Checking that he wasn't under observation, Scott stepped back and fired a single shot into the trunk. He smiled with relief.

Option one taken care of.

Scott locked the trunk and hailed a taxi.

Metcalf's assistant, Christine, was watching the elevator for Joseph and Scott.

As he approached reception, she rose to put her hand on Scott's arm. She whispered a warning to him and he nodded.

Adnan Mugabe and his aide, Solomon, were waiting. Christine led Scott into the room and pulled out a chair for him. Winston was pacing by the window turning as they entered.

Mugabe made the opening gesture.

"Mr. Marchand, please join us." He looked at Scott and the open door.

"I understood Mr. Harkness would be attending with you."

"We had a change of plans." Scott replied.

Christine helped him prop his crutches in the corner then closed the door behind her.

Mugabe's voice echoed through the room. "Gentlemen, as we are all aware, the diamond shipment retrieved from Amsterdam was short fifty carats, ten five-carat stones; half a million dollar value. After my discussion with Mr. McQuaid, I excused him from further guilt and I'm satisfied he received due punishment.

"I have a long-distance relationship with Winston Metcalf. My own empire was built on trust and honesty from my grandfather and my father. My ancestors fought in the Boer War to defend the resources of South Africa." He was satisfied he had impressed his audience with manipulated history.

Mugabe turned and faced Winston Metcalf.

Winston crossed his arms over his chest, presenting a rigid signal that he'd be unwilling to admit to anything.

"Mr. Metcalf, here is a copy of the photograph sent anonymously to me, displaying the diamonds on your desk. It is your letterhead."

In a long painful pause, Mugabe studied their faces. Scott wasn't able to control an impetuous glance toward Winston.

"I'd be interested in considering Mr. Harkness's viewpoint. Perhaps you have information concerning his whereabouts?"

"His guilty conscience! He refused to join me."

Metcalf was put off his game and saw that Mugabe's gaze didn't follow to Scott. Coughing, he cleared his throat and reached for a glass of water.

"Mr. Marchand, did you have an agreement with anyone in this room to share in the proceeds of fifty carats?" Mugabe's stare remained with Winston.

"No, Sir." Scott's voice wavered.

Mugabe turned to watch Scott. "Mr. Marchand, I've spent years studying people, searching for the truth in faces, voices and body language. Do you wish to change your answer?"

Scott stammered, "The only person I discussed the diamonds with was Mr. Harkness."

Mugabe leaned over the table and looked down directly into the soul of Scott.

"And what was the nature of that conversation?"

Scott grasped quietly for the words, but before he answered, Mugabe continued.

"It's only fair to tell you, I've had a conversation with Joseph Harkness."

"Please, Sir. I was following instructions." Scott begged, his demeanor turning to cowardice.

How would he have spoken to Joseph!

"Whose instructions were those?" Mugabe pressed.

Scott's glance went to Winston.

"You have spoken silently."

Winston proclaimed, "No Adnan, you are wrong. Scott retrieved the diamonds for you when Harkness interceded. Harkness is the guilty person."

"You do underestimate me, Winston."

"Mr. Marchand, for the last time, are you in possession of the diamonds?

"No, Sir!"

"Winston, are *you* in possession of the diamonds?"

Winston faltered. "No, Adnan, I am not." He was still stinging from the insult and his tone became abrasive.

Mugabe said, "Solomon, do you have my case?"

"Please Adnan, don't be so petty over a few diamonds." Winston mumbled.

Mugabe turned in a rage. The lion had been awakened, the affront unforgiveable.

Scott was aghast that Mugabe chose to vindicate Joseph. He looked pleadingly at Metcalf, hoping he'd be a man and confess. But Winston stood firm.

Scott said the unthinkable. "Mr. Mugabe, I had an agreement with Mr. Metcalf. He wanted the diamonds for himself, promising me a share."

"You stupid fool!" Winston spat at Scott.

"Ah ha! We have a cobra against a cobra, this is interesting." Adnan jeered.

Nobody in the room moved while Mugabe paced.

"Scott, wait in the outer room. I'll have instructions for you when I'm finished here." His black eyes burrowed into Scott's as he sneered.

Scott regained his strength and lunged toward the door dragging his cast. Christine had her head down in the outer office but it was clear she was listening.

Scott stopped at Christine's desk.

"Look Scott, I don't see this ending well, if you stay or if you go. Haven't you heard that somewhere before?"

Scott smiled back at Christine and headed for the elevator. *Option two completed.*

As the elevator closed, Christine placed a call to Paris.

"The situation has escalated. Harkness didn't show but Mugabe is on to Metcalf."

She listened for a moment.

"Yes, Sir, I'll do as you suggest."

FORTY-FIVE

Opening his eyes in the dark trunk, Joseph couldn't tell but guessed it would be nighttime. With the glow of his cell phone, his fingers ran along the seams of the trunk.

I'm in the trunk of the rental. Scott thought he'd outsmarted me.

He squirmed to check each side and felt for the locked latch for a trunk release. His foot fell into an indention with protruding bolts and a neon tag. He shone the phone light.

This is it. The lever!

He climbed out. No-one was in the lot. His hand passed over his thigh; it was sticky with blood.

It seems I've been grazed by a bullet.

He phoned Emily.

"Hi, Babe. I'm on my way back to Paris, but I've locked myself out of the rental. I'm not sure what my chances are of getting the auto club this hour of night."

"Forget the car, can you get a cab?"

"That's probably just as difficult. There's a pub next door, I'll test my luck there. Call you back."

"Joseph . . . how?"

"Later! I'm too angry right now."

Joseph walked briskly from the taxi to the Air France counter. He scanned the gate.

During the flight, his focus was on Emily's safety. He shouldn't have left her alone in Paris.

Sitting in the loft, Emily completed the accounting records. Their initial revenues were beyond their expectations. *Life is going to return to normal when Joseph gets home.*

Emily entered into her tablet the details of two disturbing voice messages at the office. The first had been left two evenings prior and the man's voice wasn't familiar. "Burn your evidence!" it said.

The second was on the machine the next morning: "Watch your back."

When she told Joseph about the messages, he narrowed it to Marchand, Webster or Charbonneau kin.

So many want us out of the way. We must be doing a good job.

Two blocks from Metcalf's building, Scott pulled a phone number from his wallet.

"Sorry, I didn't mean to leave you out of the loop. I'm tired of being given orders; it's *my* turn to take the upper hand."

The woman cupped her hand over the phone.

"It makes a difference to me," she whispered. He was flattered that she cared so much.

"What if I told you I'd be splitting the diamonds with Metcalf? What would you have done differently?"

She said, "I would have tried to dissuade you."

"I can't turn the clock back," he said.

"If that is what you want, Scott, I'll respect your wishes, you know you can count on me to back you up."

Scott returned and watched Mugabe's limousine pull away. Entering the Parkade he went back to the tenth floor.

With bold authority, he calmly strode past Christine. She made her objections but Scott gave her a wink before kicking the door open.

Winston Metcalf was standing quietly staring out into London. He watched Scott's reflection in the glass and stayed at the window.

"I thought you'd be back, Scott."

"We have a score to settle, Winston."

Metcalf turned and spurted, "The diamonds are cursed, so there is nothing to discuss. Mugabe made a bargain with me. Do you want to hear it?"

"You are going to tell me anyway."

"I've never killed a man over the years. I have assigned a few hits in my life, but never the dirty work myself. By the way, I do have a superior in New York. I suppose he already knows about this farce.

"I'm between a rock and a hard place, Scott. Every time I get in my car I expect it to blow up. The diamonds were supposed to save me but I've run out of time.

"I swore never to tell you, but you should know this."

Metcalf raised his hand to the back of his neck.

"When you joined the organization you received in-depth medical observations. A chip was embedded; it left a scar on your neck. Your life is on record."

Winston tilted his head. "See here is mine." His fingers ran over the raised flesh.

"I wonder what it's like to squeeze the life out of a man, to watch his desperation and pleading. Those last precious moments before life eases from his body."

Winston moved over to his desk. "Every inch had a calculated purpose. Any man with a conscience would be afflicted with nightmares the rest of his life."

Scott touched the back of his own neck. "Did you sell me out to Mugabe?"

"I didn't have to."

"What are you talking about?"

Winston looked resigned. "The price is much greater than money." He reached for his desk drawer handle.

"Why are you telling me this?"

Winston withdrew a revolver from the drawer. Before he raised it, Scott's pistol was ready.

Staring into the eyes of a desperate man, Scott could see that Winston was prepared to shoot. Without waiting for a test of morals, he fired into Winston's chest. Winston fell back into his chair and Scott walked closer to him.

Winston muttered, "It was either me or you—that was my choice. You lose—you get the nightmares." He closed his eyes.

The cell on Winston's desk vibrated. Scott picked up the phone.

"Winston is it taken care of. Who is this?"

The American listened to Scott's plea and hung up.

Scott was about to flee when an idea came to him.

"I knew it!" Scott mumbled out loud.

He rang the number back.

"Hello, this is Scott Marchand, are you surprised to hear from me?"

"Scott, my man, congratulations you've beaten the odds!" the voice answered.

"You were expecting Winston Metcalf, weren't you?"

"This didn't need to happen, Scott. You were contracted by the firm, in good faith, to fulfill a service and for that you were paid an extraordinary sum. We've been aware of your skimming in recent months. This was a final test to prove your innocence. You failed—it was time to clean up loose ends."

"It never occurred to me that the devil would have an American accent."

"I'll take that as a fear evoking compliment."

"You know that I'm finished with the firm."

"Yes, I know."

Winston's desk drawer was still open. In plain sight was a blue bag filled with the missing diamonds.

Option three completed.

Scott looked at Christine standing in the doorway. Her hand over her mouth, she tried to scream but nothing more than a whisper came.

"Scott, what have you done?"

"Christine, I need you to be calm. Take some deep breaths."

She slumped into a chair to regain her composure.

"I need to call for an ambulance, or police."

"Yes, you do, but first I need your help."

He held his hand in the air and checked under the desk for a bug, then dug into the planter. He cursed on finding Joseph's transmitter.

Drat! Too late! I wonder where the feed went.

Scott whispered instructions to Christine. He gave her a gentle shove out of the way and charged through to make a hobbling escape on the stairway.

Christine waited momentarily then whisked past the group and called the police.

She cleared the onlookers and barred the entrance to Metcalf's office, then paced at the door, guarding it until a police swat team swooped in.

Breathing heavily, Scott's adrenaline propelled him down several flights before he heard the chase from above, then voices from below. His walking was a disadvantage and the aching overwhelming.

Scott got out of the staircase on the fourth floor, leaving him with nowhere to go.

Cornered!

He submitted, lying face down on the floor with his hands locked behind his head. Policemen were on him with guns in seconds.

"Don't move!"

Two officers from the stairwell burst to the lobby. One gruffly searched Scott's back pocket for his ID.

"Mr. Marchand, you're under arrest."

The officer Mirandized and cuffed him.

"In that case, I choose to remain silent until I speak with an attorney."

Scott was yanked to his feet by both arms and held at the elevator. He limped in pain.

Daniel dialed New York. "The interference was Winston Metcalf, just like we calculated. His greed cost him his life. Scott Marchand has been arrested, however it appears he may have recovered the diamonds from Metcalf's office. Do you want me to continue the chase?"

"Daniel, I'm amazed no one has discovered those diamond are fakes with the exception of one genuine stone. What have you done with the cash and real gems?"

"They are safe, like you asked. I have fully recouped Metcalf's $400,000 that should square his debt with the firm."

In spite of Scott's handicap, the London police mercilessly shoved him into the back of a police wagon.

Christine identified the man fleeing Metcalf's office as Marchand. She politely avoided answering further questions.

Statements were taken from the employees who saw Scott departing, but without witnesses to the murder it would be impossible to determine premeditation or self-defense. Security cameras were forbidden in Metcalf's boardroom and office, preventing any video record. When the shot was fired, it created only the echo of a sharp pop, barely audible even to Christine.

Detective Jones headed the site investigation.

Well, that Tom fellow was telling the truth! It was Winston Metcalf.

Jones searched the office for a bug Tom might have left. He found one on the ficus stem of Metcalf's plant.

"There's much more here than first meets the eye,"

Tom warned him that someone in authority was interfering with criminals who were released quickly on bail.

I need to get Tom's number from my files. He's a viable witness, who can I trust? I'll stay with the informant for now.

He garbled and tucked the bug into his pocket.

This could be a detective's dream to fame. There could be a strong case for self-defense and I could blow the lid off an international cover-up.

The reporter's tank at the London Times buzzed with the news of the infiltration within the international courier operation run locally by Winston Metcalf. The clues and gossip spread quickly, and within hours, Metcalf was described as a desperately greedy man and Scott Marchand as his scapegoat.

Rifling through his desk notes, Detective Jones came upon the pink telephone message.

Tom's number.

FORTY-SIX

The Webster divorce hearings were next on Emily's agenda. It was a sunny February day and her spirits were high. On the way to the office, she stopped in the fancy shops on the Champs-Élysées.

A millinery shop lured her inside by the displays. The windows were bursting with fashionable hats, winter woolens and new spring colors. The choice was difficult, however Emily picked a Nordstrom grey wool Cloche with a narrow brim.

Emily imagined she was skipping as she walk. She was happy and it was the time of day when she could be truly alone in her thoughts.

Jack Webster had been agonizing over the upcoming divorce hearing. His wife was outraged by his infidelity and demanded an extraordinary settlement, plus voting shares in his company. It was her intention to ruin the man and the

246 | SHIRLEY BURTON

reputation he'd established long before their marriage. He berated himself for not having a prenuptial agreement.

The reduction in his social invitations irked him, and he felt the weight of shunned looks when he entered his membership clubs.

Meanwhile, his wife was the gossiping butterfly of many women's clubs and luncheons. She was generous in divulging details, knowing the information would travel back to their spouses and the boardrooms of Paris.

Webster's lawyer advised him to settle out of court and maintain a low profile. Based on photos and the witness testimony of Emily Harkness, he anticipated the judge would favor Mrs. Webster. The aftermath of publicity could cost him his seat on the Boards of some noble institutions and removal from elite society guest lists where his ego thrived.

Jack Webster seethed with rage, with a vendetta to get even. His plan wasn't rational, but the stress pushed him to it.

He spent the prior evening in his basement with diagrams, explosive plastic and wires. On the black market, he'd acquired a half dozen sticks of explosives and putty. Twisting the wires into place, he lifted the contraption to a cardboard box, with a timer in his pocket.

For several days, he had monitored Emily's arrival at the agency knowing she wouldn't be expected until close to 9 a.m. He ignored the restraining order against him.

Webster checked his watch at 8:00 a.m., calculating an hour to install the device. The building's main door was open for the neighboring print shop. Webster crept upstairs.

The floorboards creaked under his expansive weight while he pressed into the banister.

At the second floor, Webster was out of breath, panting as he fumbled with the lock pick. Leaning closer to the mechanism, he heard a welcoming pop. The handle released and he invited himself in.

Webster hadn't been there before, but knew he could improvise with the bomb placement. He found his way to the alley kitchen, a cramped space with a refrigerator and microwave. Without daylight, he affixed the bomb to the back of the refrigerator wiring the timer to the light switch. The first person at the switch would be the victim of a ferocious blast.

Surely the dame will want to make a cup of coffee first thing.

Jack Webster spent forty-five minutes setting the bomb, a painstaking process for a novice. With everything in order, he returned to his car down the block to watch for Emily's arrival. Anticipating an explosion and fire, he bided his time.

At 9:30 a.m., Emily arrived on rue Euler wearing her new cloche. She stopped at the corner for a coffee to go.

Coming up the stairs, she heard the phone ringing inside. Unlocking the office door she ran to her desk. It was Eloise.

"Emily! Did you hear about Scott? He's been arrested in London for the murder of some bigwig."

"No Eloise, I hadn't heard."

Jack Webster kept looking at his watch; it was 10:45. Several customers had walked in and out of the building but there hadn't been an explosion or an alarm. He was clenching his jaw and his fists, second-guessing his tactics. Going over the details of making the bomb, he visualized each step to account for every intricate detail.

What could have gone wrong? Maybe the connection in the switch.

Webster muttered as he worked to an anxious frenzy, and erratic actions overruled his common sense.

Slamming the car door, he bolted from the vehicle and charged up the walk to the detective agency. In a flash, he became an obtuse monster seeking vengeance. Rushing up the stairs, he kicked in the office door. The hinges heaved and cracked.

Startled by the crash of splintering wood, Emily turned to the ominous man. Webster glared at her in an insane rage.

Emily was dumbfounded by the aimless actions of a deranged man, and instantly speed-dialed emergency.

Feeling invincible, Webster didn't say a word but barged to the alley kitchen. Expecting a dud, he flicked the switch.

An explosion tore through the walls, creating a heat inferno and bursting light. The refrigerator door careened off the hinge. Emily dove under the pedestal desk, her arms cradling her head. The sound was deafening with echoes of shattering glass, as the beams and ceiling collapsed around her. Debris rained over the desk, trapping her as flames crept toward her.

She flexed and tried to move her arms and legs without leverage. The heat enclosed her like a blanket. Over the roar of the flames, she wasn't sure if it was her imagination that heard distant sirens.

Emily uttered a desperate prayer that they'd find her before the building was consumed.

She couldn't remember if her last words to Joseph were 'I love you'.

FORTY-SEVEN

Joseph landed in Paris, disconcerted by Scott's betrayal. The cab worked its way through the congested traffic in the streets around the agency.

By eleven a.m., a circus of fire trucks and emergency vehicles had invaded the zone, with cars unable to move. Joseph walked the last blocks to rue Euler. Panic and fear surged as he ran toward the building.

Police tried to prevent Joseph from entering the taped area, until he protested his wife was working on the second floor. With identification he was referred to Captain.

"What happened? My wife is in there on the second floor."

"We are dealing with a bomb blast and we're still in the midst of recovery. There are several injured victims we haven't evacuated yet."

Joseph could barely feel his body. His mind took over, floating above the scene. He'd never felt this desperation. His lips uttered repeated silent prayer words for Emily's safety, wanting to get to her but his feet were like lead.

Firemen held off the flames while a crew worked to extract her. In fleeting moments of consciousness, she could answer a few questions, but suffering from acute trauma, her hearing was intermittent with ringing and deafness.

"Ms. Harkness, where is your primary pain?"

Her eyes were still closed from the smoke and she motioned her hands. Almost silent, she mouthed the words.

"All over."

"How about your legs?"

"I'm sure I am wiggling my toes."

Emily's shoes had been blown off in the explosion and her toes were visible.

"Please do that again, Emily."

Still no movement. The medic signaled for a body brace.

A fireman yelled, "Get out of here! Now! The ceiling is caving!"

The rescue crew pulled her to the hall as the beams heaved and folded over her desk. As two stretchers made it to daylight, the wall sections fell to fuel the inferno. Sirens blared from every direction to save the doomed building.

An officer called to Joseph, but he barely heard his own name. He rushed to Emily's side; she was semi-conscious.

"Hey, Babe. I'm here." Joseph leaned over and kissed her on the lips.

Emily's eyes fluttered open and she silently mouthed the word, "Joseph".

The other gurney was removed with a black sheet over a lifeless body.

"Mr. Harkness, we're taking her to hospital right away, but would you remain a few minutes for a statement?" He desperately wanted to be with Emily, but he shrugged to comply with the police process.

"Do you know a man by the name of Jack Webster?"

"I've never met him but I know about him. A restraining order was issued to stay away from my wife. She filed assault charges when he attacked her at the office.

"Emily worked on a divorce case for his wife and took incriminating photos. She received a summons recently and is supposed to appear as a witness in divorce court on Wednesday."

"Did he make any verbal threats toward her?"

Joseph relayed Emily's story leading to the assault charges. "He deliberately pushed her and used physical force. It's not a nice thing to say when someone loses his life in a tragedy like this, but he caused this by himself. I heard he planted a bomb in our office?"

"It looks like Webster may have rigged a home-made explosive to your refrigerator, and panicked when it didn't detonate. He foolishly rushed in to test the dud and the door of the refrigerator killed him instantly."

"It looks like most of the building will need to be demolished. Did everyone else get out alright?"

"Yes, we have accounted for everyone. Here's a copy of the preliminary report. Call at the station tomorrow, Mr. Harkness. We'll have a few more questions."

Joseph phoned his insurance agent, but his thoughts were too focused on Emily to worry about recovering his business.

In a partial trance, he flagged a taxi to Paris Memorial Hospital.

FORTY-EIGHT

Eloise bustled inside her Branly Quai home, preparing to fly to London to visit her imprisoned husband. She had been permitted a telephone call with Scott before leaving Paris. He was firm with her, giving her explicit instructions to put the garden suite up for sale.

During the last two years, while living the life of a secret agent's wife, Eloise became a minimalist. She cut her attachments to family photos, heirlooms and never saved a Christmas card or anything sentimental.

Her packing was precise and neat. Leaving the keys with a property agent, two large Pullman suitcases were packed for her flight. An upstairs tenant would keep an eye on the place and tend to the planters until the unit was sold.

Unlike Winston Metcalf's accomplices, no one posted bail or provided an attorney for Scott. Although he had ample financial resources stashed away, he took pains to keep that information from his wife.

With mug shots taken, Scott remained in a holding cell awaiting a hearing on the murder charges. Humiliated and ungraciously put in line-ups with other felons, Scott felt it wasn't for identification, but for insult.

Stripped of integrity, he vigorously denied it was premeditated murder and pleaded self-defense. From his prison cell, he negotiated representation with a London lawyer.

Assuming Eloise was under the radar, he took steps to remove her from harm in Paris. Scott's fateful decision in Metcalf's office put him on a daring path, without room for Eloise in his future. In spite of his chosen direction, he wouldn't be unkind to her and was determined to protect her during the trial.

Arrangements were made with a fund administrator to provide a monthly pension to generously cover her expenses. Evidence mounted, depicting Scott as an international courier who had double-crossed Metcalf. It would be a heavy burden to prove self-defense.

Scott's lawyer waited in the interview room. Scott was led in for his first session, and quickly sized the lawyer up as arrogant and over-confident.

He's far too young for this job.

"Hello, Mr. Marchand, I'm Kenneth Dowd."

Scott was handcuffed with his hands clasped together across the table.

"Should I thank you for considering my case?"

"I'll do the best I can. However, I insist you tell me the whole truth."

"How many cases have you lost throughout your career?" Scott was being facetious.

"I don't proclaim to have a perfect record. I've lost a few. Each time, it was the fault of the client for withholding information."

"That's easy for you to say."

"Look, Mr. Marchand, if you're not pleased with my record, you are free to choose another attorney."

Scott retaliated, "I'll give you the lowdown and you tell me if you can get me off. If you don't think so, then we're finished right here."

Dowd's arrogance subsided as he leaned back in his chair.

"I don't have first-hand knowledge about what happened to the diamonds, but the photographs verified they were returned to Metcalf." Scott gulped on his lie.

"Why did you kill Winston Metcalf?"

"I returned to his office to have it out with him. He inched toward his desk to his drawer. What would you suppose he was planning on doing?"

"You tell me, Scott."

"He pulled a gun on me. I took action to defend myself. I guess I was faster or I wouldn't be here."

Dowd opened the police report. "It says here, your fingerprints are on Metcalf's phone."

Scott answered boldly. "I don't remember touching the phone. I may have moved it on the desk."

"Obviously, he pulled his gun on me or I wouldn't have shot him. Isn't that self-defense?"

"We'll plead self-defense, but it depends on how much mud the prosecutor has to discredit you. Can a witness to corroborate any part of your story or character?"

Scott thought about Joseph. He could be relied on to tell the truth, however he'd already taken care of loose ends.

They will never tie me to Joseph's murder. No witnesses.

He certainly would not bring Christine into the matter. "No one."

Dowd was satisfied with the first visit. Scott wasn't yet convinced with his lawyer's strength, but agreed they would follow-up.

As Dowd left, Scott asked the guard for permission for a private call and was allowed five minutes.

FORTY-NINE

Joseph was unable to get a doctor's update on Emily's surgery. He paced the triage waiting room, wrestling with a new burden of responsibility.

Should I call her family? Her sister Amy? Is this life-threatening?

Haunting thoughts circulated, bringing him to the revelation that neither had Living Wills or even a regular Will.

As soon as Emily is well enough, we'll attend to that. No question, everything goes to Emily.

An orderly in scrubs broke his focus.

"Mr. Harkness."

Joseph raised a hand. "Here."

"Come with me, your wife is in Recovery. We'll hold her in ICU for a few hours before she's admitted upstairs."

"How is she?"

"The head nurse will be able to tell you."

Joseph followed through the halls, passing medi-stations on wheels, outside curtained roomettes. His eyes were transfixed on the small frame of Emily lying on the bed, with two nurses leaning over her.

He longed to take her in his arms to cradle and protect her. He ached at the sight and the horror of almost losing her.

"Mr. Harkness is here."

The orderly nodded to Joseph and disappeared.

"Your wife has been asking for you, Mr. Harkness. I assume your name is Thomas."

"That's a pet name between the two of us, my name is Joseph."

Joseph smiled affectionately as Emily struggled to keep her eyes open. He squeezed her hand and she responded with gentle pressure.

An oxygen mask was over her mouth. He moved in close beside her and brushed a few wayward strands of hair from her brow to kiss her forehead.

Joseph turned as the surgeon arrived.

"How is she?"

"She has a collapsed lung and will need the mask for a few days, then the tubes should be sufficient until her breathing is back to full capacity. Her spinal cord is bruised but if she has the determination, she should be able to walk in a few days."

Joseph relaxed his shoulders.

"Did she have a concussion?"

The doctor nodded. "Yes, and she'll have headaches and dizziness. But surgery was successful in attending to her internal bleeding; she'll be good as new with some rest.

"Considering she's the victim of a bomb explosion, your wife is in remarkable condition. Her left arm is broken and the bruising to her spine is causing intermittent paralysis; but that will subside. I heard she owes her life to a big old-fashioned desk."

"Oh no, is my desk ruined?" He laughed trying to get a reaction from Emily.

Her eyes were closed, but forced the words, "Joseph, don't make me laugh, it hurts."

Relieved to hear her voice, he planted another kiss on her forehead. "Squeeze my hand once for 'yes' and twice for 'no'. Save your energy for healing, Babe."

The doctor and nurses had moved to the next cubicle.

"What happened?" Emily mumbled.

"I know your curiosity won't take a rest until I tell you. It appears Mr. Webster broke into the office before you arrived and planted a home-made device behind the refrigerator. He watched from outside hoping you'd turn on the light switch.

"Eventually he barged in to check on the bomb, expecting it was a dud. Logic left him to his own devices. Without concern, he turned on the switch."

Emily squeezed Joseph's hand tightly as tears streaked down her bruised cheeks.

"I'm sorry," she whimpered.

"Oh, Babe, it's not your fault. Webster was a deranged man who couldn't face losing his power and reputation. This didn't have to happen."

"Joseph, I know he's dead."

"There is good news, Em. We'll be on vacation for several weeks or maybe longer. Our office has taken a hiatus from its foundation but our insurance will pay for a temporary set-up. Your phone was destroyed however I was able to retrieve your contact numbers."

She nodded her approval and closed her eyes as the nurse returned to take her vitals.

"Mr. Harkness, your wife needs sleep. Why don't you get yourself a coffee?"

Joseph stopped her. "Nurse, please understand. This woman is my whole world; she is always sacrificing for my benefit. I promised I would be here." He eased up, embarrassed. "I'll grab a take-out coffee but I'll be right back."

He felt better for letting his heart speak, and the nurse lingered. "She's a lucky lady. I once had a man like you. One morning many years ago, I let him leave without telling him I loved him. He was killed in a car accident on his way to work." Her voice faltered.

"I'm so sorry." Joseph said.

Slipping into the washroom on the way to the cafeteria, Joseph cleaned the bullet graze.

There isn't anything Scott can do to me now. I should never have wasted my time with him. I should've seen the devil in him.

In the corridor, Joseph caught a glimpse of Daniel in a leather jacket at the nurses' station. The hall wasn't easy to navigate and Joseph held his focus on Daniel, dodging stretchers and porters.

The two men locked eyes and Joseph shouted to wait. Daniel nodded to him, but had the audacity to wave as he darted to the stairwell. Joseph let him go.

This is not the time. Emily needs me here.

On the second day, Emily was moved from ICU to a private room on the fifth. Through the waking hours, Joseph stayed at her bedside. The last spinal x-rays were hopeful and the doctors gave her approval to take a few steps at a time.

With Joseph's help, she managed a few steps in the corridor on her first try before spasms left her exhausted. Plumping her pillows and tucking her in with a warm blanket, he pulled his chair to the bed.

His face was solemn. He'd been waiting for Emily's spirits to improve before telling her about Scott's arrest in London.

But Emily raised it. She said, "Have you heard from Eloise this week? She must be overwhelmed."

Emily looked at his face as he thought.

Now's the time to talk about my night in the car.

"Em."

He paused again, not to alarm her, then whispered, "Our association with the Marchands is over."

"Joseph, don't be so harsh. Eloise called me right before the explosion to tell me Scott's been arrested for murder."

"Hear me out. We were pawns. It was Scott's plan all along to steal the diamonds and frame me. His final manipulation to get me to go to London with him was not to help him in the boardroom, but to kill me. He intended to eradicate the only credible witness!"

"Joseph! That can't be."

Emily sat forward on the cushions, her brow tight as Joseph relayed the incident.

"Thank God you're alive and safe. Does Scott know you're alive?" She leaned into his shoulder.

"I don't know. But we need to stay alert. With Metcalf dead and Scott arraigned, we still need to be guarded."

The next morning, Joseph was en route to pick up Emily at the hospital. His cell rang and he put it on speaker and kept driving.

The voice said, "Hello, Tom?"

Joseph came to a full stop hearing a heavy British accent.

"Who is this?" He pulled to the curb.

"Detective Jones calling from London."

Joseph paused for a fast decision. Should he end it now by saying it was a wrong number, or admit his knowledge of the scheme?

Joseph's voice was standoffish.

"What do you want, detective?"

"I believe I talked with you about a week ago. You were facing a dilemma and asked for my assistance."

Joseph said, "If my memory is correct, you said you couldn't help me without concrete evidence."

"Let's not pussyfoot, Tom. You know we have the evidence now." Jones elevated his tone to sarcasm.

"I have nothing to offer that you haven't already discovered about Winston Metcalf and Scott Marchand."

"You can be summoned as a hostile witness."

"Look here, Detective Jones. I'm on my way to an urgent appointment and I don't have time to talk. I doubt that you'd be calling me, if you didn't already have possession of the bug. You can find a disk chip taped behind the security camera at the tenth floor exit door. Summons me if you like."

"Please, Tom, I need corroboration . . ."

Joseph clicked off without offering his real identification.

Did I commit contempt of court?

Four days later, Emily was home resting at the loft. Her paper files were gone, but most data was in her Cloud. Other research was on a flash drive in her handbag that was recovered in the rubble.

"Emily, with such a hectic month, let's consider a research assistant. You'd have flexibility to join me when we travel outside of Paris."

Emily's face lit up.

"I like that idea. What about the freelance detective, Carter. He was a great support in Normandy." She put her hands behind her head. "Thanks for doing that, Joseph. It's a true comfort."

Joseph said, "I'm meeting with the insurance agent this afternoon; they want us to get set up. I transferred incoming calls to my cell, but we need a place to plant our feet. They gave us a leasing agent who has another office space in the same area. Want to come?"

He knew the answer, and she stood up on her own.

FIFTY

Scott was led to the courtroom in shackles and handcuffs, carving humiliation into his already weakened spirits. The bailiff urged him along to the defendant's table where Kenneth Dowd was waiting.

In flagrant contrast to Scott, Dowd was in an expensive silk suit, like the quality Winston Metcalf wore when he died.

The jury filed in, each evaluating the tall handsome man, now with weathered cheek bones and sad green eyes. The women jurors took pity on him, the men distrustful.

Eloise pushed her way into the row immediately behind the defendant's bench. She called to Scott in a low voice. He turned, startled to see her there, and whispered to his lawyer.

"What is my wife doing here? She's a wild card."

"I'm sorry Scott, I didn't know she was coming. I certainly would have discouraged her."

The bailiff ordered the audience to rise and the Judge entered through a door beside the podium.

The declaration stated the case number and the charge from the Queen's Bench against Scott Nathaniel Marchand for second degree murder in the death of Winston Maynard Metcalf.

Dowd and Marchand remained standing as the judge requested a plea.

"How do you plead, Mr. Marchand?"

"I plead Not Guilty, your Honor."

Scott kept his head down and his eyes closed reciting lyrics he had heard on the radio in the common room. He knew hope was at the end of the tunnel.

I stand accused of all my sins. I must answer for my life. My fate is in the Judge's hands. My verdict Not Guilty; I stand in awe.

He repeated it silently with his eyes closed. Kenneth Dowd nudged him back into the moment.

I'm not guilty. It was self-defense. I'm trained to be evasive and fleeting.

"Please, Scott, listen attentively to the prosecution and let me know if anything is untruthful or fabricated, before I make my challenge."

"Yes, Sir," Scott said calmly.

The prosecution painted a villainous picture of Scott, an angry man without remorse for taking the life of a human being.

Scott was sickened by the description, doubting any good he had done in his life. Remaining motionless with his head down, he closed his eyes to shut out the world.

Thank God I didn't kill Joseph too!

Turning the tables on the prosecution, Dowd described the calculating Winston Metcalf as a man without morals who intentionally set up his client. Dowd's eyes burrowed down the row of jurors as he spoke.

"Scott Marchand faced that moment. It's when life flashes before your eyes and you make a fatal decision to save yourself."

As Eloise watched, she thought of Scott as spineless and incapable of defending himself. He had wanted respect from Metcalf's organization, and when this assignment came up, Scott and Eloise had discussed setting up a scapegoat. To Eloise, it should have been simple—they decided together on a random freelance detective, and she was instrumental in setting the trap.

On the first day of the trial, Scott's pistol was identified as the murder weapon.

Christine was called to the witness stand.

"Was Scott Marchand the man arguing in Winston Metcalf's office, before you heard the gunshot?"

"I called the police while Mr. Marchand exited to the stairwell."

The lawyer persisted. "Was Mr. Marchand hostile towards her or any of the staff?"

Christine replied, "Mr. Marchand was always a courteous gentleman when he came to the office. Yes, I did hear Winston Metcalf verbally accosting the defendant. It was Mr. Metcalf that was irate and talked over Mr. Marchand."

Dowd was pleased with the secretary's cooperation.

"In your opinion, would you say Mr. Metcalf was the aggressor?"

"Yes, that would be correct. Mr. Metcalf was often talked about around the office as a bully." She was relieved to get that out.

The prosecution objected, requesting that her answer be stricken, but from Dowd's viewpoint it was too late. Winston's credibility had been tarnished. The defense had nothing to argue about until the prosecutor went to motive.

A late adjournment brought the day's testimony to an end. Eloise tried to press through the crowd to get to Scott, but the bailiff had already led him to the exit door. He didn't turn to look for her but thought about her manipulation.

She's playing me, how could I not have seen it earlier.

FIFTY-ONE

Joseph stepped out of the rue des Saules loft and turned downhill to pick up Chinese food. The Twizy was still being babied for special excursions. It was dark and the light bulbs glowed in the cafés. Pulling his collar up, he scurried toward St. Pierre.

By the bottom, he was aware of an echo of feet in sync with his own.

Metcalf's dead and Scott's behind bars; who else did I cross?

He took a sidelong view; the street behind was clear other than a news boy on his bike and a cat skulking in the ditch. The echo had abated.

Joseph idled his time waiting for the food. Outside the window, pedestrian traffic seemed a blur. Across the street, a man in a checkered woolen jacket was leaning over the railing, enjoying the view.

Joseph felt for his leg holster.

The one time I don't have it!

"Ah, Mr. Harkness, your order is ready now."

Joseph eased closer to speak to Marvin, the manager; he'd known him since he moved to Montmartre. Marvin wiped his hands on his apron and took him to the kitchen.

"Sure, you go out back door; or better, Mr. Joseph, you take the scooter and bring back tomorrow."

"You're a true friend—one in a million."

Joseph put the brown paper bag in the basket and revved up the Vespa before wheeling down the back lane. At the turn in the lane he screeched to a stop. Another scooter was waiting at the end; the woolen jacket watching for his next move.

If I can get to the Basilica, the gendarmes should be in the area. I'll have to count on my memory of these lanes.

Halfway up the Basilica hill, he parked Marvin's scooter, just before the parks. Stopping above the familiar terraces, he looked down on his pursuer.

It's the student from the metro. Whose payroll is he on? I'll teach him a good lesson.

Joseph uprooted a loose metal pole from a broken windmill. Taking off his jacket, he rolled up his sleeves and took a running leap, vaulting the pole to the opposite building. Bracing his hands, he vaulted again to the corner square. The rust from the pole was embedded into his palms stinging as if he put his hands in a fire pit.

I can't do any more of this.

Joseph buckled over to catch his breath. The revving of Simon's bike got closer, and the engine cut out.

Dusk had turned to darkness, making it difficult to find the kid, but as hard for Simon to find Joseph.

If I can get to the roof below, I can land on the ground.

He watched as the student parked at an apartment building. As the plaid jacket disappeared behind heavy doors, Joseph lurched for the scooter.

Simon stood inside in the darkness watching. The side door opened inches, exposing the silhouette of the assailant raising his gun.

Ping, Ping, Ping. Three bullets hit the scooter.

Emily was pacing by the balcony window for any sign of Joseph. More than an hour passed when she decided to call the Chinese restaurant.

"Marvin, did Joseph leave with the take-out? He hasn't come home yet."

"So sorry, Ms. Emily. A stranger was following your husband so I loaned him my scooter to go the back way. I haven't seen him since. Do you want me to send out one of the boys to look for him?"

"Oh, no, Marvin, that won't be necessary. He'll be along soon, I'm sure of it."

Another half hour passed.

Panic gripped her stomach. *Where are you Joseph!*

She checked her phone, but no messages, then opened the balcony door to watch and listen.

"Em . . . Emily."

The gasps were from the back where the ladder rose from the alley. She unlocked the door. Joseph was on his belly in a crawl position, his shirt soaked in blood.

She crouched to grasp him with both hands. "Joseph, what happened?"

He muttered angrily.

"It was the fellow who jumped me in the tube. The opportunity to ask who hired him didn't come up."

"How bad is it?" Emily propped him on a kitchen chair and cut off the sticky shirt. She ran her fingers over his shoulder.

"Let's see. You've lost a bit of blood but it seems to be drying up. I can see where the bullet went in. Looks like it was right through and out the front. There's a hole on this side too."

Emily dabbed antiseptic into the wound causing Joseph to grimace, biting down on his lip.

"If you patch me up, I'll be okay."

"I called the Chinese place and they said you were being followed. I'm scared silly."

"Always have faith in me, Emily. I've gotten out of other situations close to the wire."

Emily worked on his wounds using stitch tapes to close the hole and stop the bleeding.

"And how many times have you been shot since I've known you?"

"Should I be keeping notches on the edge of the kitchen door?"

Joseph and Emily picked a two-room office a block from the rue Euler agency, with elevator access to the third floor. It was larger than the old office, with space for a reception desk.

Emily's mobility was hampered by her injuries, but her spirit revved as she planned for the new location. She was deliberate in her sentimental need for oak pedestal desks.

Joseph, with a bandaged shoulder, spent the final days painting the walls with one arm in a sling. With Emily's design advice, they jiggled and shifted the furniture that had been delivered at the expense of the insurance claim.

Emily set up a makeshift conference area to interview candidates for the dual role of Receptionist and Research Assistant. An ad ran in the local weekly, and was posted on the bulletin board at the café. Of six resumes, Emily selected the best three.

Madge Bitteridge was punctual, arriving ten minutes early. She took the staircase and introduced herself from the door with a strong voice. She was middle-aged, with experience in an attorney's office.

"Hello, Mrs. Bitteridge. Thank you for coming." Their voices echoed in the bare office.

Emily motioned to the folding chairs. She was charmed by Madge, caving to her first impression and kindly smile. Madge straightened the jacket of her grey woolen business suit, and with both hands adjusted her shaped tam with a short plume of colorful feathers correctly positioned.

"It's my pleasure, Ms. Harkness."

She placed her black folio case on the folding table. "Please call me Madge; it makes me more at ease."

"I'm Emily . . . and the man in the paint coveralls over there is my husband, Joseph. Please don't mind the chaos; we are in the midst of moving in."

"Yes, I heard about the fire. I hope you're not offended that I searched your agency on the internet. I was astonished to see the circumstances for your relocation.

"Not at all. I like it that you are curious; that's the business we are in. May I offer you a cup of coffee?"

"Thank you, just cream."

Emily returned with two mugs.

"Please tell me about your past work and how it would enhance your work with us."

"I was last employed with Chartrand & Baynes. It was difficult working in a large law firm where justice and morals differ—I find satisfaction comes when the truth is discovered. You're welcome to call Mr. Chartrand for a reference; I worked for him for the last five years. He encouraged me to come here and said you were a fine detective."

"I am flattered, Madge. Are you concerned that the work here might not be as stimulating as your previous assignments?"

"No. I see this as a ground floor, to be part of this team. I'll work long hours whenever I'm needed. My family is grown. My husband died some years ago, so I don't have other obligations or responsibilities to interfere with my my job. I am financially secure, so I'm not asking for a high wage, just whatever you suggest."

"Madge, what would you consider as a possible weakness in this type of work? Something to develop?"

"That's a fair question. Perhaps I care too much about the victims. They are all real people and deserve the best from us."

Emily smiled to herself, noticing how coyly Madge had inserted the words 'us' and 'team'.

"Well, Madge Bitteridge, we are opening on Monday. Can you start then?" Madge was about to answer but Emily continued. "Joseph has hired a freelance detective, a Jebb Carter, and the four of us will make a good team."

Madge burst into a broad smile, rallying wrinkles at her eyes. "Thank you, Emily. I promise a good job."

FIFTY-TWO

The Dutch couple boarded the flight to London, the Amsterdam assignment now complete. They broke into laughter, their excited behavior contrary to their actions at Scott's hotel and her subsequent surveillance at the Swiss Bank.

The man became silent, his brow tightening as he raised his remorse.

"I think we lit the fear of God into that fellow in London. But I really didn't mean to hit him that hard. Did you see the welts on his face?"

His hand touched his forehead, then rubbed his jaw. "Was I too forceful?"

"We did what we had to do."

"Het is voorbij. It is done."

"Yes, it's over."

They looked forward to the meeting in London.

Amelard and Pascal drove the armored truck from the coast of Normandy, then made the channel crossing to England. Once the truck was secured in the hold of the ferry, Amelard unlocked the padlock to check on the load. With a sharp crank of the bolt the door heaved open.

The truck's equipment box was stuffed with goggles, wigs, hats, and painters overalls. Behind the boxes, wardrobes and trunks were strapped to the walls in rows down each side. Prop panels portrayed a boardroom backdrop, pushed to the wall by an array of tables and chairs.

Amelard called out.

"Eh bien! All is good Pascal."

His cell vibrated.

Two men packed up their window washing equipment in west end London. Reeling the scaffolding down to street level, they checked out with the weekend foreman.

"Have you ever been to South Africa?"

"Nah! I like to stay close to home. London is full of adventure if you look for it, mate!"

"I'll be going up to Normandy when the weekend is over."

"You lucky sot!"

FIFTY-THREE

The days were shorter, and by five o'clock it was already dark when Joseph and Emily locked the office.

Exiting to the street, Joseph scrutinized each car in the vicinity and scoured the pedestrians waiting under the street lamp for the bus.

He whispered to Emily and raised his hand.

"Over there, at ten o'clock. The black sedan. It's Daniel."

Emily flushed. "Our Daniel? But why?"

Closer to them, a man's footsteps were running toward the bus stop. As he passed, he banged headlong into Joseph.

With a sudden stop, the man pushed the tip of a knife against Joseph's neck. His message was clear.

"If you move or shout, your missus will be harmed."

The man then moved his knife to Emily, scratching her skin on her face. With his left arm, he dragged her to an idling taxi. The car squealed to the road leaving Joseph in the dark.

Daniel opened his car door, across the road. "Joseph, what's going on? Who took Emily?"

Joseph ran to Daniel's passenger side and looked back. "I don't know, Daniel. Follow them."

They sped into the intersection, with the cab in sight. Within seconds, Joseph's iPhone beeped with a text.

Get all of Ms. Harkness's notes and documents on the Tessier case. Don't discuss this with anyone or she will suffer.

Joseph read it silently, then aloud to Daniel.

They stayed in pace behind the taxi, but Daniel's mind was also now focused on the text.

"You need to tell me what he's talking about."

Joseph said, "A law firm hired Emily to find a beneficiary for a provisional Will. She was thorough and filed court papers declaring the rightful inheritor. The lawyer wasn't too keen on the outcome, and his client was left with egg on her face and a pending prison term."

"Could this be a disgruntled member of the family?"

Daniel stepped up his speed, following down a dark lane, but the taxi vanished in the next block.

Joseph said, "It could be the Charbonneau nephew or repercussion from the Webster family. I ran into a kid the other night intent on giving me a message. It could be him."

"Take a deep breath, Joseph, you think better when you're calm."

"I'll kill him if he hurts Emily. She's still not well, Daniel. She's only been out of the hospital a few days."

"I guess we're partners on this manhunt, Joseph! In one way or another I've been part of your life since Albany."

"Did you get the cab's number?"

Daniel said, "In the haste, I didn't see it. I'll call some cab companies to see if any vehicles were hijacked; it was a Peugeot E7. They must have GPS tracking."

They pulled back to park on a main road. Joseph got out and paced as the taxi companies ran the search. Twenty minutes later, Daniel started writing. He shouted to Joseph to get in.

"Good. A stolen cab was just recovered. I've got the street; come on!"

They sped up behind the taxi as the front end was being hoisted by a tow truck.

"Hold on!" Joseph yelled as he flung the door open.

"Did you forget to pay your fare, buddy?" the truck driver said sarcastically.

"Put it back down! My wife was kidnapped in this vehicle. Do you want to let us have a look now, or should we all wait for the police to come?" Joseph bargained.

"No problem."

The driver cranked the tow bar back to the ground.

Opening the passenger door, Daniel looked in the front section through the driver's side.

"She was pulled into the back seat by the man. I know Emily would have left some sort of clue." Joseph said.

Daniel mused, "I wonder if the driver was a cabbie or a bribe."

"The driver's photo is here on the seatback; name is Mohammed Habib. I'll call the dispatch for his home address." Joseph picked up his cell to call.

"Did you find Emily's clue?"

Joseph nodded and pursed his lips. "Her lipstick, to let us know this was the car."

Mr. Habib's rental flat was on the outskirts of town, a thirty minute drive. Daniel and Joseph had little to say; Joseph knew it wasn't the time.

Daniel slowed while they looked for the house number in a row of brick and tar paper flats, each with an asphalt drive.

Joseph pounded on Habib's door and waited.

"Check with the neighbors. The dispatch said he was to take the cab home last night, but didn't check in this morning."

Joseph put his hand up for silence and leaned his ear against the door.

"Someone's in there. It's a muffled voice, calling for help."

Joseph checked the mail box and door mat for a key.

"There it is." He muttered as his fingers locked on a key tucked over the door jamb.

He positioned his gun, and opened the door an inch. The TV was on and Joseph listened for any noise above it. He pushed the door all the way with the revolver in both hands. Mr. Habib was tied and gagged, lying on the carpet.

Daniel leaned over him and untied the gag. "It is okay, Sir. We're not the bad guys."

Habib's eyes were wide with fear. "The fare seemed nice at first, but then turned violent. Did he take my car?"

"He also took my wife!"

"Mr. Habib, can you give us a description, or anything to help us? Your cab has been recovered without damage."

"He was young, early twenties. Tall with blonde spiky hair. Had a Harvard sweatshirt."

"Would you come with us, Mr. Habib? Could you pick him out of a line up, or a year book?"

"Oh yes. He must be stopped!"

Joseph was convinced there'd be clues at the scene of the abandoned cab. He got out there, leaving Daniel and the cabbie to search the internet for Harvard clues.

The abductor was enjoying Emily's anguish, reveling that she was now at his mercy.

Standing over her, he tossed her to the ground. He threw her head back with an angry grip on her long hair.

He spit his words. "Well, Harkness lady, did you destroy the Tessier file like I asked?"

Emily took a moment to choose the right reply. Again, he grasped her hair and pulled her head to the side. His anger was growing and he placed his boot onto her side.

She said, "It is all gathered together." The pain drilled into her ribs.

"I asked if you destroyed it. Apparently the answer is no!"

He raised his arm as a threat to her and tightened his fist.

"You haven't asked who I am," he said.

"I know who you are."

Emily regretted her words as soon as they were out.

"Then you understand that I agree with my Aunt's warning to old Baynes. No witnesses! He actually called me before he died and asked me to take care of you." Simon's outrage changed to laughter.

"You know, Miss Harkness, I've already taken matters into my own hands. I used my nighttime finesse to enter Mathias's home. He won't survive as a beneficiary." He laughed. "Arsenic in their coffee supply!"

Emily pleaded, "Simon, you won't get away with this. Stop before someone else gets hurt."

"I was promised old Benjamin's estate for years. You weren't supposed to meddle. Just let the time lapse happen; that's all Verona wanted. You haven't seen her, tied in a straightjacket, medicated to the hilt and ranting like a child. She is ruined."

"I'm truly sorry Simon, but your Aunt caused the trouble for herself by putting poison in Mr. Tessier's tea. You have nothing to gain by harming Mathias."

"You fool. Don't you see? If I get rid of him, the Normandy property reverts to me."

Simon wrapped tape over the ropes on her hands and ankles. With her arms secure, he blindfolded and dragged her to the lower deck of the houseboat, and threw her to the damp teak floor. He tied a gag around her mouth.

"I'll be back for you!"

His footsteps retreated and the hatch was slammed shut.

Joseph searched for tire marks where the taxi had been abandoned, then looked through the darkness toward the rows of houseboats along the Seine.

She must be nearby. In her condition, she couldn't walk too far.

He lowered to his knees, feeling the drag marks left from the toes of her shoes. He crouched as he followed them to the boardwalk where they stopped. In plain view on the concrete was Emily's universal driver's license.

Joseph picked up his cell and dialed Daniel.

"I've found a track in the dirt near the houseboats, where the taxi was found. Did you have any luck with the yearbook?"

"Not yet, I'll need more time. Stay where you are and I'll come and catch up."

Joseph called out to two dock workers repairing a houseboat near the path.

"Bonjours, mes amis! Have you seen a woman who may have been pulled along here in the last few hours?"

Both shrugged negatively, but Joseph doubted their honesty.

He continued past some boats, and interrupted an elderly woman tending to her flower boxes. This time he tried a sympathetic approach.

"Excusez-moi, madam. Did you see a woman being forced along by a young man? She was taken against her will and is in need of medication."

"Eh bien, monsieur. They passed as you describe. She needed assistance to walk. They went some distance further down the riverbank. I don't know where they stopped."

Joseph cringed in fear that Emily was suffering.

"Do you know of any that are empty?"

"Come, I will take you."

She came around to a brightly colored set of red steps and a handrail, and hoisted herself to the boardwalk. He reached in a gentlemanly way to help her, but she refused.

"This way!" She gestured for him to follow.

Four moorings down from her boat, they stopped. Joseph leaned down to feel the dirt. It appeared to be secure, with no muddy footprints coming aboard.

Another two spots and they stopped again.

"This one has a young fellow who comes and goes. Sometimes I don't see him for months."

"Was he the man you saw with my friend?"

She paused and scratched at a whiskered chin.

"It could have been, but I didn't look at him. It was the woman who created the attention. I hope you find her."

Joseph walked her back. Returning to the suspect houseboat, he examined each window and the door.

He was considering the door latch when his cell rang.

"We're looking for Simon Charbonneau! That's our man! We found him in a database, I'm sending you the picture now." Daniel said.

Joseph said, "Yep, that's the kid. If she hadn't been such a good detective, the provisional limit would have passed."

"It is clear that is sufficient motive," Daniel said. "I'm almost there. I'll turn my lights down as I approach you."

"Daniel, one boat looks suspicious, but that's all I've got. There are no tracks directly to it, but I brought a sound transmitter to attach to the hull, and put a motion camera in the bushes. It could be any of the boats; we can check more in daylight. It's tempting to continue in the darkness, but there could be a trap tonight."

Daniel's sedan pulled up and he was alone. Joseph got in and they drove fifteen minutes to a brasserie. After only moments of silence at the table, Joseph broke the ice.

"Daniel, why are you following us?"

"I can't answer that right now, Joseph. Let's get Emily back and we'll discuss everything when she's safe."

Daniel dropped Joseph at St. Pierre before midnight with an offer to pick him up before breakfast.

With little sleep, Joseph's mind was on the docks, to find Emily in the houseboats.

Joseph was waiting by the St. Pierre Museum with a coffee in hand at 6:30 a.m. when Daniel pulled up.

"Daniel, I retraced everything in my mind. My gut tells me to start first at the boat transmitter. I brought lock-pick tools. We should board it."

Emily wasn't sure if it was lack of circulation or the spinal bruising that took away the feeling in her legs. The tape was over her mouth and her bonds in place; she was grateful Simon hadn't returned.

I know Joseph will come for me.

In the bowels of the boat and out of sight and sound, Emily was overcome with pain and helplessness. Shivering, she relented to the sway of soft waves splashing between the boat and the moorings. She had no concept of time but concentrated on sounds, hearing gulls and crows in search of their morning meals.

She perked up at a familiar shrill whistle, undeniably 'Que Sera Sera'. She laughed at her imagination and fell into a darkened sleep.

The changing boat's movement awakened her. It seemed like hours to her.

Someone has come on board. I would rather stay in this dark dungeon than see Simon. There are two people!

FIFTY-FOUR

Simon's voice roared into the phone. "The Tessier files? By noon, or you won't see your wife again."

"You don't understand who you are dealing with, Simon." Joseph heard stuttered breathing, having surprised him by name. "You harm my wife, and you'll wish you were dead."

"Noon!" The line went dead.

"We're not waiting until noon; we're going to find her this morning. I feel it."

At the houseboat, Joseph whistled a tune he knew Emily would recognize. Climbing aboard with Daniel they cased the windows and doors, all locked, bolted and chained. Moving the transmitter to pick up any sound below, Joseph listened closely. Nothing.

Daniel took the aft section, stopping at each step to listen.

"Joseph!" Daniel waved. "Whistle again."

Daniel sensed a muffle. "She's kicking! I'm sure of it."

Without waiting, Joseph smashed the fire box to release the hatchet. The axe made its mark and Joseph kicked with his full force. The door splintered whole at midpoint, opening into the cabin. In their haste, they overlooked a silent alarm triggered by the door.

"Emily, where are you?" Joseph checked the lower deck without any sign of her.

"I've only been onboard one of these once before, but I recall an engine room and bunk somewhere below," Daniel said. "You take the bow and I'll take the stern."

"Emily! Emily! Joseph yelled.

Wondering if it were a dream, Emily writhed in pain, gagged and struggling to pound her numb feet.

I can hear footsteps of two men. One has to be Joseph!

Simon had taken all measures to prevent her escape, and a padlocked hatch to the lower deck drew Joseph's attention.

"Ahoy, Daniel, over here!"

Joseph shouted at the hatch. "We're here Emily." He hammered at the lock with the axe.

"Stand back, Joseph, we'll shoot it off."

Daniel fired a shot into the door jamb and Joseph was the first through. He crouched over Emily gently removing the gag.

"It's Simon Charbonneau," she said.

"We know, Babe."

Emily looked past Joseph's shoulder and was surprised to see Daniel.

"For heaven's sake, Daniel. What are you doing here?"

Not sure whether to be embarrassed or proud of his involvement, Daniel smiled back.

"Remember, Emily. It seems to be my lot in life to watch over the two of you."

Emily sagged into Joseph's arms then became rigid again.

"I almost forgot. Someone has to get to Mathias Tessier. Simon put arsenic in their home coffee supply. It's urgent!"

Daniel said, "I'll call Mathias, but we have to get out of here."

The first to surface up top was Daniel. As he emerged, gun fire whizzed past his head. Taking a defensive position in the captain's cabin, he searched the bush.

From a vantage point above the boardwalk, Simon set the rifle lens to lock on the deck, ready for any movement. He was unaware of Daniel's training as a marksman with Interpol.

From down below, Joseph spotted Simon. "Daniel, see the green boat trailer parked in the lot above? He's in the cabin."

Training his eyesight on the mark, Daniel fired one shot. He put down the rifle and dialed Mathias Tessier at his office.

"Mathias, your home coffee supply has been poisoned. You should alert your wife too, right away."

Mathias breathed heavily. "I am grateful, Mr. Boisvert. Fortunately no-one has used our coffee in the past few days. I'm appalled that life can be taken so routinely. My poor grandfather."

Daniel nodded but his focus was on safety and not sentiment.

"Mr. Tessier, a police squad is on the way to your home and office to make sure everything is recovered. Don't disturb anything, there might be fingerprints. Be careful."

FIFTY-FIVE

Scott dreaded the approach of this day and the hour when he would hear his verdict. The morning was foggy and grey but he was unaware without a window to the outside. Through a slot in the door, he accepted a breakfast tray.

Until sentencing, he was kept alone in a holding cell. Integration into the prison population would happen after sentencing, and he was troubled about new threats facing him.

In his orange jumpsuit and shackles, Scott was marched through the halls. Inmates jeered and spit at him, and a piercing voice stood out as he passed.

"Hey, Scottie. I wouldn't be in here if it weren't for you. You better watch your back."

Scott turned to face the scarred eye of Manny Leach.

"Leach, I thought you had legal connections to keep you out of a place like this."

"I did! You murdered him!"

Scott was helped into an armed prison security van to be transported across town to the courtroom.

The prosecution was concerned, as public opinion was considering that Scott was a scapegoat. They had negotiated with the defense down to a charge of manslaughter.

Scott's defense lawyer, smelled success and gambled firmly on 'Not Guilty' on behalf of his client. The jury had been out for two days, sending questions to the judge for clarification of manslaughter and self-defense.

Scott's heart pounded awaiting the outcome.

The Judge asked if the jury had reached a verdict while Scott stood stoically beside Kenneth Dowd. He turned toward the foreman, and watched in slow motion as a folded paper with his destiny was handed to the judge.

"In the case of second degree murder of Winston Metcalf, the defendant has been found Not Guilty. In the case of Involuntary Manslaughter the court finds the defendant Guilty."

Crestfallen, Scott turned to look at the audience, but not for Eloise. It was as he hoped, that she wouldn't be there.

"Do you have any presentencing statements, Mr. Dowd?"

"Your Honor, my client, Scott Marchand, has pled Not Guilty to the murder of Winston Metcalf. Mr. Marchand acknowledges his actions and has demonstrated great remorse. The defense asks for leniency and consideration for the time already served."

"Thank you Mr. Dowd, your statement will be taken into consideration. The jury is excused. I'll take a ten minute recess before I announce sentencing."

Voices buzzed and raised across the audience, but were hushed on the judge's return.

"I am directed to uphold the laws of the United Kingdom where the most serious of crimes deserve the most serious sentences. I have concluded a sentence of five years less time served, at the Thameside Prison."

"Thank you, Your Honor."

During his incarceration, Scott's physical stature had eroded, now slumped and defeated. With few friends, he knew that had been his choice; living his life in disguises and always in the shadows.

Scott was delivered to Thameside after sentencing, to a private cell with an iron bed, sink, toilet, and a foot locker. He had barely adjusted to the tiny quarters when he was notified his wife was in the interview room. Not wanting to face Eloise, he assumed she came to demand money.

Eloise was waiting in the visitor's chair with her blonde hair tied tightly in a twist. She wore an old coat and had no makeup. Scott felt a pang of pity for her as he was led into the room without shackles.

"What brings you here so soon, Eloise?" His compassion for her was evident in his tone. "Is something wrong?"

"No, Scott. I haven't talked to you for weeks. You mentioned a while back if anything happened to you, there were arrangements for a pension."

"Eloise, I can see you're not happy. I'll likely be here for a long time—too long to leave you waiting. I can see the strain is too much. Why don't you see a lawyer to draft up a divorce petition? I won't contest. Anything you want."

She stroked her eye as if it had a tear, to evoke self-pity.

"Scott, I can't endure the humiliation of being married to a murderer."

"Eloise, you'll be fine; you're strong and capable, a beautiful woman with courage. Months ago, I made arrangements with my lawyer in Paris to secure my financial affairs. His business card was in the living room desk; I assume you know where those papers would be now. You'll receive a generous monthly supplement. If the time comes and you want to remarry, I'll not oppose it."

There it was, said. A sigh of relief overcome both of them.

"You told me to put the garden suite up for sale. We made a nice profit, but the money is all tied up in escrow waiting for you to sign. I have moved to a suitable apartment near Hyde Park but I'd like to move back to the States.

"Don't fret. I'll call my accountant and get the pension started. You'll continue to receive monies until you re-marry. See, that was simple enough." Scott sighed with relief.

"What about the garden suite? It's still in escrow?"

"I'll sign the entire title over to you, Eloise."

After an awkward embrace, Eloise was gone with a sprightly walk, her demeanor elevated.

On the first day's initiation, Scott was assigned to laundry duty. He reported to a room with machines running at a high pitch. It was humid with little ventilation; the walls were lined with double decker washers and dryers. Metal tables were in the middle with canvas bags of soiled garments and hotel bedding, piled for sorting.

At the door, workers were handed mandatory disposable paper caps to keep hair from the clean linens.

Scott surveyed the room and smiled.

They contract to outside laundries. With this cap, they'll never know one new inmate from another.

A laundry truck labelled 'Mountain Rain' was in the receiving bay, unloading carts and sacks. The inmates hustled around dealing with the heavy loads when Scott saw the chance to chat with the driver.

Another van was waiting for Mountain's truck to leave. Returning the empty carts to the back of the truck, Scott crouched then slipped into one of the bins pulling a cover on top. Ten minutes later the truck was across town.

Routine continued in the laundry room until the shift finished at 4:00 p.m. The checkout monitor sent up alarms of a missing inmate, and a shrill siren was triggered, sounding throughout the prison. With the laundry room doors locked, a roll call was taken and three guards came instantly to assess the escape. Four trucks had come and gone during the afternoon.

The official radioed to security. "It's Scott Marchand!"

Leaving the orange suit in the bin, he slipped on jogging clothes from the laundry. Jumping from the back door at the delivery point in the west end of London, he was planning ahead to get to the border crossing.

Scott entered a drug store and carried a newspaper around to block the camera's view. Pacing as he conversed with the clerk, he pocketed hair color, a box cutter, gauze, disinfectant, tweezers and bandages. With his supplies hidden in his clothes, he returned to the clerk and handed him the newspaper.

Scott walked a few blocks watching for an abandoned building, and broke into in an empty boarding house. He dyed his hair dark brown then cleaned and disinfected the box cutter. Leaning over the bathroom sink, he let his fingers feel for the scar. Detecting a lump, he made a small incision. Using the mirror, he could see the chip. After several minutes of struggling with the tweezers, he pulled out the tracking chip.

Why didn't I notice this years ago? It always nagged me about this lump.

FIFTY-SIX

Joseph was alone in the office when the call came. "Mr. Harkness, I need your help. It's Christine!" She waited for a response. "From Metcalf's office."

Joseph got a notepad.

"Where are you, Christine? What's the problem?"

"I'm calling from London. To make my story short, I'm being hunted by Metcalf's mobster. My intention is to go underground with a new identity, but I need help in getting to a safe place in the North of France.

"I can take the hydrofoil from Dover across the English Channel to Calais. I have a forged passport to get me across, but when I arrive, I need to disappear. Please, Mr. Harkness, I need your help. Daniel said you would help."

Joseph interjected. "Christine, I won't participate in illegal activity. What makes you a fugitive?" He ignored the reference to Daniel.

"Some mobster thinks I know about Metcalf's debts and wants me to make good." She had rehearsed her script and sounded convincing.

Why should I help her? Could I be another pawn? Why should I care what Daniel thinks?

"When do you plan to leave England? Have you thought of an alternate appearance or an alias?"

"Yes, I'm ready. I've mailed a money order to your office for 5,000 euros. Please Joseph!"

He put her on hold and called Emily on his cell. In less than a minute he was back.

"Christine, I can meet you in Calais in five hours. I'll wait at the ticket booth exit towards Ramsgate."

The woman at the Calais crossing was plain in appearance with a stronger jaw than he remembered. She had an inadequate disguise with a grey wig and heavy rimmed glasses.

Her makeup was heavy, but her bright blue eyes and warm smile broke through. Christine saw him first and as she approached, he recognized Metcalf's secretary.

"Mr. Harkness?"

"Hello, Christine. My wife, Emily, made arrangements for a few days. You'll have the façade of a nurse in a seniors' guest house. Mrs. Marceau, the house matron, is trustworthy."

"Thanks, I appreciate what you've done. I'll be meeting my travel companion in a few days and we plan to go undercover."

She stopped, reasoning that she had said too much.

"Christine, what about your testimony at the Marchand trial . . . don't you have to stay in the country for the appeal?"

"Yes, I heard about that. Personally, I believe the young man, Scott Marchand." Her eyes looked away. "In my opinion, he's innocent."

On the drive, the scenery changed to open farmland on the rise above the ocean. The sky was azure blue and the sandy beaches were as white as pearls. Rocks and boulders distorted the surf that bounced in to splash against the strand.

"The Flower by the Sea has about a dozen seniors, and with the grey wig, you'll blend in as a nursing aide. Have you had any experience treating patients or with first aid?"

"Life experience will get me by. This is one of the most beautiful places I've ever been to; the ocean air is so invigorating."

On the veranda, Jeanne Marceau was waiting for them in a rocker. She waved as Joseph pulled to the entrance and he got out quickly to greet her.

"Hello, Jeanne. It's a pleasure to finally meet you. This place is picture perfect."

She gushed, "Bonjours! I'm glad to meet the other half of the Harkness team."

"Jeanne, thank you for taking my friend in for a few days."

Christine appeared shy at first, but stepped forward with her bag and greeted Mrs. Marceau with an unexpected hug.

"Come in. I've arranged for tea for us. What shall I call you?"

"Just Chris."

Joseph excused himself and walked to the beach for privacy. He needed to talk to Emily.

"Em, there is something not right about Christine. I'm going to hang out in Saint-Germain-Sur-Ay for a few days. I'm skeptical of the situation. Will you be okay with Madge?"

"Trust your instincts, Joseph. That's what makes us detectives."

Chris fell into the pace at the guesthouse and Joseph bunked in at the old lighthouse that stood high on the shore with its ocean beacon. It was within sight of the Flower of the Sea mainhouse but far enough that his movements would go unnoticed. An old telescope was fixed on the Milky Way.

In the first two days, Christine didn't step beyond the veranda. Joseph watched with binoculars, and with Jeanne Marceau's permission he secured transmitter in Chris's room.

She made a call to England the day she arrived. Her only words were 'Flower of the Sea, Saint-Germain-Sur-Ay'. No-one spoke at the other end.

Two days later she made another call, simply saying, 'Beach seven'.

Joseph was convinced her timing was running out, that her partner's arrival was imminent. From the upper window he scanned the landscape. A farm truck puttered down the road toward the village, but otherwise the sleepy town was silent.

He jumped to his feet.

What is that? That drone.

Then to the other window.

It's getting closer. Not from the road; it's from behind the tower.

With his binoculars, Joseph scanned the shoreline and the sea. No boat lights were visible, but the noise was getting louder.

Darting to the other window, he saw Christine walking across the road, with a flashlight toward the beach in the darkness, her silhouette barely visible.

Joseph checked his watch. It was 7:00 p.m. He nodded.

The coded rendezvous hour.

Turning back to the ocean, he heard the distinct sound of an idling motor. In the moonlight, he made out the shape of a cigarette racing boat with a dim running light. A lone man anchored the boat near the protruding rocks and swam the few feet to shore. Christine was waiting.

Joseph zoomed in and snapped photos of the pair. Christine had abandoned her disguise but her silhouette was the same, except her brown hair now hung loosely over her collar. She ran toward the man on the beach and they locked in an embrace.

Feeling sheepish that he was suspicious of a romantic reunion, Joseph phoned Emily to give her an update.

"Em, the meeting has taken place on the beach across from the guest house. In the darkness, the man is familiar but I can't pinpoint it."

She said, "Joseph, Madge and I are convinced the man is Scott."

"Preposterous! He's in London." Joseph gasped and reset his emotions.

"Look at him again. Breaking news on the radio indicates he broke out of prison."

Joseph centered his binoculars on the man's face.

"You're right, Emily. He's tried to disguise himself, but it *is* him. I can't believe I had the wool pulled over my eyes. I'm not sure if I should oppose him or leave well enough alone. I'm going in closer."

"Call me back, Joseph."

Joseph ran down a rocky slope to the sand. The couple waded into the ocean, satisfied they were free.

"Scott!" Joseph yelled.

Scott snapped his head around and squinted to focus on the intruder. He recognized the voice.

"Go home, Joseph, or I'll shoot you!"

The pair splashed on through the water on foot, slowing over the slippery rocks.

"I don't want to have to kill *you*." Joseph threatened.

Scott and Christine halted, putting their hands up as if to surrender. Joseph was still on land and stepped slowly along the rocky shore.

"Joseph, you're getting to be a bad scab. Can't you leave me alone?"

Christine pleaded, "We haven't hurt anybody. We're just two people wanting to escape the madness. Walk away!"

"You both have the diamonds don't you, Christine?"

"We hid them in the boardroom planter? Yes, I retrieved them, but does it really matter to you, Joseph?"

She turned and took Scott's hand. They swam to the boat.

Joseph put his gun down and watched as their silhouettes climbed into the boat. The motor revved, and the roar of the inboard disappeared into the horizon.

She's right, there isn't a crime. The diamonds were never reported missing. The case of Christine aiding a criminal—no one will ever know.

Silence settled over the beach. Joseph squatted to sit in the sand watching the moonlight and the diminishing spot of freedom he gave to Scott.

FIFTY-SEVEN

Elijah McQuaid sat in the waiting room at a doctor's office in Yorkshire. He'd been wearing a glove over his right hand, so anyone familiar with his penance would not ask questions. It would only be a few more days.

Dressed smartly in a suit, his memories went back to the events in Metcalf's office with an angry Mugabe.

The words still echoed. "Take a deep breath, now!" Then the command. Elijah barely had time to react with a scream when Solomon tied a white towel over his hand. The crimson staining was immediate and profuse. Solomon's finesse was almost thrilling.

Mugabe had affirmed to Metcalf that Elijah's soul had been emptied of his sins; however when he excused Elijah from the room, he tucked a note into his pocket.

Since that day, Elijah hadn't seen nor heard from Mugabe, Scott Marchand or Joseph Harkness.

His train of thought was broken by the nurse. "Mr. McQuaid?"

Elijah stood up and followed the nurse to an examining room.

The man said, "It's good to see you my friend." They laughed and embraced in a gentleman's hug. The doctor offered a claret of wine to his patient.

"Good job," he said.

Elijah dropped the glove to the floor, showing the man his hands.

The two men laughed again. "Well done," the man said.

"Here's to ten fingers.

FIFTY-EIGHT

Marie was arranging the flower pots when Emily stepped out of the loft.

"Bonjours, Emily! A man was here and left me with tickets for you. He insisted I tell you it is extremely important for you to attend an event tonight. He was such a gentleman; he left a box of chocolates for me."

Marie rooted into her apron for the envelope.

"Thanks, Marie, but I'm not sure if I'll be up to entertainment tonight. What did the man look like?"

"Mais, oui! An outing after a tragedy is the best medicine. He was tall, dark and handsome." Marie giggled.

Emily smiled and kissed her.

"I'll mull it over while I get Joseph his favorite pastries."

She tucked the envelope into her bag and disappeared to the St. Pierre Bakery.

At the loft, Emily roused Joseph out of bed.

"Marie said a man left this for us. I thought you should open it."

She laid the envelope on his chest and gave him a kiss.

"Coffee first! I'll come out to the kitchen."

Joseph said, "Two theater tickets for tonight—in London. Also two air tickets in our names for this afternoon and a hotel voucher. There's no note to explain it."

He looked at his watch. "Can we go that fast?"

Emily said, "Marie said the man was very insistent that we attend. I'm game for a couple of days in London."

"It could be another trap." Joseph said and watched Emily's face dimple with disappointment.

"Alright, pull out the satchels."

They stood at the front door of London's Copthorne Hotel in Kensington, waiting for their taxi.

"This inevitable curiosity will be the death of us someday," Emily muttered.

She was elegant in a floor length blue pearl dress draped from a single strap on her left shoulder. Wearing Joseph's earrings, she pinned her hair up the way he liked it best. Her new sapphire ring sparkled.

"This will be one of those older theaters that still holds the revered charm of yesteryear," Joseph noted.

A lone usher stood at the door, awaiting their arrival. They paid the cab and approached the usher.

"By gosh, Randy, you're moonlighting."

Randy winked. "I am, Mr. Harkness. I love my work here." He led them to red velvet seats in the front row and handed them programs. They were early, however enthusiastic theater goers quickly filled in the seats around them.

The lights turned down and the curtain rose.

In the first set, an American philanthropist discussed a business plan involving the purchase of a diamond shipment from a South African mine owner.

Joseph's face reddened. He looked at Emily.

"What's the name of this play?"

"The Rogue Courier."

"Sounds too coincidental," he said. "We've been tricked."

The play continued with an unsuspecting courier hired to follow clues to secure the rescue of a kidnapped man.

Joseph's face showed his fury and embarrassment. Then the actor playing the kidnapped man came on stage for his lines. It was like an earthquake to Joseph.

"Emily, that's McQuaid! Elijah McQuaid! He has all his fingers!" He pulled the program close in the darkness to read that the role of Elijah McQuaid was played by actor Elijah McQuaid.

"Actors, Emily! They're actors. Emily, this really is the man who had his finger cut off in the boardroom!"

He was shushed from a patron behind.

An unfamiliar actor then came out, playing Scott Marchand, and another played Winston Metcalf.

Joseph whispered his sarcasm. "I'm surprised he's not back from the grave."

The story continued with the diamond cutter from Amsterdam walking on in a painter's suit. Then the actors from 'The Amsterdam Dungeon', who appeared again playing the captors of Scott Marchand.

Joseph sat back into the plush seat. It was making some sense now.

They were just actors, except Scott, and Metcalf and his thugs.

He opened the program again to check the roles.

CAST		PLAYED BY
London Boss	Metcalf	Nathan Boyce
Courier Agent	Marchand	Marcus John
Thug #1	Winchester	Lou Samms
Thug #2	Leach	Aaron Lamb
Thug #3	Dillon	Tim Dallas
Kidnap Victim	McQuaid	Himself
Diamond Owner	Mugabe	Jim Webster
Mugabe Aide:	Solomon	Sol Kemp
Boss's Secretary	Christine	Minnie Walsh
Dutch Spy:	Woman	Joanne Nilsson
Dutch Spy:	Mugger	Peter Nilsson
Shoe-Shiner	Daniel	Daniel Boisvert
Prop Manager	Amelard	Amelard Boisvert
Stage Manager	Pascal	Pascal Charest

For most of the audience, the play was entertainment, mostly a tragedy about lives lost needlessly over greed.

Joseph hung onto every word, knowing his own part in flushing out Metcalf and Scott, the two criminals.

As the curtain fell, Daniel stepped to the front removing his fedora.

"Ladies and Gentlemen. Perhaps you saw this play as a comedy, or a tragedy of life. Or a romance."

Daniel's eyes were on Joseph and Emily.

"This has been the story about a greedy man who tried to intercept diamonds and replace them with fakes.

"His assistant, Christine, cooperated fully with us and with Scotland Yard in real life and in the caper. But she is now in America on the run with our unwitting rogue courier, Scott Marchand. We don't know for sure if he understands, in reality, that he murdered for fake diamonds. It's possible he is clinging to the fantasy that he is a wealthy man, but we hope it is the opposite and he has found true romance.

"The victims in this story were Winston Metcalf whose greed caused his own death, and Scott Marchand, a convicted murderer bearing the cost of an escaped prisoner.

"The character of Mugabe was played by a doctor in the East of London, and his assistant Solomon was played by a banker at the Swiss Bank in Amsterdam. Neither have ever been to South Africa. More than half of the people you encountered throughout this ruse are hired actors. However, Metcalf, Marchand, Winch, Leach and Dillon were deceived into reality. Life is full of consequences."

Daniel removed his dark toque and gestured for Joseph to stand.

"I'm sorry for the ruse, Joseph. The organization had to find the thieves among its couriers, and we found it in two men, Metcalf and Marchand. That was achieved thanks to our cast. There never was more than one genuine diamond in play. The originals were switched for fakes at the bank by Mr. McQuaid. The $400,000 US was recovered from Mr. Metcalf and placed for charitable distribution. Our worldwide work is much greater than a simple play."

Daniel paused.

Encouraged by the audience applause, Joseph nodded to the crowd. He turned back to Daniel. "Preposterous that you're even the shoe-shine guy. But why did you let me risk my own safety?"

"Joseph, you were never in danger. I made sure of it, and you must admit I tried to warn you off multiple times."

"I was shot twice! Who are you?"

"You know who I am."

"No, tell me." Joseph revealed an edge toward anger.

Daniel took another step closer.

"I'm part of an international courier organization recreating the values of Robin Hood. We're known as 'The Angels of Providence'. We're Samaritans; we take from criminals for the benefit of world charities. Our assets are intended for distribution to the poor and needy. By protecting our assets, these proceeds will enable us to fund medical supplies to the flood ravaged Philippines."

"Today's theatrical production wraps this case. It's our way to thank you, Joseph, and salute the actors who helped us dupe these criminals. Tonight they get the curtain call in these roles one last time."

After an encore applause, Joseph and Emily joined a small reception back stage to celebrate a successful mission.

FIFTY-NINE

Their new employee, Madge Bitteridge was in the outer office when Eloise's call came.

"Harkness Detective Agency," she said.

"I demand to speak with Joseph Harkness."

"I'm sorry, Ma'am, but they're out of the office."

She screamed into the phone. "This is Eloise Marchand. It is imperative I speak with Joseph."

"I'm sorry, Mrs. Marchand. I explained they're not in the office right now."

"Listen, Ms. Bitter, my husband paid well for services performed by Joseph Harkness and I'm not satisfied we've come to a conclusion. Joseph must call me! I demand it!"

"Mrs. Marchand, I'll pass your message on when I speak with him."

Eloise slammed the phone. The news of Scott's escape had startled her. She rifled through all his papers looking for clues to secret accounts but it only fuelled her anger and frustration.

Pacing her flat, she cursed and avowed to herself to confront Joseph.

Scott must have been in cahoots with the Harknesses.

Grasping her coat and handbag, she slammed the door. The tube was a blur; she exited on the Champs Elysses charging along rue Euler.

Standing in the doorway with her strawberry blonde hair askew, she looked wildly beautiful with her intent on a vendetta.

Madge was busy working in the outer reception area.

"Are they here?" she demanded.

From the inner office, Joseph heard the sudden outburst. He recognized Eloise's voice and rose from his desk to come to Madge's assistance.

Emily came to her office door and her eyes met Eloise's.

"Where is Scott? I was all set up with a nice pension. He's got a lot of money stashed away and I'm entitled to my fair share." Eloise was irate. "Invest wisely was his advice. Ha!"

Emily's compassion overtook her. "Eloise, we've never known anything about Scott's affairs. I'm sorry you are left in a spot."

Eloise stamped her foot. A nasty rash rose up her neck.

"I don't need your pity, Emily. You and Joseph live in your fairy tale world of romance and adventure—it's too much. It's just not fair, what has happened to me."

Reaching deep into her handbag, Eloise drew out a long pearl handled double-barreled .45 caliber pistol and raised it to her eye level. Clasping the gun with both hands, her aim was on Joseph's forehead. Her hands trembled.

"Eloise! What are you doing?" Emily yelled.

Emily inched toward the desk, wondering if she had returned the revolver to the drawer.

Eloise continued the rampage. "Don't think for one minute I don't know how to use this! I spent all week practicing at the gun club's firing range. I'm good."

Emily glanced at Joseph with panic. She was afraid to move in case it spurred Eloise.

Joseph stood calm, like a soldier in front of the firing squad. His gun was within his reach, but Emily knew he was unlikely to go for it if it would risk her being shot.

Madge inched to a phone and dialed emergency, with Eloise too focused on Joseph and Emily to take notice.

"It's your fault, Joseph, that my Scott is gone."

Eloise turned to Emily. "I want you to know what it feels like. I want you to see the life disappear from him. You should suffer like I have."

While Eloise prepared in slow motion to pull the trigger, Emily glanced at Joseph—calm but rigid. She felt numb and cold, it was happening so fast.

In the same instant, Madge stealthily rose from her desk and mounted a footstool, now in line with Eloise. Her gun was drawn and locked in position behind Eloise.

Emily saw Madge in the corner of her eye. Madge was in control, with a fierce look on her face. She was mama bear protecting her cubs.

The pause was deafening before the sound of the hammer striking the firing pin. Two pistols fired simultaneously.

Joseph's face was white as he fell to his knees, his shirt spattered. Eloise slumped to the floor.

On his knees, Joseph trembled while faces closed in and peered at him.

They must be the angels coming to get me.

Emily's face faded from over him.

Holding a scrap of paper with a phone number, Emily dialed.

"Daniel! Daniel . . . can we talk?"

"Emily, what is it?" Daniel's voice softened with concern.

"We're going back to New York."

Daniel was suddenly distracted by flashing lights ahead.

"I'll call you back, Emily! Looks like an accident ahead."

Daniel was heading to the North of France with Amelard and Pascal. He eased on the brakes and came to a stop at a roadblock with flares.

The reason for the detour wasn't apparent, except for the flashing lights of a tow truck, orange cones and emergency workers.

Three crewmen with neon jackets waved them down.

"There's been an accident, gentlemen, could we ask for your help?"

Daniel climbed out of the passenger seat. He didn't see anyone in distress and turned to look at the road crew. It was too late; a black hood was placed over his head, and his hands and feet were bound. Amelard and Pascal were put in another car.

Within seconds all signs of Daniel disappeared.

THE END

PREVIEW OF

SECRET CACHE

**BOOK FOUR OF
THE THOMAS YORK SERIES**

SECRET CACHE

SHIRLEY BURTON

SECRET CACHE
BOOK FOUR OF THE THOMAS YORK SERIES

Daniel Boisvert's dalliance in Paris intensified his relationship with Joseph and Emily. But under his façade as an Interpol agent and his passion and commitment to righteousness with The Angels of Providence, his appearances and disappearances became a growing enigma.

Beckoned to California by Emily's aunt, Joseph and Emily rush to America to deal with her uncle's murder at the Napa Valley vineyard, revealing lingering threats from his mysterious past.

With aliases left behind in France, they decided to take a risk by returning to their real names from America, Thomas York and Rachel Redmond.

Unaware of forces against them in the States, they gamble that they'll be safe from discovery by their former antagonist David Sanderson and his sinister world.

The California murder investigation unravels explosive family secrets and a murderous plot brewing at the vineyard. The mansion leads them through passageways and caves to a Brazilian cache and a trunk of ancient silver coins.

The loyalty of the vineyards is challenged by a family member with a destructive scheme of his own.

I hope you'll join me in the fourth book of the series, now available.

Reviews are appreciated on Amazon.com and goodreads.com, and I welcome comments at shirleyburtonbooks.com

About the Author

Shirley Burton lives with her husband in Calgary, Alberta, Canada, with a view of the magnificent Rockies. Inspired at a young age to write stories for children on her street, she became driven and motivated to write, starting with research for a ten-generation family saga.

"There comes a time in life to take the leap into writing. It's that time for me. I hope readers will become as attached to my characters as I have."